GABRIELLE MEYER

A Mother in the Making

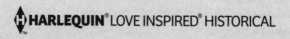

HARLEQUIN® LOVE INSPIRED® HISTORICAL

Recycling programs
for this product may
not exist in your area.

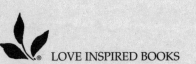

LOVE INSPIRED BOOKS

ISBN-13: 978-0-373-28377-4

A Mother in the Making

Copyright © 2016 by Gabrielle Meyer

www.Harlequin.com

Printed in U.S.A.

"Miss Baker came to supper tonight."

Marjorie wrapped her arms around her waist. "That's nice."

"That's nice?" John wished he could concentrate on reprimanding her. Instead, he could only think about her curls and her beautiful voice as she sang to Laura. "You had no right to invite a guest to my home to dine with me."

She was quiet for a moment and then she spoke softly. "I have a confession to make. She's not the only woman coming to supper this week. Miss Addams and Miss Fletcher will also be coming."

"But—why?"

She took a step toward him, and he pulled back. He could smell the lilac scent she wore and it made his mind a jumbled mess. Why was he responding to her this way? She was the governess. He must keep that in mind.

"You said you're looking for a wife," she said. "I thought each of them would be a good candidate."

"What gives you the right to do that?"

"I care about your children—and you."

She cared about him? He swallowed the rush of surprise that surfaced at her statement.

He couldn't allow himself to dwell on Marjorie Maren, or his growing attraction to her.

The sooner he found a wife, the better.

Gabrielle Meyer lives in central Minnesota on the banks of the Mississippi River with her husband and four young children. As an employee of the Minnesota Historical Society, she fell in love with the rich history of her state and enjoys writing fictional stories inspired by real people and events. Gabrielle can be found at www.gabriellemeyer.com, where she writes about her passion for history, Minnesota and her faith.

Books by Gabrielle Meyer

Love Inspired Historical

A Mother in the Making

A man's heart deviseth his way:
but the Lord directeth his steps.
—*Proverbs* 16:9

To my children, Ellis, Maryn, Judah and Asher.
Thank you for being my biggest fans.
I love you with all my heart.

Chapter One

Little Falls, Minnesota, November 1918

John Orton stared at Anna's portrait, his grief nothing compared to his pulsing guilt. How could a physician let his own wife die?

"Papa?" Charlie entered the office, his heavy gaze lifting to John's face.

John put the photo in his desk drawer, wanting to spare his son the reminder of his pain. "Yes?"

"The new governess has arrived—"

A young woman stepped over the threshold without an invitation, her blond hair in a mass of curls under a wide-brimmed hat. She glanced around the neat interior before she dropped her bag on the floor and proceeded to take off her gloves in quick succession. Her bright green eyes found John and a smile lit her pretty face. "Where shall I begin?"

John stood, grappling for a foothold of familiarity. This was not the sensible woman he had expected his mother to send from Chicago. Standing before him, in layers of lace, and a cloud of flowery perfume, was a woman far too attractive and impractical to raise his children.

"Are you—?"

"Marjorie Maren." She grasped his limp fingers in her right hand and lifted her left hand above her head in a great flourish, her gloves flapping in the air. "A governess by day—and an actress by night."

John glanced at Charlie, whose eyes grew wide with interest.

It would be impossible to replace Anna, but surely there was a more suitable governess to take care of his children—one with the same gentleness and competence Anna had demonstrated.

This lady would not do—would not do, at all.

"You must be Charles." Miss Maren dropped John's hand and turned to the ten-year-old boy. "My, but you look like your mother."

"You knew my mama?" Charlie asked.

Miss Maren offered a kind smile, and dimples graced her cheeks. "Your grandmother showed me her picture."

"You know my grandmother?" Charlie looked even more impressed with Miss Maren.

"I know your grandmother and your uncle Paul. They are my neighbors in Chicago." Miss Maren removed the long hat pin from her hair, and slipped off her hat. Her curls looked like golden silk and for a fleeting second, John wondered how they could look so disheveled yet perfectly arranged. "*Were* my neighbors," the young lady amended. "I don't expect to return to Chicago— I'm going to California to become a film actress."

"You're going to be in the movies?" Charlie's face filled with awe.

It was time for John to take control. He rounded the

desk, finally finding his voice. "Miss Maren, I think there's been a mistake."

She turned her gaze on John, and he was startled again by her pretty face. If she wanted to be an actress, she would be a charming one—but what reasonable woman wanted to be an actress?

"A mistake?"

"I expected—" How could he tell her he had expected an older woman, who wasn't quite so...fetching?

"You expected what?"

When she looked at him with those big green eyes, he couldn't recall what it was he had expected—but certainly not her.

"Your room is connected to the night nursery, on the second floor, with Lilly and the baby," Charlie said. "Petey and I sleep on the third floor, next to the day nursery." He picked up Miss Maren's bag. "You can follow me."

"Charlie, would you please leave for a moment so I can speak with Miss Maren alone?" John usually appreciated his son's hospitality—but at the moment he needed Charlie to put down the bag until he knew what he would do with the young woman.

Charlie was a perceptive boy and he studied John's face now. His grip tightened around the handle of Miss Maren's bag. "I'll just bring this up to the day nursery."

Miss Maren ran her hand over her blond curls and smiled at the boy. "Thank you, Charles."

The boy's cheeks filled with color and he dipped his head. "You can call me Charlie."

John lifted his eyebrows. The boy rarely gave people permission to use his pet name—and never so soon.

Charlie left the room—with the bag in hand—and

Miss Maren turned her charming smile on John. "He's a lovely boy."

"Would you please have a seat?"

She lowered herself into the leather chair facing John's desk. Though she had just spent a few days on a train, she looked as fresh as a bed of flowers after a summer rainstorm. "I'm eager to meet the other children," she said. "Your mother and brother spoke of them so often, I feel as if I already know each one. How old is Laura now? Six months old?"

"Yes—six months." He dropped to his chair and tried to pull himself together. He was a physician and he prided himself on staying calm in every situation. Surely he could manage something like this. He would have to be direct and honest—two attributes he appreciated in business dealings. "Miss Maren, do you have any experience with children?"

She tucked a curl into her bun with a great deal of nonchalance. "I'm afraid not—but your mother said the children are so well behaved I won't have any troubles."

"My children are well behaved, but they are still children—and my mother is a bit biased."

Miss Maren laughed.

If he had been in a different frame of mind, he would have enjoyed the sound. It had been absent from his home for far too long. Instead, he cleared his throat. "I had expected someone with experience—and maturity."

She shrugged. "How do you gain experience if you aren't given your first job?"

That was fair enough. "What types of skills do you have?"

She waved the question away with her hand. "Oh, this and that… Who has been caring for the children since your wife's passing?"

"My wife's mother and sister."

"Do they live close?"

"Too close…" He paused, embarrassed at the hasty words. "They live across the street."

Miss Maren frowned. "Why do you need a governess if you have their help?"

"I…" He paused again. He was the one interviewing her, wasn't he? "What led you here to be our governess?"

She blinked several times. "Didn't your mother tell you?"

"Tell me what?"

"This is a stopping point for me on my way to California. I need the money, and you need a governess, so your mother thought it the perfect solution."

John steepled his hands on his desk. What had his mother been thinking? Normally she used better judgment, and he had no reason to question her advice—but now he could see he should have asked her more questions. Had she sent Miss Maren in the hopes of matchmaking? If she had, Mother would be sorely disappointed. "I'm afraid I'm in need of someone with experience raising children. My work is very demanding and I must have complete confidence in—"

"You can be completely confident in me." Miss Maren's face and voice became very serious.

She would make a convincing actress. He almost believed her.

"I have some questions for you, too," she said.

He leaned back in his chair. "Oh?"

"How long will you need my services? I won't be able to stay permanently—but I don't want to leave until the job is done."

He wasn't sure he would need her past this conversation. "I had intended to employ a governess until—" He hated to admit his plans, but what did it matter what this young woman thought of him? "Until I find a wife."

She leaned forward, her voice lowered as if she didn't want anyone else to hear. "You'd marry again so soon?"

Irritation flashed warm under his collar. Who was she to question his decision to remarry? It had been a month since Anna died. Not nearly enough time to think of a second marriage in the traditional sense—but more than enough time to realize his children needed a mother. "My concern is for my children."

"But surely it will take some time for you to grieve—and then fall in love again."

He stood abruptly. Fall in love again? He could never love another woman the way he had loved Anna. "I would never dishonor my wife's memory by marrying for love. This is purely a practical decision on my part."

She rose, as well. "Practical?" Her voice was filled with passion. "Marriage should be everything but practical! It would be dreadful to be married for practicality's sake."

Her response was unnerving. He leaned forward, his hands on his desk, and couldn't help asking, "What is marriage, if it isn't practical?"

She put her hand over her heart. "It should be whimsical and utterly romantic. It should be entered into for love, and no other reason."

"You are young and naive, so I will forgive you."

"Forgive *me*?" Ire rose in her countenance for the first time since entering the room, and he had a glimpse of the spark beneath all the fluff. "I know something about practicality, and it is overrated." She put her hands on her hips and stared at him—and he suddenly felt like a schoolboy being reprimanded. "You need a bit of whimsy in your life. I could tell the moment I entered this room that you're much too serious for your own good."

He crossed his arms and offered her the stern look he gave the children when they were being impertinent. "You may have time for whimsy, Miss Maren, but I do not." He was a widower, as well as a doctor with a pandemic on his hands. He had no time for anything resembling whimsy—and Miss Maren was at the top of his list.

He dropped into his chair and pulled a piece of paper out of his top drawer. The picture he had studied earlier peeked out at him. Anna had been as pragmatic as they had come—and he had admired her. Never once had she demanded anything else but practicality from him.

He began to scribble a note to his mother, informing her that sending Miss Maren was a mistake, no matter what her intentions. "I'm sorry, Miss Maren, but I will have to send you back to Chicago."

The lady lowered herself into the chair, wilting like a plucked rose. "I can't go back."

He didn't bother to look at her. "I need a steady, levelheaded woman to care for my children until I find a wife." He would put her on the next train back to Chicago—and tell his mother exactly what he thought of Miss Maren.

Marjorie stared at the doctor, never imagining her day would end like this. "I've cut all ties to my life in Chicago—I can't possibly return."

Dr. Orton didn't look up as he continued to scribble on the paper. A lock of brown hair fell out of place and brushed his forehead. "That's not my concern."

"But it is."

He lifted his head, his brown eyes filled with frustration. "How is it my concern?"

"You asked me to come."

"My mother sent you."

"At your request."

"At her suggestion."

"Your mother told me I would be welcome." Mrs. Orton had said that Dr. Orton's family needed someone like Marjorie to bring joy back into their lives.

Dr. Orton paused and he looked as if he had to concede. "Everyone is welcome in my home."

Marjorie toyed with a silk flower on her hat. "I don't feel welcome at the moment."

He sighed, put down his pen and then rubbed the bridge of his nose. "I suppose I can't make you return home tonight. You'll need to rest."

Home. What a strange and lonely word at the moment. After Marjorie had left Preston Chamberlain at the altar, her parents had turned her out of their house and withheld her allowance, unless she marry him. But Preston did not love her. To him, she was an advantageous match—a business deal. Out of fear, she had almost caved to her parents' demands, but then she was reminded of their own loveless union. They had married to strengthen social and financial ties, and they had been miserable.

Marjorie could never marry a man who didn't love her.

If it hadn't been for Mrs. Orton's suggestion, and Dr. Orton's need, Marjorie would have nowhere else to go. "I have no home to return to."

He looked at her as if he didn't believe her. "My mother told me you are a neighbor, from a good family."

"Yes, they are good people."

"Then surely you have a home."

She needed to change the subject. She stood and ran her hand over the walnut mantel on the large fireplace. "You have a beautiful home. Your mother told me all about it. Actually she told me a great deal about you and the children."

"That's interesting," Dr. Orton said as he crossed his arms. "She told me very little about you."

Marjorie lifted her shoulder, trying to sound blasé. "What's there to tell?"

She wished to say she had led a boring life, but the past few weeks had proven otherwise. Hopefully he hadn't read the Chicago newspapers recently. They had covered the jilting and Marjorie's subsequent departure from her parents' home. But why wouldn't they? Who would deign to reject Preston Chamberlain?

Marjorie, that was who.

Dr. Orton stood and motioned for her to follow him out of his office. He was a tall man, exuding confidence and authority as he strode to the door. "I will see that our cook sets a plate for you to join us for supper, and then you're welcome to sleep in the governess's room, but I will put you on a train to Chicago in the morning."

"I beg you to reconsider your decision." Marjorie wanted to put her hand on his arm and stop him from making plans to send her back—but she refrained. "I'll show you I'm the right person for this job."

"I doubt you could convince me to change my mind."

Marjorie clutched her hat in her hands. "Give me until the end of the year—and if you're unhappy with my work, I'll leave." In those two months, she might raise enough money to go to California.

"The end of the year?"

She nodded and offered him an innocent look. "What harm could I do in two months?"

He lifted an eyebrow, his face filling with skepticism. He stepped out of his office and Marjorie followed him into the front hall.

The home was stunning, inside and out. Three stories tall, with deep gables and large windows, it stood like a stately queen on the tree-lined street. Redbrick covered most of the house, with white bric-a-brac and trim gracing the windows and eaves. Inside the dark wooden trim and wainscoting gave it a warm feeling, while oak flooring and expensive—yet practical— furnishings reflected the status of the owner. It wasn't quite as elaborate as Marjorie's childhood home—but it was comfortable.

"Mrs. Gohl, the cook, and Miss Ernst, the maid, live in the servant's quarters at the back of the second floor," Dr. Orton said as he passed through the front hall and up the stairs. "Charlie is the only child home at the moment. The other three are across the street at my mother-in-law's home…"

Marjorie followed close behind, her gaze feasting on a beautiful stained-glass window above the landing of the curved stairs. Rays of brilliant colors depicted a glorious sunset. She had tried her hand at working with stained glass, but the unfinished project was tucked away in her room in Chicago along with dozens of other half-completed ventures.

Dr. Orton stopped at the top of the stairs and Marjorie bumped into his back.

He turned, barely concealing his frustration. He pointed down a long, carpeted hallway. "The night nursery is at the end of this hall, to the right. You'll find your room attached to it."

She didn't want to beg, but she needed reassurance that she would be given a chance. "I hope you'll consider my offer. Please give me two months to prove I'm the person for this job."

He studied her with an analytical gaze just as the downstairs door opened and voices drifted up the stairwell.

"Papa, we're home!" A little girl's voice filled the hall.

"John? John, where are you?" An older female voice pierced the air. "Peter wet his pants once again. I've told you to put your foot down with him, John. The child needs more discipline."

Dr. Orton closed his eyes and let out a long sigh.

Marjorie raised an eyebrow and whispered, "Your mother-in-law?"

He opened his eyes and she could see exhaustion behind his weary gaze. "You might as well meet her and get it over with."

"Get it over with?"

"John!" the lady yelled up the stairwell, her head peeking around the banister. Her gaze narrowed when she spotted Marjorie. "Who are you?"

Marjorie pasted on her biggest smile. "I'm the new governess."

The lady's blue eyes grew enormous in her wrinkled face. "The what?"

Dr. Orton gave Marjorie a warning glance as he stepped past her on the stairwell.

Marjorie tried to hide a giggle as she followed him down the stairs and faced the lady standing in the foyer. She wore a black mourning gown, with a black hat pinned tight against her gray hair. She held a baby in her arms, while a little boy peeked around her skirts.

A girl of eight or nine stared at Marjorie with open curiosity, a spark of animation glistening from her eyes.

"This is Miss Marjorie Maren," Dr. Orton said. "She is my mother's neighbor from Chicago."

"*Was* her neighbor," Marjorie couldn't help adding as she nodded a greeting at the older woman.

John gave her another warning look and Marjorie snapped her mouth shut. If she was going to keep this job, she must be vigilant about guarding her tongue.

"Governess?" the woman asked. "You don't need a governess, John—you have Dora and me."

John took the baby, a smile lifting his lips when he looked at his child—but it disappeared when he glanced back at Marjorie. "Miss Maren, this is Mrs. Scott, my mother-in-law."

Marjorie extended her hand, but Mrs. Scott only stared at her. "Maren? Why does that name sound familiar?" She openly examined Marjorie with a critical eye. "I don't like it, John. These things should stay in the family."

Marjorie lowered her hand.

The little boy raced away from his grandmother's skirts and clung to Dr. Orton's leg, eyeing Marjorie with big blue eyes.

"I can't impose on you forever," Dr. Orton said. "You and Dora have been helpful—but it's best if I hire a governess to take care of the child—"

"If you would do as I say and marry Dora, you wouldn't be an imposition. It would become her duty."

"Please," Dr. Orton said, pointedly looking at the children. "I don't want to discuss this right now." He looked at Marjorie, relief suddenly lighting his face. "And since I have a governess, this conversation is pointless."

Mrs. Scott crossed her arms over her ample bosom. "You trust this lady? We don't know anything about her."

Dr. Orton looked as if he was trying to control his irritation. "Thank you for your concern, but Miss Maren is from a good family and is highly recommended by my mother."

Mrs. Scott raised her eyebrows in disdain. "*Your* mother?"

John moved to the front door and opened it. "Thank you for all your help. Please extend my appreciation to Dora, as well."

Mrs. Scott ran her gaze over Marjorie one more time, her displeasure evident, before looking back at John. "I'm right across the street if you need me."

He nodded and opened the door wider. The woman stepped through it with her nose high in the air.

Dr. Orton closed the door behind her with a decided thud.

"Are you our new governess?" the girl asked.

"Miss Maren, this is my oldest daughter, Lillian. And this—" Dr. Orton put his free hand on the head of the little boy who still clung to his leg "—is Peter." He lifted the smiling baby in his arms, his voice softening. "This is Laura."

"You can call me Lilly," the girl said with a shy smile. "Will you sleep next to our room?"

Marjorie looked to Dr. Orton and posed a question with her eyes.

The doctor lifted the baby to his shoulder, lines edging his mouth. "For now." He hugged Laura and then handed her to Marjorie, saying under his breath, "Until the end of the year, Miss Maren—and don't let me regret my decision."

Relief washed over Marjorie as she took Laura—trying to look as if she had held a baby before—and smiled. "You won't—I promise."

"The children are required to have at least one hour of exercise every day," Dr. Orton said, "and the two oldest are to spend an hour reading. Petey needs to practice his numbers, letters, colors and shapes every day, as well. There is a schedule posted in the day nursery for you to follow. Laura's feedings and nap times are listed beside the others. I don't like the children to deviate from their schedule." Dr. Orton paused and his face became grave. "If you fail at being a governess, you'll prove my mother-in-law right—and I hate when she's right."

Marjorie jostled the baby in her hands, trying to remember everything he was saying. For a brief moment she thought she might drop the precious bundle—but she held her tight. "Come, Lilly and Peter, and show me your nursery."

"First you'll need to change Petey's clothing." Dr. Orton disengaged the child from his leg and put him near Marjorie. He turned toward the office but then pivoted back to face her. "One more thing, and this is the most important—the children are to take ten drops of cinnamon oil in a glass of water every morning with their breakfast."

"Cinnamon oil?" Marjorie wrinkled her nose.

"It's a preventative measure to ward off influenza. I've been studying the effects and they're promising. I'll require you to take the oil, as well."

"Of course."

Petey stood close to Marjorie, his eyes filled with apprehension.

Dr. Orton looked at his son, and then back at Marjorie. "If you need anything, don't hesitate to ask."

Marjorie swallowed her anxiety. At the moment, she needed someone to tell her how to take care of four children—but the last person she would ask was Dr. Orton.

Chapter Two

Marjorie stood in the water closet facing Petey. Laura was in her arms, chewing on her fist, and Lilly stood behind Marjorie quietly observing the scene.

Petey stared up at Marjorie with defiant blue eyes and she didn't blame him.

First, he had lost his mother, and then he was presented with a strange woman who didn't know the first thing about child care. How could she make him trust her—and feel comfortable in her presence?

She smiled—it was the only thing she could think to do.

He didn't blink.

"I'm Miss Maren," she said with a happy tone to her voice. "I'm here to take care of you."

Still, he scowled at her.

"I need to help you out of your soiled clothes, and then I'll give you a bath and put you in something clean."

"His clothes are upstairs in his bedroom," Lilly said. "Shall I get him something to wear?"

Marjorie could have sighed in relief. "Yes, thank you, Lilly."

Laura began to whimper in Marjorie's arms and she awkwardly bounced the baby to quiet her.

"I need to help you get your clothing off," Marjorie said to Petey.

The boy took a step back and shook his head.

Laura's whimper turned into a cry, close to Marjorie's ear. She bounced her faster, but the baby refused to be soothed.

How would she hold the baby and take off Petey's clothing?

"I'm going to put Laura in her cradle, and then I'm coming back here to help you. All right?"

Petey didn't respond.

Marjorie turned from the water closet and stepped across the hall to the night nursery, where she placed Laura in her cradle. The baby's cries increased at being set down, and Marjorie's heart rate picked up speed. What would Dr. Orton think if this baby continued to cry? And how could she stop her? What did she need? Was she hungry? Was her diaper soiled?

She offered the baby a rattle lying in her cradle, but Laura cried even harder.

A flash of movement caught Marjorie's eye.

Petey ran out of the water closet and down the hall toward the stairs.

Marjorie left the crying baby and rushed out of the room. Petey turned the corner and Marjorie raced after him. She grasped the little boy as he reached the stairway landing where the beautiful stained-glass window had caught Marjorie's eye earlier. She held his arm to stop his escape and tried to sound calm. "We haven't bathed you, Petey. You must wait for me."

Laura's wails filled the upper hall and met Marjorie on the stairway.

Petey tried to pull free from Marjorie's grasp, his own whimpers filling her ears.

Heat gathered under Marjorie's traveling gown, warming her neck and back until perspiration gathered. How would she get Petey back to the water closet? His clothing smelled of urine. If she lifted him, her dress would need to be cleaned, as well.

"Miss Maren?" Dr. Orton appeared at the bottom of the stairs, his eyebrows pulled together in a frown. "Do you need help?"

Petey reached for his father, but Marjorie held tight.

The doctor gave Marjorie a disapproving look. "It appears you are off to a poor start."

Marjorie had little choice but to lift the child into her arms. His wet clothing penetrated hers, and she had to breathe through her mouth. "I'm fine."

"Why is Laura crying? Does she need to be fed?"

Marjorie had no idea why Laura was crying—or what a person fed a hungry baby—but she couldn't tell Dr. Orton. She was on trial. She couldn't ruin her chances within the first half hour. "I have everything under control."

"Are you sure?"

She wanted to glower at the doctor, but instead, she forced a tight smile and walked up the stairs with her head held high as Petey tried to wiggle out of her arms.

Laura's cries were so pitiful Marjorie felt tears gather in the back of her own eyes. Did children always make such a fuss? As an only child, Marjorie had never been exposed to anything like this. Had she been this way for her own governess? It didn't seem likely.

Marjorie entered the water closet and set Petey on his feet. The little boy tried to push past her, but she held her hand on his shoulder. "I'm sorry, but I must get you clean and put new clothes on you."

He backed up against the stand-up radiator under the window.

The reprieve gave Marjorie a moment to study his romper, her brow furrowed. There were far too many buttons. If Petey didn't cooperate, she had no idea how she would get the wet clothing off his wiggly body.

"Mama used to sing to him while she changed his clothes," Lilly said, suddenly standing at the door.

Marjorie turned to the girl with a bit of desperation. "What did she sing?"

Lilly shrugged and set the clean romper and underclothes on a bureau near the door. "Church hymns, mostly." The girl went to the bathtub and turned on the water faucet. "It takes a few minutes for the hot water to travel up the pipe from the basement. Mama always used the time to gather her bathing supplies." Lilly went to the bureau and pulled out a clean towel and washcloth.

Petey stopped squirming and watched his sister work.

Lilly stepped onto the closed toilet seat and reached for a bar of pink soap, high on the top shelf. She paused for a moment, her hand hovering over the soap. "Petey always asked Mama if he could use her rose-scented soap, but she usually said no because it was a gift Papa gave her." She looked at Petey, and a tender gaze passed between them before she grabbed the soap. "It makes us feel close to her."

Petey stood still and dropped his little chin down to his chest.

Lilly set the soap on the towel and then began to

hum "Onward, Christian Soldiers" as she unbuttoned Petey's romper.

Marjorie's heart broke for the children—but Laura's wails continued to fill the house, sending gooseflesh racing up Marjorie's arms.

"Laura needs a bottle and a diaper change." Lilly looked up at Marjorie, blinking her blue, trusting eyes. "Do you know how to do those things?"

Marjorie wanted to sit on the rug and throw her hands up in defeat. Maybe being a governess was a bad idea—but she couldn't give up now. She refused to leave another job unfinished. She wouldn't let her father's parting words define her. *You're a quitter, Marjorie, and you'll never change.*

"No, but I'm a good student." Marjorie unbuttoned her sleeves and began to roll them up to her elbows. "Do you know how to make a bottle and change a diaper?"

Lilly nodded and slipped Petey's romper off his body, her young arms working with an air of confidence Marjorie wished she possessed. "You can bathe Petey, and I'll see to Laura's diaper—you do know how to wash someone, don't you?"

Here, at least, was something Marjorie did know how to do. "Yes, of course—I bathe myself all the time." She looked toward the room across the hall. "But how will I learn to change her if I'm in here?"

Lilly giggled and the sound was a welcome change from the wailing baby. "She'll need to be changed again in a few hours. You can learn then." She reached into the tub and put the plug in the drain.

"Is Petey old enough to talk?" Marjorie asked as she set the boy into the water.

"Of course he is." Lilly shook her head. "Don't you know anything about children?"

Marjorie couldn't tell her the truth—though she suspected the girl already knew. "I have a lot to learn, but you look like a good teacher."

Lilly's shoulders lifted at the compliment. "I'll change Laura and then when you have Petey clean I'll help you make her a bottle."

Marjorie smiled at Lilly. "Thank you."

The girl stepped out of the water closet and Marjorie turned to her next task, determined to do this job well.

She would not be sent back to Chicago.

An hour later, Marjorie opened her trunk lid and surveyed the gowns piled haphazardly inside.

"Your clothes are lovely," Lilly breathed beside Marjorie as they stood in the governess's bedroom. The little girl ran her hand over a purple silk gown.

The governess's room was surprisingly large, with a fireplace, cheery floral wallpaper, soft white curtains and two generous windows overlooking the front yard. Two doors exited the room, one to the hallway and one to the night nursery, where Laura was finally napping in her cradle.

Marjorie glanced down at her soiled traveling gown, memories of cleaning Petey still fresh in her mind. Thankfully the exhausted little boy was now napping. Marjorie wished she could rest herself, but she needed to unpack, and for the first time in her life there was no maid to do the chore for her.

"I've only seen dresses like this in my aunt Dora's *Vogue Magazine*," Lilly said. "Where did you wear them?"

"I didn't get a chance to wear many of them—although I did wear this one." Marjorie lifted out the exquisite green dress she had worn to her debutante ball in June of 1917, the day she had met Preston. It had been one of the last debutante balls in Chicago after the United States had entered the war. In June, the young men began to ship out of the city, on their way to fight, and a somber mood had fallen on the country. Instead of dancing and partying, Marjorie had filled her time volunteering for the Red Cross—and entertaining Preston.

After he made his intentions known, her parents insisted that Marjorie allow him to court her. She was eager to finally please them, so she agreed.

Preston was everything her parents had hoped for. With his wealth, success and good connections, it was supposed to be the match of the year. But by the time she realized Preston did not love her, it was too late to call the wedding off, and she was forced to leave him at the altar.

Lilly sat on the bed and grasped the brass knob on the footboard. She studied Marjorie, her pretty blue eyes filled with a bit of uncertainty. "Do you have any work dresses?"

Marjorie examined her trunk and put her hand on her chin. She had led a charmed life in Chicago and had very few serviceable dresses to begin with. She hadn't thought to put any of them in her luggage when she packed so hastily. "I'm afraid not. I suppose I'll have to make do with what I have."

Lilly shrugged. "I don't mind if you wear these pretty dresses."

Marjorie walked the dress across the room and hung it in the large wardrobe against the wall. She put it in the back, since she would have no use for it until she reached California.

Just thinking about the movies caused a trill of excitement to race up Marjorie's spine, and she paused for a moment. Nothing else had brought her as much joy during the past few years as the movie theater, and she wanted to bring the same happiness into other people's lives. If she could help them forget about their troubles, even for a little while, it would be worth all the hard work to get there.

Lilly lifted her finger to her mouth and nibbled on her nail. "Papa might not like you in those dresses, though. I don't think I ever saw Mama wear anything like them."

Marjorie's attention returned to her task, and she took another gown out of the trunk, this one a soft muslin morning dress. She paused. "What was your mother like?"

Lilly's face filled with sadness and she dropped her gaze. "She was wonderful."

Marjorie lowered the gown and sat next to the girl. "You must miss her very much."

Lilly nodded but didn't speak.

"I'm sure she would be very proud of how you're helping take care of Laura and Petey."

"Mama was very gentle and kind. She was never angry."

"And what of your father?"

Lilly lifted her shoulder and toyed with a loose thread on the quilt. "Papa wasn't home much before Mama died. He was usually gone by the time we came down for breakfast, and he often came home after Mama put us to bed."

"But he's home more now?"

Lilly nodded.

"Do you like having him home?"

Again, the girl nodded. "I like it very much—but

I'm afraid that since you've come, he might go back to working as much as before."

"Did your mother ever ask him to stay home more?"

"Mama always said we must never complain about how much he worked. She said he was a doctor, and doctors needed to make people well. Her father was a doctor, too, and she said it was our job to sacrifice so they could do their work."

Marjorie wanted to deny what the girl said. Yes, Dr. Orton had a demanding job, but his family should not have to suffer because of it.

More than anything, Marjorie had wanted her own father present in her life when she was a child. He had always used his work as his excuse—and Mother had never pushed him to be present.

Indignation rose in Marjorie's gut. If Dr. Orton could make time to be home with his family now, surely he could have made time before his wife died.

Marjorie looked off toward the window where the November landscape looked bleak against a pale blue sky. What kind of woman would Dr. Orton choose for his second wife? Would she be as compliant as the first Mrs. Orton? Would she keep quiet as he sacrificed his family? In the few minutes Marjorie had spent with him, she could tell he was authoritative and probably ruled with a stubborn set of principles—just like Marjorie's father. He needed a woman who wouldn't be afraid to stand up to him and tell him when he was being too rigid.

Someone she wished her mother had been.

But was Dr. Orton capable of finding someone like that?

An excited bubble fluttered through Marjorie's midsection—the same feeling she had every time she was about to undertake a new project. But this time, she wouldn't leave the task half-completed. She would finally finish something she started. She would find a new wife for Dr. Orton—and she would make sure the woman he married was exactly who the doctor and his children needed.

Marjorie could almost picture the lady in her mind now. She would be bold, vivacious and charming. She would stand up to the doctor when she needed to, and be an excellent mother to the children. Hopefully she was pretty and would look nice standing next to the handsome Dr. Orton—but that was a secondary concern for Marjorie.

As soon as she had a moment, she would make a list of all the attributes Dr. Orton's second wife should possess—and the first item on her list would be whimsical. He didn't need a practical woman. Practical women forced their daughters into practical marriages and didn't leave room for things like love and romance. He needed someone who would be his opposite, to balance his personality.

Clearly Dr. Orton needed help with this important endeavor, and Marjorie was in a position to help him.

"Don't worry, Lilly." Marjorie stood and lifted the muslin gown in her hands once again. She walked to the wardrobe and hung the dress inside. "I have a feeling your father will be around the house much more now that I'm here." She would make sure of it…somehow.

"Really?"

"Why don't you run along and play? I have some work to do this afternoon."

Lilly stood obediently and crossed the room to the door. "I like you, Miss Maren."

Marjorie paused and smiled. "I like you, too, Lilly."

A bit of Lilly's sadness seemed to disappear. She slipped out of the room and left the door open.

A new face peeked around the door and then disappeared just as quickly.

Marjorie walked across the room. "Charlie?"

After a moment, Charlie appeared in her doorway, his hands clasped behind his back and his eyes lowered to the floor. "Hello, Miss Maren."

She hadn't seen him since he took her bag. "It's nice to see you again."

He dug his toe into the plush carpet and wouldn't meet her gaze. "I brought you something."

"A gift?"

He shrugged one shoulder. "Something like that."

"I love gifts—how did you know?"

Again, he shrugged. "Most girls like gifts—at least my mama and Lilly do. Or did—my mama, I mean."

The corners of Marjorie's mouth tipped down. She couldn't imagine losing her mother as a child. What a horrible experience for these children to endure. Maybe, along with finding a new wife for Dr. Orton, God had brought Marjorie to this home to bring some life and enjoyment into these children's lives. "Have you ever been to a movie theater?"

That got his attention. Charlie looked up. "No."

"Would you like to go? Maybe to a matinee?" She didn't have any money to bring them, but surely Dr. Orton would give her an allowance to spend on the children's activities.

Charlie's eyes lit with excitement. "Could we?"

Marjorie nodded. "I'll even ask your father to come."

The excitement disappeared from his gaze. "He won't take the time to come. Especially now that you're here to take care of us, and he's so busy with all the influenza patients."

Marjorie nibbled on her bottom lip. There had to be a way to get Dr. Orton to have some fun with his children. "You leave your father to me." She offered him a smile. "Didn't you have a gift to give me?"

The tops of Charlie's ears turned red and he brought his right hand out from behind his back. Nestled inside his palm was a dried rosebud. "My mama has a rose garden behind the house. This was from the last bush that bloomed this past summer—before she was sick. Mama and I picked the roses, and she showed me how to hang them upside down to let them dry."

Charlie extended his hand, and Marjorie gently took the rosebud.

"Charlie—" Her voice caught. "This is a beautiful gift. But are you sure you want me to have it?"

Charlie nodded. "I have others. I just thought—" He let out a breath and put his hands in his pockets. "I thought, since you didn't know my mama, you might like to have something she loved here in the house with you."

Marjorie swallowed another lump of emotion. "Thank you. I will keep this on my bureau so I can look at it often. But this isn't the only thing in the house that she loved. You, Lilly, Petey, Laura and your papa are all examples of things she loved dearly."

Charlie lifted his gaze and his expression softened. Without a word, he turned and left Marjorie alone.

She stood in her doorway for a moment and fingered the delicate rosebud. It might have been plucked from life too early, but its beauty would live on—just as Anna Orton would do in her family.

Chapter Three

John sat in his home office and pulled a fresh sheet of paper out of his desk drawer. Now that he had secured a governess—even a temporary one—he could turn his attention to the next order of business on his to-do list: find a wife.

He numbered the page from one to ten. Before he started his search, he would have a clear idea of what he was looking for. He was a man who liked to plan every aspect of his life and this important list would be the backbone for his quest.

John put his pen to the page and wrote in bold letters the first thing that came to his mind: *practical*.

His second wife would be practical, just as Anna had been. He pulled her portrait out of his desk and studied it, recalling all the things he loved about her. Anna's attributes would fill numerous pieces of paper.

But how many attributes could she have written about him? Wasn't the picture in his hands proof of his many flaws?

She had asked him for a family portrait after Laura was born, but he had kept putting it off, telling her he was too busy. The last picture he had of his wife, besides their wedding photo, was this one, taken just before they were married eleven years ago.

John traced the photo with his fingertip. She had looked so young and vibrant before the cares of his medical practice and motherhood had wrinkled the edges of her eyes and created a few white hairs along her temples. Oh, how she had fussed about those hairs. But they had been a reminder to him of all her hard work and the life they were creating together. Though she had aged, she had only grown more beautiful to him.

He just wished he had taken the time for a family photo. The children did not have a picture with their mother, and he did not have a final image of how she looked just before she was called to heaven.

It was a harsh reminder of how he had failed his wife. He should have been home more—especially when she was sick—but he had been out of town attending a patient when Anna died.

A knock at the office door captured his attention and he gladly put the photo back in his desk drawer. "Yes?"

"Dinner is served," Mrs. Gohl said. "The children and Miss Maren are seated."

John put aside his list for now and pushed himself up from his desk chair with a heavy sigh.

Miss Maren was not what he had planned. But it appeared he was stuck with her—at least for the next two months.

John stepped out of his office and found Mrs. Gohl waiting for him.

"Dr. McCall phoned and said they had half a dozen new cases of influenza arrive at the hospital since last night." Mrs. Gohl wrung her work-worn hands together. Though the wave of illnesses had subsided from the initial impact that had arrived at the beginning of

October—and taken Anna's life—there were still more cases reported every day. "He asked if you could go to the hospital after supper to consult with him."

It would be another long night. He would have to put off his list making until he returned home. Maybe tomorrow at church he could start the search. He really had no idea what his prospects were, since he had not considered another woman since he had laid eyes on Anna for the first time.

John nodded his thanks to Mrs. Gohl and then walked through the front hall to the dining room.

Miss Maren sat at Anna's regular spot.

John paused in the doorway, his stunned gaze riveted on her. "What are you wearing, Miss Maren?"

The governess held Laura on her lap and moved the baby aside to look down at her luxurious dress. She glanced back at John, innocence in her gaze. "It's just a simple evening gown."

The dress in question was definitely not simple. "Don't you think it's a bit too fancy for a quiet family meal?"

Lilly hid a giggle behind her hand, and Charlie opened his mouth to comment—but John silenced both of them with a look.

"It's all I have," said Miss Maren.

"You have nothing less…ostentatious?" Or attractive?

She shook her head. Laura reached for the silverware, and Miss Maren gently pulled her hand away. "This is what I wore for meals at home."

He cleared his throat, trying to avert his eyes from the beautiful woman seated at his table. "Meals in this home are much less formal." He took his seat and Petey jumped off his chair and ran around the table. John lifted the boy into his arms while he addressed Miss Maren. "I must ask you to put on something more… suitable."

Miss Maren's free hand slipped up to her neck and hovered over the exposed skin. "I only have one other evening gown—and it's not much different."

"She's right," Lilly said. "I saw her dresses."

He ran his finger around his collar, suddenly feeling a bit awkward having this conversation. He tried not to stare as he lifted his hand and indicated her dress. "Surely you have something else you could wear."

"I suppose I could put on one of my morning gowns—but it's hardly the thing to wear for sup—"

"Does it show so much skin?" His voice sounded much gruffer than he intended.

She had the decency to blush.

Miss Ernst entered the dining room with a steaming tureen of tomato soup and must have sensed the tension in the room. Her green eyes darted to Miss Maren and then back to John. Red hair stuck out in disarray behind her white maid's cap, and a spot of soup stained her apron.

"It will take me a moment to change," said Miss Maren.

"We'll wait."

Miss Ernst set the soup on the sideboard just as Miss Maren stood and handed the baby to her.

Miss Maren exited the room and John couldn't help watching her leave.

No one said a word until she returned ten minutes later in a modest gown—though this one was made of a gauzy material, and just as impractical as the first. She took Laura from the maid's hands and sat quietly in her seat.

John said grace and then Miss Ernst ladled the soup into everyone's bowls. The savory scent spiraled into the air making John's stomach growl.

They ate in silence for a few moments, and then Miss Maren spoke. "Lilly has been a great help today with Petey and Laura."

John looked at his eight-year-old daughter, always the mother of the group, especially since Anna had died. "Thank you, Lilly. Did you show her how to make Laura's bottles as I instructed with the infant formula?"

"Yes, Papa."

"Good." John smiled approval at his daughter. "But I expect Miss Maren to do the work from here on out."

Lilly nodded.

John handed Petey a dinner roll and then dipped his spoon into his soup.

Miss Maren spoke again. "I'd like to have a party."

John's spoon fell into his soup, splashing the white tablecloth with the red liquid. "A what?"

Miss Maren lifted her spoon to her lips and sipped on her soup. When she was done she offered him a dimpled smile. "A tea party."

"Why?"

"I'd like to see the prospects."

Charlie and Lilly looked between John and Miss Maren, their interested gazes never dropping.

John frowned at the strange woman. "What prospects?"

Miss Maren opened her mouth and then closed it again, as if she wasn't sure what to say. Finally she pulled Laura's hand away from the silverware again and spoke. "I'd like to make some friends. I thought I would host a tea party to do so."

The older children swiveled their gazes to John.

"I don't have much experience with governesses," John said. "But I've never heard of one hosting a tea party."

Miss Maren lifted her free hand with an air of nonchalance. "There's always a first for everything."

"I didn't employ a socialite. I employed a governess. Your first priority is not to entertain—but to take care of my children."

"I would never neglect my duties, if that's what you mean. I will host the party on my day off—I do get a day off, don't I?"

"Of course. Sundays."

"Then I will plan the party for next Sunday. May I use the parlor?"

Petey squirmed in John's lap, and John put his hand on his son's knee to steady him. "I still haven't decided if you should have the party."

The children looked at Miss Maren.

"It would be an educational opportunity for Lilly," the governess said. "What better way to teach her social graces? You do want her to learn how to be a hostess someday, don't you?"

"Of course—"

"Then it's settled." Miss Maren sipped her soup once again.

He hadn't given permission—but one look at Lilly's face, and he knew his daughter loved the idea. How could he say no? "Fine."

"Who will you invite?" Lilly asked.

Miss Maren dabbed at her mouth with a napkin. "Anyone I think who would make a good match for…" She paused.

Lilly waited for a moment and then asked, "A good match for what?"

Again, Miss Maren looked unsure if she should say something, and John was growing weary of this conversation. "You and Lilly may discuss your plans away from the dinner table."

Miss Maren's green eyes sparkled in triumph—until Laura grabbed her spoon and splattered red soup down the front of Miss Maren's delicate gown.

Maybe now she would understand why practical clothing was needed in his home.

John waited until Miss Ernst helped clean up the mess, and then he spoke again. "After supper I'm going to the hospital. I probably won't return until it's time to bring the children to church in the morning. See that they are put to bed by seven thirty. If you have any trouble, ask Mrs. Gohl or Miss Ernst for assistance."

Miss Maren took Laura's hand off her buttered bread, a sigh on her lips. "I'll do my very best."

He hoped her very best was good enough.

Marjorie's head dropped toward her chest—but she snapped it up and blinked her burning eyes several times to stay awake. She needed to use this time as she listened to the sermon to study the ladies in the congregation. Maybe one or two might be suitable for Dr. Orton.

Her eyes started to droop again, but she fought the exhaustion and lifted her head.

Out of the corner of her eye, she saw Dr. Orton glance at her—but if it was with sympathy or disapproval, she couldn't tell.

She sat between Lilly and Charlie on the family pew, with Laura asleep in her lap. Dr. Orton sat beside Lilly, with Petey on his lap.

Though Marjorie tried, she could not keep her eyes

open. Laura had woken up at least half a dozen times through the long night, demanding Marjorie's attention. Marjorie's only consolation had been the knowledge that Dr. Orton was at the hospital and could not hear his daughter fussing. Surely he would have been angry that she didn't know how to quiet the baby.

Now Laura slept peacefully—and Marjorie wished she could join her.

The pastor droned on and on…

Lilly poked Marjorie in the rib and whispered, "You fell asleep."

Marjorie's cheeks flamed with heat. What would Dr. Orton think of her, falling asleep in church when she should be listening to the reverend?

She readjusted her position, trying not to disturb Laura. Her neck and back ached, but she dared not try to rub out the knots.

The sermon finally ended and they rose for the closing song.

Marjorie stole a look around the crowded church. Colorful stained-glass windows allowed a muted light to fall on the congregation, and she was happy to see so many young women in attendance. Surely someone in this room would make a good wife for her employer.

Dr. Orton's gaze lingered over the congregation, as well. Was he also surveying his prospects? He had an advantage over Marjorie, since he already knew which of these ladies were single.

The final song ended, and the family moved out of the pew. Marjorie turned just in time to see Mrs. Scott marching up the aisle, pushing aside anyone who stood in her way.

Marjorie couldn't hide her groan.

Mrs. Scott pointed her finger at Marjorie. "What kind of example are you? Falling asleep in church."

"Laura was awake all night—"

"Excuses, excuses—"

"Laura is teething," Dr. Orton said in Marjorie's defense as he stepped out of the pew with Petey in his arms. "And Miss Maren was put to work immediately after her long journey. I imagine she's exhausted."

Marjorie blinked up at him in surprise. He wasn't angry at her lack of propriety during the service?

Mrs. Scott appeared to ignore Dr. Orton as she turned to the young woman walking up the aisle behind her in a black mourning gown. "Dora, what is taking you so long?"

The young lady looked exactly like the picture Marjorie had seen of Anna Orton, although Miss Dora Scott was probably ten years younger than Anna.

"Hello, John," Dora said with a gentle smile. She put her gloved hand under Lilly's chin, her cheeks filled with a healthy glow. "Hello, dear."

Lilly wrapped her arms around her aunt's waist, and Petey reached for her from Dr. Orton's arms.

Dora took the little boy and snuggled him close.

"It's nice to see you, Dora." Dr. Orton smiled at his sister-in-law.

Dora turned her pretty blue eyes to Marjorie—eyes the exact shade of the children's. "And you must be the new governess, Miss Maren."

Marjorie extended her hand and Dora took it. "I'm pleased to meet you," Marjorie said.

"We're going to have a tea party." Lilly clapped her hands. "And Miss Maren has said I will help her plan the whole event."

"How nice," Dora said. "You will have such fun. I love tea parties."

"A tea party?" Mrs. Scott tsked. "How utterly ridiculous. Whoever heard of a governess hosting a tea party? What will people think, John? It would be one thing if you had a wife in the house to act as hostess—but the governess? People will think she's taking on the role of mistress of your home."

Marjorie's chest filled with embarrassment. "I have no such intentions—"

"John, think of your reputation!" Mrs. Scott said. "Even now the ladies in the church are looking at this woman with disdain." Mrs. Scott looked out the corner of her eye and lifted her nose. "I think it's disgraceful."

Marjorie's eyes grew round and she opened her mouth to protest, but Dora laid her hand on Mrs. Scott's arm.

"Mother, no one thinks such things." Dora smiled at Marjorie. "I think it's wonderful that you are teaching Lilly how to be a hostess. I, for one, would be honored to be a guest at such a fine party."

Marjorie glanced at Dr. Orton to gauge his reaction to Dora. His demeanor had softened at her arrival. He watched her with a mixture of affection and appreciation.

"Of course Lilly will invite you to her tea party," Dr. Orton said.

Lilly looked up at her aunt and grinned. "You'll be my guest of honor."

"What a wonderful privilege." Dora squeezed Lilly's shoulders. "I shall take great care with my appearance that day."

Dr. Orton took Petey from his sister-in-law's arms. "You always look beautiful."

Dora looked up at Dr. Orton, her eyes shining. "Why, thank you, John."

Marjorie glanced between them. Was he considering Dora for his next wife? It wouldn't be uncommon for him to marry his wife's sister—but Marjorie could already tell she was too much like Anna. Gentle, soft-spoken, compliant...

Mrs. Scott glared at Marjorie. Could she discern Marjorie's thoughts?

"We must be off," Dr. Orton said. "I was at the hospital all night and I need to sleep before my shift tonight."

"You're going back to work so soon?" Marjorie asked.

All eyes turned to her.

"Of course he is," Mrs. Scott said. "My late husband was at the hospital more than he was at home."

Marjorie wasn't surprised.

"With the pandemic, we're overburdened and understaffed," Dr. Orton explained. "I will be working long hours. It's one of the reasons I hired you to—"

"Don't you dare explain yourself to her." Mrs. Scott wagged her finger at Dr. Orton. "She's your employee. Dora would never question you."

The blush in Dora's cheeks turned crimson, and Dr. Orton cleared his throat. He nudged his children toward their grandmother. "Say goodbye."

Charlie, Lilly and Petey obediently kissed her wrinkled cheek, and then Dr. Orton and Dora began to walk down the aisle.

Mrs. Scott put her hand on Marjorie's arm and stopped her. "I saw the way you eyed up John and Dora." She narrowed her eyes, and her hand tightened on Marjorie's arm. "I'm warning you not to intrude on their budding romance—do you hear me? John needs a woman like Dora, and the children need her, too." She looked Marjorie up and down. "You, on the other hand, are completely unnecessary."

Marjorie clenched her jaw. No one had ever talked to her in such a manner. "I'm sorry you feel that way, Mrs. Scott."

"It's clear you're only here to secure John for yourself. I'm sure that's why his mother sent you."

Marjorie opened her mouth to deny the claim, but Mrs. Scott interrupted her.

"I'm watching you—don't think you'll get anything past me."

Laura began to stir in Marjorie's arms and she put the baby to her shoulder and bounced. Would Mrs. Scott discover the reason she had fled Chicago? There had been so many rumors flying about. Would they believe the lies? And if they did, would Dr. Orton allow her to stay, or would he put her on the next train out of town?

She swallowed the lump of apprehension growing in her throat. "Good day, Mrs. Scott."

Marjorie walked down the aisle to join the Orton family, refusing to glance over her shoulder to see if Mrs. Scott was still glaring at her.

She needed to focus on meeting the other ladies in the church. If she only had until the end of the year with the Ortons, she had a lot to accomplish.

Dora turned to Marjorie. "Since you're new to town, would you allow me to introduce you to some of my friends?"

"Oh, would you?" Marjorie couldn't hide the appreciation from her voice.

"I'd be happy to." Dora took Laura from Marjorie's arms and handed the baby to Dr. Orton. "You go ahead with the children, John. Mother and I will bring Miss Maren home later."

Dr. Orton's face was lined with fatigue, but he took the baby without complaint.

"Maybe I should go home with Dr. Orton and allow him to rest instead," Marjorie said, torn between meeting potential brides and offering the doctor a bit of a respite after a long night of work.

"Sundays are your day off," Dr. Orton reminded her. "The children and I will be fine." A yawn overtook his last word and he shook his head in embarrassment. "Pardon me."

Dora linked her arm through Marjorie's and led her away from Dr. Orton and the children before Marjorie could protest further.

Marjorie glanced behind her and met the blue eyes of all four children. She experienced a strange mixture of relief at having a few moments to herself—and sadness at being away from them.

What an odd feeling.

Chapter Four

John switched on his desk lamp and glanced out the window. Soft snowflakes fell from the gray sky and landed on the cluster of tall Norway pines just outside the hospital. Usually he didn't like the onslaught of winter, but this year was different. Hopefully the cold air would force people to stay inside, and they could keep the influenza from spreading. Just this morning they had lost another patient, this one a young man who had recently returned from France after surviving an injury on the battlefront. He had died at the hands of the flu— and on the very day world was celebrating the signing of the armistice, which had formally ended the war.

It didn't seem fair.

A knock at the door brought John's musings to an end. "Come in."

Nurse Hendricks opened the door. Bags hung beneath her light brown eyes, and her round face looked pale against her white cap. Though she had not contracted the flu, the constant demands on her time and energy had done damage to her health. "Your last patient has arrived. Shall I show her in?"

"Yes, please."

Nurse Hendricks nodded and then slipped out of the room, quietly closing the door. She had been at the hospital almost around the clock serving in any capacity she was needed.

John scanned the list on his desk. He had quickly come up with ten characteristics he wanted in a wife—and he was chagrined to realize the first six were a direct result of his two days with Miss Maren.

He tapped his pencil against his oak desk and leaned over the page, squinting as he scrutinized each item.

> Practical
> Experienced with Children
> Modest
> Sensible
> Cautious
> Levelheaded
> Caring
> Wise
> Patient
> Reasonably Attractive

He flipped his pencil over and poised the eraser above the last item. Did it matter if his second wife was attractive? He did not intend to have a marriage in the traditional sense, but he was smart enough to know he would be married for a long time, and it might help if his wife was pleasing to look at.

He started to erase the last line but lowered the pencil. What would it hurt to keep it on the list? He was the only one who would see it.

The door squeaked open and John flipped the paper over. He stood from his desk just as Nurse Hendricks led Winifred Jensen and her four young children into his office.

The widow's weary face matched the anguish in John's heart. "Hello, Mrs. Jensen."

"Hello, Dr. Orton." Winnie offered John a nod, but no smile turned up her once jolly mouth. She had been a good friend to Anna, and John had been a good friend of her husband, Calvin. The two couples had spent many happy hours together picnicking along the banks of the Mississippi River and riding through the countryside in John's Model T.

He would ask how she was doing, but he detested the platitude he so often received from well-meaning friends and neighbors. It was plain Winnie was not doing well since Calvin had died of the very same disease that had taken Anna.

Instead, he smiled at the twin boys he had helped deliver just four years ago. They wore identical gray coats and stared at him with identical hazel eyes. Even their freckles, which covered their nose and cheeks, were almost identical. How Winnie could tell them apart was a mystery.

But it was the two toddlers she held on her hips that drew John's attention. Another set of identical twins had been born to Calvin and Winnie two years ago. Girls. Their cheeks were rosy and flushed with apparent fever. Was it influenza?

"Please have a seat." John indicated the wooden chair across from his desk and took the chart Nurse Hendricks held out for him. He opened the file, expecting to see the girls' names. Instead, it was Winnie's name listed there.

He glanced up at her and quickly assessed her outward appearance. She didn't look feverish, just worn

down and filled with grief. Her jet-black hair had lost
its shine and her brown eyes were lined with premature
wrinkles. According to her chart, she was just twenty-
five years old, but Calvin's death had aged her.

Nurse Hendricks took a seat just behind John, her
hands busy with rolling bandages. She always stayed
in the room with John when he saw a female patient,
even ones he considered a friend, like Winnie Jensen.

"How may I help you today?" John asked.

The two boys stood on either side of their mother,
watching John closely. Winnie set one of the girls on
her feet, but the child began to fuss. Winnie sighed and
picked her back up. She looked at John and her chin
began to quiver. "Something terrible has happened."

John laid his forearms on top of his desk and leaned
closer. "What?"

Winnie's face crumpled and she dropped her head,
great sobs shuddering through her body.

John rose, his instinct to heal coming to the fore-
front of his actions. "Nurse, could you please bring the
children to a different room while I speak with Mrs.
Jensen?"

"Of course." Nurse Hendricks rose and lifted first
one girl into her arms and then somehow managed to
take the other. "Come, boys, I will show you where the
cook keeps the cookie jar."

One of the boys willingly went with Nurse Hendricks, but the other watched his mother cry, his own
eyes filling with tears.

John took his clean handkerchief out of his pocket
and handed it to Winnie, then ushered the second boy
out of the room, closing the door softly.

He turned back to his friend. "Winnie, what's the
matter?"

He hated to see her in such distress.

She looked wretched as she bent over, her body shaking. "It's awful! I don't know what I will do."

John took his chair from behind his desk and brought it out to sit in front of her. He took her hand in his. "Are you sick? Is there something I can do for you?"

She looked up, and her brown eyes were awash in tears. "I didn't know where else to go. I have no family in town, and I have no money to travel back to Rhode Island to be with my father. I've been living on the kindness of neighbors and the church, but I don't know how much longer I can rely on them."

John rubbed the top of her hand. "Slow down and tell me what happened."

The tears began again and she put her face into the handkerchief. "I'm pregnant."

John sat up straight. "Pregnant?"

"I've been denying it for months. I suspected it when Calvin became sick—but I didn't have time to think much about it after he died—" Her sobs choked off her words.

John moved his chair so he was sitting beside her and put his arm around her shoulder. He couldn't imagine if Anna had been left to care for their four children. At least she would have had her mother and sister. Winnie was all alone.

She clutched his hand, her eyes wild with fear. "What if I have another set of twins?"

John patted her shoulder. "Don't borrow trouble, Winnie. You must take everything a day at a time. If you don't, you won't be able to bear it."

"I can't." She shook her head, a hiccup escaping her mouth. "I can't do this. It's too much."

"What are your other options?" John pulled away

from her and offered her a little space. "You must do what you're called to do."

She wiped at her cheeks and bit her trembling lip. "I'm considering something drastic."

"It's never a good idea to make a drastic decision when we're upset."

"I'm thinking about offering up—" She began to cry again.

"Shh." John tried to soothe her. "Winnie, I promise, everything will work out."

"I'm thinking about giving some of my children up for adoption."

"Adoption? You're not thinking straight."

"But how will I provide for them? I have no means of income. My only option is to marry again, but who would want to marry a bereaved woman with five or six children, all under the age of four?" She stared at him, her face splotched and swollen.

John sat up straight. If Anna was still alive, she'd insist they help Winnie, and he liked to think that Calvin would have helped Anna in the same situation. But how?

"Will you help me, John?" Winnie reached out and took his hands. "I'm desperate. I can't go through this alone."

"Is there anyone?"

"Anyone to do what?"

He lifted a shoulder. This was an uncomfortable conversation to have with a friend. If she had been a stranger, perhaps it wouldn't be so hard. He pulled his hands out of her grasp and stood. "Is there anyone who might…?"

"Marry me?" She also stood. "Who? The war, and now the influenza pandemic, has left no family untouched." She wadded up the handkerchief. "I would not dream of being so presumptuous to ask…and it embarrasses me to even admit why I came here…"

She wanted John to marry her.

He took a step back and bumped into the desk. The list he had made earlier was still facedown, waiting for his attention. Winnie fit most of the criteria on the list, if not all—but she was Anna's friend, his friend—and she had four children to care for, more on the way. She was clearly overwhelmed with her responsibilities and her grief. Could she be a stable mother for his children?

Charlie, Lilly, Petey and Laura were John's first concern. He needed a woman who would love them like Anna had.

Was it Winnie?

"Winnie—"

"Don't say no right away." She had stopped crying and was now looking at him with an intense gaze. "Please think about it, for me—for Calvin and Anna."

What was the harm in thinking about her as a prospect? Before Calvin had died, Winnie was a happy young woman who was quick to laugh and offer help where needed. Maybe, when her grief subsided, she could be the mother his children needed.

Maybe.

"Would you and the children like to come for supper this week?" It was the very least he could do for an old friend. Why hadn't he thought of it before?

Her shoulders loosened, and she let out a long breath. "Thank you. We would love to come."

"Wednesday night?"

She dabbed at her cheeks again, her hands shaking, and suddenly looked embarrassed. "I'm sorry about all this—"

He put his hands on her shoulders and looked her in the eye. "You don't need to be sorry, Winnie. We're friends. I'm happy you came to me."

She put one hand on his and offered him the faintest smile. "Thank you, John. I knew if anyone could understand, it would be you. I look forward to Wednesday."

He nodded and opened the door for her. "Me, too."

She walked down the hall toward the waiting room and looked over her shoulder one last time before he stepped back into his office.

He closed the door and stood for a moment. It wasn't enough that he was grieving his own loss, and treating dozens of patients who were dying every day, but he was also grieving the loss of friends.

He walked back to his desk and turned the sheet of paper over. Winnie might fit the criteria, but could he marry her? He would share a meal with her and get to know her better before making a final decision. If he didn't marry her, he would have to find some other way to help.

Miss Maren's smiling face suddenly appeared in his mind, and for some reason he couldn't identify, he was eager to get home and see her. Was it because he was worried she couldn't handle his four children, or was it because he longed for her cheery disposition right about now?

He surmised it was the former. Of course.

"You're sure she isn't married?" Marjorie put Laura on her other hip and leaned down to ask Lilly, "That one, over there?"

Lilly looked across the mercantile and nodded vigorously. "That's Miss Baker. She teaches Sunday school at church."

After picking the two older children up from school, Marjorie had brought them downtown to see if she could spot anyone who might make a good bride for the doctor. She and Lilly had extended half a dozen invitations to their tea party in just an hour—and they were about to extend another.

Marjorie straightened and peered around the display of ladies' handkerchiefs. The woman in question was perusing a rack of sheet music, flipping through the songs in quick order. She wore a trim black coat and a jaunty purple hat, tilted just so on her brown curls.

Miss Baker must have sensed Marjorie's gaze, because she suddenly looked her way.

Marjorie smiled and took her cue to approach. "Come, Lilly, I'd like you to introduce me."

Laura chewed on her bonnet strings, drool dripping down her chin and over the fist holding the strings, while Lilly walked beside Marjorie, her navy blue sailor coat and hat complementing her pretty blue eyes. Charlie had Petey in the corner of the store looking at a display of toy airplanes.

"Hello, Miss Baker," Lilly said as they approached.

Miss Baker offered Lilly a smile, her whole face lighting with the gesture. She put her hand on Lilly's shoulder. "Hello, Lilly. Have you heard the war is over?"

Lilly nodded, a grin on her face, and looked up at Marjorie. "This is Miss Maren, my new governess."

Marjorie extended her hand. "It's nice to meet you, I'm Marjorie Maren."

Miss Baker shook Marjorie's hand. "It's a pleasure to meet you. I saw you in church on Sunday." She laughed, and the sound made Marjorie warm to the young lady. "I saw you nodding off and I was jealous! Once, I came home with a black-and-blue mark from where my mother pinched me when I fell asleep in church, and I've never done it again."

"I think Papa would have pinched Miss Maren, too, if he was close enough." Lilly joined in the laughter.

Marjorie wasn't inclined to laugh with them, though she offered a complimentary smile. She still hadn't slept well since coming to the Ortons' and was barely standing upright at the moment. This was their last stop before going home and she wanted to be done with the chore. "We're going to have a tea party this Sunday after church and would like for you to join us."

Miss Baker clasped her hands. "Oh, that sounds lovely. I've always wanted to see inside Dr. Orton's home." She leaned closer to Marjorie and put up her hand to shield Lilly from her next words. "I feel so terrible about his wife. It must be awfully sad there. What I wouldn't give to bring a little joy into their lives right about now."

Marjorie glanced at Lilly and found the girl quietly watching them, though she didn't ask Marjorie what was said.

"I do hope you can come to the party," Marjorie said to Miss Baker. "Three o'clock."

Miss Baker nodded and pinched Laura's cheek. "I'll be there."

"Good. Now we must be off." Marjorie shifted Laura into her other arm, surprised at how tired her arms felt from holding the little girl. "Come, Lilly."

"It was nice meeting you, Miss Maren," Miss Baker called out in a singsong voice.

"And you, too." Marjorie walked over to the boys and tapped Charlie on the shoulder. "It's time to leave."

Charlie stood straight, but Petey didn't look at Marjorie. He continued to fly the plane, making a motor sound with his lips.

"Petey, it's time to leave," Marjorie said. "Please put the airplane down."

He lifted the plane high in the air and then dipped it low, acting as if he didn't hear her.

Charlie and Lilly both watched Marjorie.

She would not be with this family long, but she owed it to Dr. Orton, and his future wife, to discipline the child. But how did you get a child to listen and obey?

Marjorie squatted down to be eye level with the little boy and tapped him on the shoulder.

He turned to look at Marjorie, his airplane coming in for a landing.

"Do you like airplanes?"

Petey nodded.

"Have you ever seen a real one? In the air?"

He shook his head.

"I have, when I lived in Chicago. It was flown by a pilot named Glenn Curtiss. I even went up in the airplane for a ride with him."

Petey's eyes grew wide. "Really?"

Marjorie nodded. "I'll tell you all about it tonight when I put you to bed, all right? But now it's time to go home, so you need to put the airplane back on the shelf for the next little boy who wants to look at it."

Petey hesitated for a moment and Marjorie sent up a quick prayer, hoping he would obey, because she had no other ideas.

He placed the tin airplane on the shelf and then stood.

Marjorie sighed with relief and pulled herself up, not an easy task with Laura in her arms. She led the little group out of the mercantile, the bell over the door jingling as they walked through.

A festive air filled the streets. The signing of the armistice in France was a boost for the community's morale.

"Didn't you need to buy something in there?" Lilly asked.

Marjorie readjusted the bonnet on Laura's head to protect her from the cold air. "Not today."

"But you didn't buy anything at the millinery, the cobbler's, the dress shop or the mercantile."

"I'm just looking over the selection before I make a final choice." Marjorie smiled, tickled that she had told the truth, if somewhat evasively.

Large snowflakes fell gently from the sky, like little feathers from heaven. They landed on their hats and shoulders, and the three older children opened their mouths to try to catch them on their tongues.

The children must have sensed the lighter mood about town. They laughed as they ran around chasing the flakes, their feet leaving prints in the fresh snow gathered on the sidewalk. Tall storefronts stood on either side of Main Street, and green streetlamps dotted the idyllic downtown. More than one person stopped to watch the children, though not everyone smiled along with Marjorie. Some of the older women looked downright mortified by the children's behavior.

Marjorie considered stopping them—but she remembered the joys and wonders of childhood, and didn't think it would hurt to let them revel in a carefree moment.

"Are those Dr. Orton's children?" One lady stopped by Marjorie's side and squinted at the trio. "No…they couldn't be."

Marjorie didn't know if she should bother to answer,

but when the woman turned her beady glare on Marjorie, she didn't have a choice. "Yes, they are."

The older woman put her hand over her bosom. "Haven't you heard the old adage children should be seen and not heard?"

It was one of Marjorie's least favorite sayings— something her parents had said to her all the time while growing up. "I have."

"Well?" The lady lifted her eyebrows. "Why can I hear them?"

Charlie and Lilly stopped, but Petey continued to dance in circles, his face tilted to the sky, laughing and blinking as snowflakes landed on his eyelashes and cheeks.

"You can hear them because they're having fun." Marjorie lifted her own face to the sky and opened her mouth. A frosty snowflake landed on her tongue and promptly melted. She looked back at the matron and grinned. "You should try it some time."

The lady stared at Marjorie as if she had grown three heads, but she didn't say a word.

"Come, children." Marjorie extended her hand to Petey. "Supper will be ready soon and your father should be coming home."

Petey stopped twirling and stared at Marjorie's proffered hand, and then he looked up into her face. His soulful eyes studied Marjorie, and he must have found her lacking, because he slipped his hand inside Lilly's and hid his face against his sister's sleeve.

Marjorie stood up straighter and started walking home. She couldn't force Petey to like her…but she wouldn't give up trying.

"Papa's not going to like that," Charlie said as he glanced at Marjorie.

"What?"

The boy pointed over his shoulder. "That was Mrs. Kingston."

"It's not polite to point, Charlie—and who is Mrs. Kingston?"

"The mayor's wife."

Marjorie quickly glanced over her shoulder. The lady still stood next to the mercantile, her perturbed gaze following Marjorie's retreat.

"He'll probably hear about this before we get home." Charlie sighed and offered Marjorie a shake of his head. "Papa doesn't like to be talked about, especially by Mrs. Kingston, because she tells everyone everything."

"I heard Mama say that if Mrs. Kingston didn't like you, then no one would like you," Lilly added.

Marjorie frowned. "Really?"

"Really." Lilly's mouth turned down at the corners. "No one will come to our tea party now."

"Because of her?" Marjorie pointed over her shoulder—recalling what she had said to Charlie just a moment ago—and then promptly put her hand by her side. How was she to ever teach these children proper manners when she didn't display them herself? "I don't think we have anything to worry about. She's only one person."

Lilly and Charlie shared a glance. "But she knows everyone in town," Charlie said.

Marjorie was beginning to realize she didn't know the first thing about small-town life.

Chapter Five

John stalled the engine of his Model T and opened his door, grabbing his medical bag as he exited the vehicle. He kept his gaze on his home as he strode up the field-stone path, through Anna's dormant rose garden and onto the back stoop.

No doubt Miss Maren would have the children seated at the dining table, awaiting his arrival. He had told her he would be home at six o'clock, and it was now ten minutes past the hour.

His discussion with her would have to wait until after supper ended. The dining room, with four children listening, would not be the best place.

He stomped the snow and mud off his shoes and pushed open the heavy oak door, shaking snowflakes from his hat and coat as he passed into the back hall.

The aroma of pot roast and simmering root vegetables greeted him upon arrival. He paused for a moment to inhale a whiff of the delicious scents. If his nose didn't deceive him, there would also be spiced cake for dessert. His favorite.

John set his medical bag on the back hall table and then paused. A strange sound filled his ears. It was a combination of thumping and grinding, followed by… laughter. Children's laughter—and Miss Maren's.

He took off his overcoat and set it on the hook next to his fedora.

"I won," called Lilly.

"You didn't beat me," Charlie said. "I won, just like last time."

Lilly's joyful laughter seeped through the door. "You're a sore loser, Charlie. Don't you like to be beat by a girl?"

"Let's go again."

How long had it been since he'd heard his children sound so carefree? He paused, reveling in the moment, and yet—it didn't quite seem right to be so happy with Anna gone.

"All right, children," Miss Maren said. "On your mark, get set…go!"

The same thumping resumed, this time coming closer to the back hall, and then moving farther away.

What in the world?

John opened the door and stopped short.

Miss Maren stood near the front door in a filmy pink gown, her blond curls piled high on her head. Her cheeks were rosy red and her green eyes shone.

She saw him standing in the doorway and grinned, the ever-present dimples gracing him with their appearance. "Hello, Dr. Orton."

Lilly and Charlie halted on their trek down the front hall in their roller skates and sheepishly turned to look his way.

"Hello, Papa," Lilly said with a squeak.

Mrs. Gohl stood just inside the dining room, a smile on her face. The moment John looked at her, the smile dropped and she scurried off to the kitchen.

"Miss Maren—" He couldn't find the right words to convey his astonishment. What had she been thinking? The children had a nursery filled with toys—why were they scuffing up the front hall with their roller skates?

"They should sleep well tonight," Miss Maren said, a triumphant look on her face. She cocked a wry eyebrow. "I wish I could say the same for Laura."

"What is the meaning of this?" John finally demanded. "Why are my children riding roller skates in the house?"

Miss Maren looked toward the window and waved her hand. "Because it's snowing outside."

"I know it's snowing outside—but what does that have to do with my children roller-skating *inside*?"

"Surely you wouldn't want them roller skating outside right now, would you?"

He crossed his arms. "I don't see why they need to roller-skate at all."

Her expression became perplexed. "Because they're required to spend an hour in physical activity every day, and they chose roller-skating."

Charlie and Lilly hadn't moved a muscle as they stared at John, and he recalled his earlier decision about reprimanding Miss Maren in private. "Children, take off your roller skates and prepare for supper."

"Are we in trouble?" Charlie asked.

They knew better, even if Miss Maren did not. "Yes—"

"No," said Miss Maren.

Lilly and Charlie looked at one another, their own confusion evident in their tilted eyebrows. Anna had never contradicted John in front of the children.

Never.

John looked at the governess, his voice as even as he could manage. "Please join me in my office."

Miss Maren still looked a bit bewildered, but she nodded her assent and followed him across the hall and into his domain.

When they were both inside, he closed the door. "Have a seat."

She clasped her hands in front of her gown and sat in the chair he indicated. Her dress was covered in lace and looked as out of place in his home as the lady who wore it. Anna had only dressed in such a fashion on rare occasions when they went out in the evening. Why Miss Maren dressed this way was a riddle to John—but he wished she would stop. It was far too difficult not to notice how attractive she was when she looked like this.

"Have I done something wrong?" she asked, her eyes beseeching him.

He took a seat at his desk. "Maybe the question I should ask is if you've done something right today—" The moment the words left his mouth, he wished he could retrieve them. "I apologize. That was unnecessary."

Miss Maren's innocent expression fell and her face was filled with pain. "What have I done?"

He hated to see the pain he had caused her—but he needed to address his concerns. "I have three grievances I'd like to discuss with you."

"Three?"

"I had an interesting phone call from Mrs. Kingston this afternoon."

Miss Maren's mouth opened in surprise. "Did she really call you? I didn't believe Charlie and Lilly when they told me she would." She put her hand up to cover a giggle. "Doesn't the woman have anything better to do?"

John wasn't laughing.

She sat up straighter and her giggle disappeared.

"She said my children were running about the streets, acting like hooligans."

Miss Maren's brow jumped. "Hooligans? They weren't causing any problems. They were just catching snowflakes on their tongues."

"Mrs. Kingston said when she approached you to deal with them, you mocked her."

"Mocked—?" She looked stunned.

John had never met a woman with such vivid expressions.

"I didn't mock her, I simply told her the children were having fun catching snowflakes and she should try it sometime."

John wanted to groan. "Mrs. Kingston is a very important member of Little Falls society, and when she's displeased with you, everyone is displeased with you. If she had a mind to, she could easily destroy my medical practice with a few flicks of her tongue."

"That's ridiculous."

It was, but John wasn't in a place to change the intricate societal web Mrs. Kingston had spun. "If you are still planning to have the tea party with Lilly on Sunday, I'd advise you to make a call on Mrs. Kingston in the morning and apologize for any misunderstanding."

"Me?" She pointed at her chest. "Apologize?"

"I will not have Lilly's heart broken when no one comes to your party."

"Would people really snub me because of Mrs. Kingston's opinion?"

John leaned forward, wanting to make himself clear. "Yes. Don't you have women like her in Chicago?"

Miss Maren's heavy expression filled with more

pain. "Of course we do." She sat for a moment, as if contemplating her options.

"There's nothing to think about," John said. "Either you apologize to Mrs. Kingston, or your plans for the party will be ruined—and Lilly will be devastated. I cannot allow that to happen."

"I would never want to hurt Lilly."

"Then you'll go?"

She nodded, her face sincere. "Right after I drop Lilly and Charlie off at school."

"Good—now for the other items we need to discuss."

She sighed. "What other transgressions have I committed that I'm unaware of?"

"Mrs. Kingston—"

She unclasped her hands. "Mrs. Kingston, again—?"

"Mrs. Kingston," he said slowly, "told me you had come out of the mercantile."

"And?"

"What were you doing in the mercantile? Or downtown for that matter?"

She closed her mouth and didn't answer, studying him as if to gauge his response to an unspoken confession.

"Miss Maren?"

"Where's the harm in going downtown?"

"That's not an answer."

"But it's a legitimate question. Isn't it my job to exercise the children and expose them to things outside this home?"

John stood suddenly. "That's the problem." He walked over to the mantel and looked at the portrait he had set there the previous night. Anna's picture reminded him of the dangers just outside their door. "I don't want them exposed to anything. We still have a disease running rampant through the state. I had considered bringing a tutor into the home to teach the children, and keep them out of school, but they've already been through so much that I didn't want to upend their entire lives." He turned and looked at her. "I don't want them unnecessarily exposed to the general public."

"But they're taking their cinnamon oil—and aren't they exposed at church and—"

"Those places are necessary. The mercantile is not." He walked closer to her and sat on the edge of his desk, his hands on either side of him. "Now tell me why you were there."

She hesitated.

"Miss Maren, I am losing patience."

"I was inviting ladies to the tea party."

He frowned. What was her fascination with this tea party? Was she really that desperate for friends, even though she would be leaving soon? "For now, I do not want my children taken out in public, unless absolutely necessary."

She nodded and folded her hands in her lap once again. "And the third grievance?"

"Isn't it obvious?"

She shrugged in her nonchalant sort of way. "Apparently not."

"My children are not allowed to ride their roller skates inside the house." She opened her mouth—but he put up his hand. "Never."

She let out a long sigh. "Very well. Is that all?"

"For now."

He had a sneaky suspicion this would not be the end of his grievances toward her.

* * *

A soft floor lamp glowed in the corner of Marjorie's bedroom as she sat at the secretary and looked over the list of ladies she had invited to the tea party on Sunday. She yawned as she absentmindedly ran a brush through her blond curls and reviewed each name, studying the notes she had written beside them.

So far, Miss Baker and Miss Addams, the owner of the millinery, were the forerunners in Marjorie's mind—but she'd had so little time to get to know either one that it was hard to tell. If everyone came to tea, there would be fifteen ladies to choose from. She intended to use the party as a place to weed out the undesirable prospects.

But, for now, her bed beckoned. She stopped brushing her hair and offered up a simple prayer. "Please, Lord. Let Laura sleep through the night."

A gentle knock sounded at her door.

She tossed her curls over her shoulder and set the brush down on the desk. Her wrapper was draped over the footboard, so she picked it up and slipped it on. No doubt one of the children needed something, though all four of them had been in bed for an hour. Hopefully Petey hadn't had another nightmare.

Marjorie opened her door and then abruptly closed it again.

"Miss Maren?" Dr. Orton stood in the hallway, probably bewildered by her abrupt greeting—or lack of one.

She touched her hair and closed her robe. Why had he come to her room? Since she had arrived, he had not even walked past her room. Marjorie opened the door once again—just a crack. "Yes?"

He stood in the dark hall, holding a children's book in his hands, his tired face outlined in the shadows. He studied her for a moment and then looked down at the book, swallowing a few times before he spoke. "I'm sorry to bother you, but I just got called into the hospital and I will be leaving for the night."

She opened the door a little wider, concern softening her voice. "But you've only been home for three hours. When will you get some rest?"

He ran his hand through his hair and sighed. He lifted his brown eyes and shrugged. "Hopefully in the morning, though I might catch a few minutes of sleep on a cot in my office tonight, if I get a chance."

"But aren't you at a higher risk of getting sick if your body is exhausted?"

The weary lines of his face disappeared and he offered her a tender smile.

The gesture took Marjorie by surprise and made her close the door just a hair more.

"That's usually what I tell my patients, but I'm not known for taking my own advice." He lifted the book and extended it toward her. It was a copy of *Peter Pan and Wendy*. "I was just reading this to Petey. He came into my office crying after another bad dream. I read to him until he fell asleep and then I put him in my bed." He lifted the book higher and nodded to her to take it. "In case he wakes up again."

Marjorie took the book from Dr. Orton and hugged it to her chest. "Will you be home in the morning before the children go to school?"

He slipped his hands in his pockets and shook his head. His eyes followed the outline of her face and he cleared his throat. "I don't think so. Dr. McCall lost two patients this evening and needs to go home and rest, so I'll be there until he can relieve me. I told him to take all the time he needs." He took a step back. "Good night,

Miss Maren." He paused and offered her another smile.
"Thank you—and be sure to give the children their cinnamon oil in the morning."

Marjorie closed her bedroom door and leaned against
it for a moment, the book still warm from his touch. It
was a few heartbeats before she heard him walk away
from her door.

The man was a study in extremes. He could be hard
and demanding—yet gentle and kind. He disciplined
his children with a rigid set of ideals, yet they ran to
him for comfort and acceptance.

For the first time, she genuinely liked him.

Another yawn overtook her, and her eyes watered
from its force. She dragged her feet across the room and
switched off the floor lamp. She would think about the
good doctor in the morning when she had control over
her thoughts and emotions.

She slipped *Peter Pan* onto her nightstand and took
off her wrapper. She kicked her slippers off and pulled
back the covers. With a sigh, she climbed between the
sheets and allowed every muscle in her body to relax
as she sank deep into the mattress.

Her eyelids fluttered closed as a soft smile tilted her
lips. Bed had never felt better in her life.

Laura's whimper drifted into Marjorie's bedroom.

Marjorie's eyes opened. "Please, no," she whispered
into the dark room.

She held her breath as the baby quieted. The ticking
of the hall clock was the only sound.

Marjorie let out the breath and closed her eyes
again—but this time Laura's unmistakable cries filled
the night.

Marjorie flipped onto her stomach and pulled the pillow over her head. "No," she fairly cried. Why couldn't the baby sleep for longer than two hours at a time?

Laura's cries grew in intensity and Marjorie finally pushed the covers back and practically fell out of the warm bed. Her slippers were somewhere in the abyss of darkness, and her wrapper had fallen off the end of the bed and was probably pooled on the floor.

She flipped on the light, frustration making her movements quick and awkward. If she didn't quiet Laura, Lilly would soon be awake, followed by Petey, and then she'd be up much longer reading to the little boy to put him back to sleep.

Marjorie quickly located her slippers and tossed her wrapper on as she exited her room and tiptoed into the nursery. Lilly's bed was against the far wall, where a swatch of moonlight filtered into the room in an elongated rectangle from the window. The girl was still asleep.

Laura's cries grew louder and Marjorie's own eyes filled with tears. She just wanted to sleep.

Marjorie arrived at the cradle and peeked over the edge. Laura's face was scrunched up and she was wailing at the top of her lungs.

"Shh," Marjorie whispered, jostling the cradle.

Laura immediately quieted and her eyes opened. She looked at Marjorie and a sweet smile lifted her chubby cheeks, a coo bubbling from her mouth.

Marjorie's shoulders relaxed and her tension melted away. She put her hand over Laura's chest and felt her heart beating a steady rhythm.

So this was what unconditional love felt like.

"You silly baby. You're just lonely."

Laura gurgled and grinned.

Marjorie's eyelids felt heavy and her mind was

foggy, but she smiled back at the little creature inside the cradle. Affection replaced the irritation, and Marjorie reached in and lifted the baby into her arms. She put Laura up to her shoulder and began to sway, patting her on the back as she hummed a lullaby her governess had sung to her as a child.

Pain filled Marjorie's chest as she thought of her childhood, and her parents, and all the disappointment Marjorie had caused them before she left Chicago.

Would her parents ever forgive her for rejecting Preston? If their initial response was any indication, the answer was no.

Laura's downy head fit perfectly into the crook between Marjorie's neck and shoulder, and she nuzzled in. Marjorie laid her cheek against Laura's hair. She wouldn't think about her parents or Preston right now. Instead, she would enjoy the sweet innocence and acceptance from the little girl in her arms.

In just three days, Marjorie had somehow fallen in love with these children. Though it was the hardest work she had ever done in her life, and she was exhausted beyond all reason, she had never felt so accomplished.

Her father's words visited her again. *You're a quitter, Marjorie, and you'll never change.*

Would she quit on the Orton family? It seemed everything in her life had eventually become too difficult to deal with, and it was easier to just walk away.

But this time it felt different. This time, the idea of leaving these precious children and their grieving father didn't hold any appeal…at least not until she helped Dr. Orton find a wife.

Chapter Six

Marjorie stood outside the impressive home of Mayor and Mrs. Kingston, Laura on her right hip and Petey standing to her left. The little boy still refused to hold her hand, but at least he came with her willingly. He wore a wool cap on his sandy-blond hair and a thick wool peacoat hugged his body. In his hand was a toy airplane with a gray fuselage and red wings that Marjorie had just bought for him at the mercantile. Despite Dr. Orton's warning, she had taken the two children back to the store—but this was a necessary trip, and under his specific instructions, she was allowed to bring the children into public for necessary purposes.

The way Petey's face had lit up when she handed him the toy was crucial for the health and well-being of their relationship, even though it did eat into the modest allowance Dr. Orton had given her for the children's expenses. And in a way, it felt like a bribe.

"Now, you'll be on your best behavior?" Marjorie asked Petey.

He pulled the airplane to his chest and looked at Marjorie without smiling.

It was the only answer he would give—though she didn't know what it meant.

Marjorie took a deep breath and knocked on the Kingstons' front door. Their ornate Queen Anne Victorian boasted a large wraparound porch, deep bay windows and extravagant trimmings.

Oh, if only this chore was finished! Marjorie hated to grovel, and she detested women who wielded their power in such a shameless manner. Marjorie had been the victim of many society ladies when she jilted Preston, and she had wanted to be done with them forever. That was yet another reason she was going to California.

But she also hated the idea of Lilly, and ultimately Dr. Orton, suffering. How would Marjorie find a new wife for the doctor if no one came to her party?

The front door was opened by a maid in a black-and-white uniform. "May I help you?"

Marjorie took a deep breath. She wanted to be an actress, didn't she? Well this would be a perfect time to practice. She could pretend to be contrite, and even boost the woman's ego, if need be. Anything to get into her good graces.

Marjorie extended her calling card toward the maid. "I'm here to see Mrs. Kingston."

The maid clasped her hands in front of her apron without touching the card. "I'm sorry, but Mrs. Kingston only receives visitors on Friday mornings from ten o'clock until noon."

Friday morning? But the damage would be done by Friday morning.

Laura grabbed at Marjorie's nose and Marjorie had to push her hand aside. "But I must see her today. It's a matter of great urgency."

The maid was small and pale, her eyes too large for her delicate face. "I'm sorry."

"Is the good lady home?" Marjorie asked.

The maid hesitated. "Yes, she is, but—"

Marjorie let out a relieved breath and lifted the card toward the maid once again. "Good. Please tell her Miss Marjorie Maren is here to call."

"But—"

"Tell her I am the Ortons' governess. I think she'll want to see me." Marjorie swallowed hard before she uttered the next words. "Tell her I've come to apologize for my rude behavior."

The maid looked over Marjorie and the children shivering in the cold. She finally took the card. "Won't you step into the foyer? I'll see if Mrs. Kingston will receive you."

"Thank you."

Marjorie led the children inside and was duly impressed with the interior. A wide oak stairway ascended to their left, and a little alcove sat just in front of it with a built-in bench. Two generous archways displayed a lavish front parlor and a richly appointed dining room.

"You may have a seat." The maid indicated the bench and then looked at Marjorie's card before disappearing up the stairway.

Petey toyed with his airplane while Laura grabbed at Marjorie's bonnet. She managed to remove a silk flower and Marjorie allowed her to gum it. At least the baby was occupied.

It felt as if an hour passed, but the hall clock claimed it was only twenty minutes before Mrs. Kingston descended the stairs in a beautiful morning gown. She took her time, placing one slippered foot in front of the other, gliding her hand along the banister in what appeared to be a deliberate act of disdain.

Marjorie wanted to roll her eyes, but instead she stood and took a deep breath, pasting a smile on her face.

The woman finally stopped in the foyer. "I don't receive callers on Tuesdays, but I'm making an exception, because I believe you have something very important to say to me."

"It's so good of you to see me now. I hope this isn't an inconvenient time."

"Of course it is." Mrs. Kingston looked down her thin nose at Marjorie. "It isn't Friday."

Marjorie managed to look repentant, though she didn't feel apologetic. She might as well get this over with. "I'm here to apologize for my terrible behavior yesterday."

Mrs. Kingston lifted one eyebrow. "Go on."

Marjorie had practiced this little speech all the way over from the mercantile, but perhaps she should have practiced it even longer. Suddenly, looking at the conceited face of Mrs. Kingston made her forget everything she had planned to say.

She wished she could tell her that she had been engaged to Preston Chamberlain, the heir to one of the largest railroad fortunes in the country. Maybe that would impress the mayor's wife—but what would it matter now? Marjorie refused to use Preston's name—or draw attention to the past.

"I do hope you'll accept my apology. I'm sorry I spoke to you in such a manner, and I'm sorry the children's behavior displeased you."

"Did Dr. Orton request this meeting?" Mrs. Kingston asked.

"Yes, he did."

"It wasn't your idea to come on your own?"

Marjorie swallowed once again as Laura's drool dripped from her chin and landed on Marjorie's bare wrist. "It was also my idea. As soon as I realized my mistake, I knew I needed to make amends. I do hope you won't hold any ill will toward Dr. Orton's family."

"Will you allow the children to be so disruptive in the future?"

The children hadn't been disruptive, not in the least. They were just being children. Marjorie wanted to tell Mrs. Kingston this, but she recalled Dr. Orton's words. Her tea party must be a success for Lilly and for Dr. Orton. She dipped her head, as any good actress would do in such a scene, and spoke in a remorseful voice. "Of course not."

"Very well." Mrs. Kingston lifted a handkerchief from her sleeve and dabbed at her upper lip, as if the ordeal of this conversation had caused perspiration. "I will forgive this blunder, but only because the doctor's children are grieving, and are not in their right mind." She lifted the confounded eyebrow once again. "You, however, have no excuse."

Marjorie was grieving, in her own way, being ostracized by her parents—but she would never reveal this to Mrs. Kingston. "You're right. There is no excuse for me." Marjorie hated every single word she spoke, but she had no choice. She must pander to this society matriarch for the success of her plans. "Please forgive me."

Mrs. Kingston dipped her head. "You're forgiven. But I will be watching you closely, Miss Maren. I'm aware that you have a tea party planned for Sunday afternoon, and you've invited a number of prominent women to Dr. Orton's home. Anyone who enters into the upper echelons of my society will be expected to behave properly. See that you do."

Marjorie ground her teeth and nodded. "Thank you for taking the time to meet with me." She put her hand on Petey's shoulder. "I need to get the children home for their morning nap."

Mrs. Kingston took a step back and rang a bell on top of a hall table.

The maid appeared immediately and opened the front door for Marjorie and the children.

"I have high expectations from you, Miss Maren. See that you don't act so foolishly in the future."

Marjorie turned and offered a drippy-sweet smile. "I'll endeavor to do my best. Goodbye."

She walked out of the house, her head high, with Petey beside her. She disliked when other people brought out the worst in her.

"Now that this distasteful task is done, I will turn my full attention to the tea party once again," Marjorie said to Petey, who didn't bother to acknowledge her. "There is so much to be done."

They walked the five blocks back to the Orton home in silence. Laura fell asleep on Marjorie's shoulder and Petey plodded along, inspecting every inch of his tin airplane. The sun shone bright in a cloudless sky and though it was still chilly, the streets and walkways had melted, creating mud.

"It looks like your father is home," Marjorie said to Petey when she spotted the doctor's Model T next to the carriage house. "I hope he's resting."

"Papa!" Petey raced down the sidewalk and quickly climbed up the front steps.

Marjorie picked up her pace to catch him, not wanting the boy to barge in on his father and wake him up.

"Petey," she called, but he was already stepping through the door.

Marjorie placed her hand on Laura's back to keep her upright, and then ran the last few feet across the yard. The mud beneath her feet became slippery and before she could right herself, she slid to the ground, hitting her bottom hard against the cold mud.

Laura woke, startled, and let out a whimper.

The front door opened wider and Dr. Orton appeared, Petey at his side. His concerned gaze swept over Marjorie and he strode across the front porch, down the stairs, and arrived at Marjorie in two seconds. "Are you all right?"

Her backside stung and one of her best dresses was probably ruined, but other than that, it was only her pride that hurt. Heat filled her cheeks and she couldn't meet his eyes. "I think so."

"Here, let me take Laura." He reached down and took the baby from Marjorie's arms, quickly examining the child. "She appears to be fine."

Mrs. Gohl arrived at the front door and came down and took Laura from Dr. Orton. She ushered Laura and Petey into the house, leaving Dr. Orton with Marjorie.

He extended a hand toward her, and she finally glanced up into his worried face. She would much rather he leave her to walk the path of shame on her own, but it didn't look like he was going anywhere.

She put her gloved hand into his and allowed him to tug her to her feet. Cold fabric clung to her legs, and mud dripped from her skirt. "Thank you."

"Are you sure you're all right?"

"I'm positive."

"Do you hurt?"

She couldn't lie. "A bit."

He placed his hand on the small of her back and probed her muscles. "Did you jar anything out of place?"

His gentle hand ran up the length of her spine. Though his touch was purely platonic, it sent a warm sensation through Marjorie and she abruptly stepped away from him.

"Thank you for your concern, but I'm fine. Nothing a bath and a change of clothes won't fix."

He studied her for another moment, though she couldn't discern his thoughts. "I'm happy you're here. I'm going to the hospital again and wanted to let you know I am having a dinner guest tomorrow night. She will be bringing along her four children—I hope you'll entertain them and see that they are fed."

"She?" Marjorie temporarily forgot about her muddy clothing—or the fact that he was returning to the hospital again.

Dr. Orton stood a bit straighter. "Yes, Mrs. Winifred Jensen. She is an old family friend."

Was the doctor considering her for a wife? And, if so, would she fit the criteria Marjorie had listed for him? "Yes, I can see to the children."

She would see to Mrs. Jensen, as well.

John stood in his bedroom, staring at his reflection in his floor-length mirror. Why was he taking such pains to dress for dinner tonight? He had known Winnie Jensen for years and had never once thought about his appearance in her presence.

But tonight was different. Tonight he would interview her for the position of mother to his children. The thought still made his insides twist in grief and disbelief. No doubt Winnie was feeling the same way. Neither one of them would have chosen this course. It had been thrust upon them without consultation or permission.

John had accepted Anna's death as God's will—after all, he was a physician and was familiar with loss—but it still hurt and he had moments of anger when he wanted to demand an answer—yet he couldn't bring himself to speak to God. Not yet.

He unwound his necktie and tossed it onto his bed. It wasn't quite right for this evening. He opened his drawer and lifted another one out, inhaling the scent of Anna's lavender sachet from the drawer beneath his.

Anna's touch was still present in their bedroom. John could see her in the billowy curtains at the large windows, the hand-quilted spread on the bed and the woven rugs on the floor. Her clothes still hung in the wardrobe and her reading glasses—which she despised—were on the Bible next to her side of the bed. Would his second wife demand that he box all of Anna's things up and bring them to the attic?

If the children didn't need a mother, he would never conceive of such a plan. He had considered allowing a governess to raise them—not Miss Maren, but someone with more experience. In the end, he had concluded they needed a permanent woman in their lives. And what was more permanent than marriage?

"Dr. Orton?"

John's bedroom door was ajar and he turned to find Miss Maren standing in the hall. "Yes?"

"May I have a word with you please?"

He had hoped to speak with her about the letter he had received from his mother just that morning, but now wasn't a good time. It had been filled with gossip about life in Chicago, and news about John's brother, Paul, and his new wife, Josephine. But the letter had been strangely empty about Miss Maren until the very end. Mother had simply said: "I hope you're finding Marjorie to your liking. I knew her joyful disposition would be good for you and the children at this time. Please send her my best."

He had hoped for more information about the young woman, and had specifically written to his mother to ask what she knew—but she had chosen to give nothing away. Why?

He grabbed his suit coat and slipped it on over his shirtsleeves and then stepped out of his room. The discussion about Miss Maren's past would have to wait for a more opportune time.

Miss Maren took several steps back, so she was standing closer to the stairwell than his bedroom.

He closed his door and joined her. "I'm in a bit of a hurry." Winnie would be arriving shortly and he needed to finish getting ready. "What can I do for you? Is it the children?"

Miss Maren wore another elaborate gown. This one was a soft creamy color with lace lapels and a short train. Her curls were pulled back in a loose knot and she wore a pearl headband. She looked as if she were prepared to join him for supper—yet she was going to take care of eight children this evening. How she would manage in such an outfit was something John would enjoy watching.

Actually the thought of watching her do anything was appealing.

"I would like to talk to you about Mrs. Jensen."

John pulled his thoughts off their ridiculous course and remembered that this woman was his children's governess. Their *temporary* governess. "Oh?"

She wove her fingers together and placed her hands in front of her waist. "I don't mean to be presumptuous—"

"But you will be." John repositioned his stance and crossed his arms.

She lifted her chin in a way he was coming to recognize as defiance. "I feel I've spent enough time with your family to advise you."

He leaned forward. "Oh, really?"

"I don't want you to make a mistake."

A mistake? With Winnie? "Miss Maren, you have been in my house for precisely five days. I don't believe you're in a position to advise me about a woman you've never met."

"I don't intend to advise you about Mrs. Jensen, per se. I hope to advise you about women in general."

"I was married for eleven years. I hardly need advice about the opposite sex. You, on the other hand, have never been married."

"But I'm a woman—doesn't that qualify me to give advice?"

"In this particular situation? No."

"Things have changed in eleven years, and not all women are like your first wife. I just want to make sure you know what you're doing."

He'd had enough of this conversation. "You're presuming I don't know what I'm doing, and your assumption is insulting. Winnie is a good friend and she is a good mother. I will make the best decision for me and my children, regardless of your opinion." He straightened and repositioned his coat. "You will be leaving us in less than two months, so I don't believe you have much say in what I do."

She unclasped her hands and lifted her chin even

higher. "I just hope you don't make a grave mistake. A lifetime seems even longer when you're wrong."

"Miss Maren, save your dramatic performance for the stage—"

"Screen."

"This is real life and I intend to deal with it accordingly."

"But what if you make a mistake? You and the children will be even more miserable than you are now."

"This conversation is over. Please retrieve the children and bring them to the foyer. It's almost six o'clock and Winnie is always prompt."

She exhaled a breath and then offered a brief nod. She spun on her heels and walked toward the other end of the hall and the third-floor stairway. She opened the door and the children's voices trailed down from the day nursery.

He ground his teeth and shoved his bedroom door open. Who was she to think she could give him advice about marriage? She was young and naive and didn't know the first thing about raising a family. Over the past five days, she had shown herself competent with the children—much to his surprise—but that didn't give her the license to intrude on his personal life.

John lifted the ends of his necktie and tied it tight, surprised at how Miss Maren's words had affected him. He understood, more than anyone, what he was planning to do. He would legally, and in the eyes of the church, bind himself to another woman for the rest of his life. Even after the children were grown and gone, his new wife would still be by his side.

He would not make a hasty decision.

For the first time since Anna's death, he longed to be on speaking terms with God. He needed to vent his frustrations and ask for guidance. What if he did make a mistake and they were more miserable? It was entirely possible that his good intentions could backfire.

He walked to the window and glanced out at the bleak world. His bedroom faced west and looked out at the buildings forming downtown Little Falls. The tall courthouse tower was visible over the leafless branches and the spire of St. Mary's Church reached toward the heavens just to the left. The Mississippi River cut through the cold earth, like a steel ribbon.

For some reason, John felt closer to God when he could look out his window at the sky. He swallowed his pain and spoke from a raw place in his heart. "I'm having a hard time understanding why You've allowed all this to happen, but I'm choosing to believe You at Your word. I know You have a purpose, even if I never fully understand what it is." He rubbed his face and closed his eyes. "Please help me make the right choice. Please guide me in this important decision. I want what's best for my children. Amen."

It wasn't grand or eloquent, but it was real and heartfelt. And it was a beginning.

Chapter Seven

John entered the front foyer and found Miss Maren standing at attention with Laura in her arms. Charlie, Lilly and Petey stood like little soldiers about to get their marching orders. Gone was the gentle teasing and lively conversation they had been enjoying with Miss Maren for the past few days.

John smoothed back his hair and adjusted his tie one last time. The hall clock said it was five minutes to six. Outside the windows, the sky had begun to darken, with only a hint of light in the west.

"All of you look very nice this evening," John said to his children. "I hope you'll make me proud and be on your best behavior."

Charlie looked at John with accusation. "You're not thinking of marrying Mrs. Jensen, are you?"

Lilly turned to John, the blue bow in her hair matching her startled eyes. "You're going to get married?"

John offered her a reassuring smile and put his hand on her head. "Don't worry about what I'm going to do. You're only eight, and you don't need to be concerned about grown-up things."

Lilly put her hands over John's, and pulled his fingers off her head. She grasped John's hand and held it tight. "Don't get married again. Please."

The front door suddenly opened and John's mother-in-law entered the house. She blinked several times at seeing them all standing in the foyer. "What do we have here?"

Dora walked in just behind Mother Scott, her sweet smile already in place.

"Aunt Dora!" The three older children stepped out of line and rushed to their aunt.

"Hello, children." Dora hugged each one. "Charlie, you need a haircut," she laughed as she ruffled his hair. "And, Lilly, I love the way your bow matches your eyes." She reached down and picked up Petey. "And look at you! Is that a new toy?"

Petey held up a toy airplane, a grin on his face. "I can fly it!"

Where had Petey gotten a toy airplane?

"I would love to see."

Petey arched the plane high over his head, making the appropriate airplane sounds.

Dora tickled his ribs and the two of them giggled. She finally glanced at John. "Hello."

It was a mystery to John how Anna and Dora could be raised by Mother Scott and turn out so kind. "Hello, Dora."

"Papa is getting married," Lilly said to Dora with a scowl.

"Lilly." John said her name quickly and with force.

Lilly took a step closer to her aunt.

"What's this?" Mother Scott asked.

Dora blinked several times, but didn't say a word.

"It's nothing." John wanted to crawl into his office

and disappear. "Mrs. Jensen is coming over for supper and the children made assumptions."

Mother Scott's blue eyes narrowed. "Winifred Jensen?" She said the name as if Winnie were a leper. "Why would you marry her? I've never cared for that woman."

"Mother, please," Dora said. "Mrs. Jensen was Anna's friend."

"I'm not marrying anyone," John said evenly. "I'm simply having her over for supper."

The hall clock chimed the hour. Winnie would arrive at any moment. The last thing John wanted was for Mother Scott to be present.

"Is there something I can do for you?" John asked.

"I was just coming to check on the children." Mother Scott sent Miss Maren a withering look. "I've been worried sick about them since *she* arrived."

Miss Maren opened her mouth to speak, but John cut off her retort. "You needn't worry. Miss Maren has been doing a splendid job."

Miss Maren looked at John for the first time since he had entered the foyer, a bit of surprise in her eyes. "Thank you."

"You're welcome." John cleared his throat and took a step toward the door, hoping his mother-in-law would get the hint to leave. "You don't need to trouble yourself with checking on the children anymore—"

"I'll be keeping a close eye on this place," Mother Scott said, still looking at Miss Maren. "Don't think I won't."

Miss Maren hardly acknowledged Mother Scott, and John didn't blame her.

Over Dora's shoulder, through the open front door,

Winnie appeared on the sidewalk carrying her twin girls, while the boys trailed behind.

John nearly groaned. This was not how he pictured this evening unfolding.

"Here's the woman now," Mother Scott said, crossing her arms over her bosom.

Dora touched her sleeve. "Mother, we should take our leave."

"Nonsense. If the woman is going to be the mother of my grandchildren, she'll need to get used to me now."

John looked to Miss Maren, hoping she would somehow help, but her gaze was on Winnie as she walked up the front steps.

Winnie glanced up and found eight people staring at her. She faltered on the top step, her eyes sweeping the room until her gaze landed on John.

Poor Winnie. She was about to enter the inferno.

John took two giant steps to the door and met Winnie and her children there. "It's nice to see you again."

Winnie looked at Mother Scott, Dora and then Miss Maren. "Is everyone joining us for supper tonight?"

"No." John lifted his hand and indicated that she should enter the house. "My mother-in-law and sister-in-law were just leaving."

"Yes," Dora said, coming to John's rescue. "We were on our way out when we saw you coming." She took her mother's elbow and walked her over to the door. "It's so nice to see you again, Mrs. Jensen. Do have a nice meal."

"But, Dora." Mother Scott yanked her arm away. "This woman could very well take your place. Won't you stay and fight for John?"

Dora's cheeks turned pink and she glanced at John quickly. "Mother, please hold your tongue."

"Why am I the only one who speaks her mind?" Mother Scott asked. "I'm simply saying what you're thinking."

"I'm thinking no such thing." Dora took her mother's arm again and managed to get her outside. "Goodbye, John. Children. Miss Maren. Goodbye, Mrs. Jensen."

John could have kissed Dora right then and there for removing Mother Scott from the house. "Goodbye."

"You're making another mistake," Mother Scott said over her shoulder. "First hiring Miss Maren and now dining with Mrs. Jensen."

John closed the door tight against the woman's words. "I'm sorry," he said to Winnie and Miss Maren.

Winnie stood in the middle of the foyer, her brown eyes filled with apprehension. She looked pretty this evening with her hair styled carefully. All four children had been cleaned, their hair still slick with water.

"Winnie, this is my governess, Miss Maren." John indicated Miss Maren.

"It's a pleasure to meet you," Winnie said.

"Two sets of twins?" Miss Maren shook her head in amazement. "How do you do it?"

"I don't have much choice, now, do I?" Winnie asked with a smile, though her words were underlined with exhaustion and irritation.

Miss Maren closed her mouth and didn't respond.

John quickly intervened. "Miss Maren will take the children up to the day nursery, where they will eat a meal and be entertained."

"How nice." Winnie passed a toddler into Marjorie's available arm and then set the other girl on her feet. "I'm ready for a bit of a break."

Miss Maren jostled Laura in one arm and one of the twins in the other. Her gown was splotchy from Laura's drool, and her hair was pulled out of its pins in various places from Laura's curious hands.

She looked like a mother—a very pretty mother.

"The two older boys are Isaac and Isaiah, and the girls are Daphne and Delphine," Winnie said. "The boys will tell you who is who."

Miss Maren looked at each of Winnie's children, her brow tilted in curiosity. "Come with me children," she finally instructed. "Lilly, please take the other little girl's hand, and, Charlie, make sure Petey and the Jensen boys follow."

Miss Maren confidently walked up the stairs looking like the Pied Piper with all the children following her. She glanced back at John, her green eyes probing. But for what, he didn't know.

The foyer was now silent, save the ticking of the grandfather clock, and it was just the two of them. "You look beautiful, Winnie."

Winnie touched her brown hair a bit self-consciously. "Do you think so?"

"Yes, I do."

"Thank you."

They stood for a moment, the air feeling awkward around them. The last time Winnie had been in his house, Anna had been the hostess and John hadn't considered that one day he would be interviewing Winnie to be his wife.

"Would you like to go into the dining room? Mrs. Gohl has dinner prepared."

Winnie sighed. "It will be a treat to eat a meal I haven't cooked with my own hands."

She was much thinner than he recalled, and her skin had a pale tone he didn't like. She had taken Calvin's death hard, which didn't surprise him, and the grief had not been kind to her.

John held out a chair for her, the one directly to the left of his chair, and she took a seat. She smelled of rosewater and something else, maybe bread.

After she sat, John took his seat. "Again, I'm sorry for my mother-in-law's comments. She's grieving her own loss, in her own way." He had stood up to her once after Anna's death, and the woman had retreated in tears for almost a week. John had been very careful around her since, which meant she got away with much more than he would normally allow.

Winnie set her clasped hands on the table. "Have you given any more thought to my proposal?"

He had, a great deal, but now wasn't the time to talk about it. "Shall we enjoy a nice meal before we talk business?"

She nodded, though she looked anxious to get on with their conversation.

For now, they would try to have a normal meal and get to know each other better.

They had plenty of time to talk about marriage later.

The third-floor nursery had become one of Marjorie's favorite rooms in the house. Large and airy, with pine plank floors and a steep ceiling, it had little alcoves where the dormer windows looked out in three directions around town. To the south and east were the rooftops and trees of neighborhood homes, with a glimpse of the children's yellow brick school, and to the west, the beautiful downtown buildings and Mississippi River. Petey and Charlie's room was behind the north wall, with one more dormer window.

"One of those boys took Petey's airplane," Lilly said with her hands on her hips.

"Which one?" Marjorie asked, looking at the identical Jensen boys. They both had their hands behind their backs.

One of the little girls began to cry—but which one was it? Daphne or Delphine? "What happened to her?" Marjorie asked Charlie, who was standing near the stairway door, watching the whole circus.

"I don't know."

The other little girl began to cry, too, her head tipped back, her face red, and tears seeping out of her eyes.

Petey put his hands over his ears and tucked his knees up to his chest. He closed his eyes tight and rocked back and forth on his bottom.

"Petey." Marjorie took a step to the little boy, but Laura began to fuss from the basinet near the south window.

"Lilly, could you please pick up Laura?"

"But what about Petey's airplane? That Jensen boy still has it and won't give it back." Lilly pointed to the little boy who clutched the airplane to his chest now.

The other Jensen boy walked up to Marjorie and tugged on her dress. "I have to go."

Marjorie wanted to put her hands over her ears and join Petey on the floor. Instead, she looked at Charlie. "Could you please take him down to the water closet for me?"

Charlie sighed and nodded. "Come on." He put his hand on the boy's shoulder. "Which one are you?"

"Isaac."

They left the nursery, but the crying prevailed. Marjorie bent over and touched the first Jensen girl who had begun to cry. "What's wrong, sweetheart?"

"I want Mama!" she wailed.

"Me, too," cried the other one.

"Laura needs her diaper changed," Lilly said loudly from the south side of the room. "It leaked through and now her dress is spoiled."

It wasn't right to ask Lilly to change Laura's diaper—but it didn't seem right to ask her to stay with the crying children, either.

"Can you please get a new diaper and a change of clothing? I'll have to change her up here."

Lilly set Laura down in the basinet again and left the nursery.

Petey suddenly stood up, his face red. He raced across the nursery on his way to the stairway door.

Marjorie caught him a moment before his hand touched the doorknob, swinging him up into her arms. "Where are you going?"

Petey tried to wiggle out of her hold. "I want Papa."

"I'm sorry, but you can't go to your papa right now."

Petey's lower lip began to tremble and he crossed his arms, but he didn't try to get away again.

Marjorie set him on his feet and looked at the boy holding Petey's airplane—Isaiah. Should she tell Petey he must share, or should she insist that Isaiah return the item, since he took it without permission? How did you deal with a situation like this?

"Petey, Isaiah is a guest. Let's let him play with the airplane for a few minutes and then we'll ask for it back."

Petey's bottom lip quivered. He ran across the room and raced into his bedroom, slamming the door shut behind him.

Laura and the Jensen girls continued to cry, and nothing Marjorie could do would convince the twins to settle down. She tried pointing out toys in the room, and then items outside the window, but nothing distracted them from their tears.

Finally Lilly and Charlie returned to the nursery with Isaac, and Marjorie was able to change Laura.

"Is this what it would always be like?" Charlie asked, his face sullen. "If Papa marries Mrs. Jensen?"

"No," Lilly said. "Because if Papa marries Mrs. Jensen, Miss Maren would have to leave."

"Mama says we're going to live here," Isaac said to Charlie.

Charlie glanced at Lilly with a look of horror.

Isaac looked up at Lilly. "Mama said you are old enough to take care of us and she can have a break."

Lilly's mouth fell open and she stared at Marjorie. "Does she think I'm going to take care of her children?"

"Shh." Marjorie put her arm around Lilly's shoulder. "Maybe there's been a misunderstanding."

"I don't want to have four more babies in this house," Charlie said.

"Mama's having another baby," Isaac offered. "Maybe twins again."

"More babies?" Lilly squeaked.

The thought of another set of twins gave Marjorie the shivers—but she squeezed Lilly's shoulders. "Don't worry."

Charlie looked around the nursery. "Where's Petey?"

Marjorie pointed to their bedroom door. "He's in there."

"Because Isaiah wouldn't give him his airplane back," Lilly said as she glared at the other boy. "Am I right?"

"Papa doesn't even realize how crazy it is up here," Charlie said. "If he could see how miserable we are, then he wouldn't marry Mrs. Jensen."

The stairway door opened and Miss Ernst appeared in her black gown and white apron. Today her red hair was tamed behind her cap, but just barely. "Are the children ready for me to bring up their meal?"

Suddenly Marjorie had an idea.

"Children." She held up her hands. "I know what we will do."

Charlie was right. Dr. Orton couldn't marry Mrs. Jensen. It would be a madhouse with all these children, especially if Mrs. Jensen expected Charlie and Lilly to take care of them. Both adults were downstairs, enjoying a quiet meal together, but they needed to see what it would be like to combine their two families.

"Miss Ernst, I will bring the children down to the dining room to eat with Dr. Orton and Mrs. Jensen."

"I was told to serve them up here."

"I'm changing the plans."

"But—" Miss Ernst stuttered. "Dr. Orton will be angry."

"Leave Dr. Orton to me," Marjorie said. "Come, children."

Charlie grinned, but Lilly looked uncertain.

"I'll get Petey," Charlie said.

The Jensen girls were still crying for their mother. "Miss Ernst, can you carry Laura downstairs? I will bring the twins."

Miss Ernst looked at Marjorie with apprehension, but she picked up Laura.

Marjorie took the twin girls in her arms and Charlie came from the room with Petey.

"Papa?" Petey smiled, despite the large tears dripping down his cheeks.

"Yes. Now come along."

The ten of them descended the stairs, with Marjorie at the lead. They marched through the second-floor hall and then walked down the grand stairway into the front foyer. The twin girls were still crying, and Isaiah was still clutching Petey's airplane.

Dr. Orton appeared under the dining room archway, a napkin in his hand. He frowned at the scene. "What's all this noise? Is there trouble, Miss Maren?"

Marjorie strode right past him and into the dining room where Mrs. Jensen sat. "The girls won't be consoled."

Both girls reached for their mother at the same moment, nearly sending Marjorie head over heels.

"Children, find a seat." Marjorie deposited the girls onto Mrs. Jensen's lap, barely looking at the stunned woman's face. Both toddlers stopped crying the moment they touched their mother.

"What are you doing?" Dr. Orton asked Marjorie. His dark eyes were filled with storm clouds. "I told you to feed the children upstairs."

Marjorie helped Petey into his seat and then put her hand on the backrest and faced Dr. Orton. "The girls would not stop crying until I brought them to their mother, and Petey wanted to see you."

The children found a seat at the large table, talking all at once, but Miss Ernst stood motionless with Laura in her arms.

"I thought it best for you and Mrs. Jensen to realize what life would be like with eight or more children, day in and day out."

Dr. Orton took a step toward Marjorie, his face red. He spoke through his clenched teeth. "I will have a word with you in my office."

Marjorie leaned back, surprised at the force of his anger.

He left the room, throwing his napkin on the sideboard as he exited.

Marjorie straightened her back and followed him through the hall.

He closed the door and didn't wait for her to sit. "Who are you to defy my orders and assume you can influence my choices?"

"I was up in that nursery with eight children, four of whom were upset."

"That is your job. I am paying you to take care of my children—and children of guests in my home."

"I didn't think it right for you to consider marriage to a woman without knowing what life would be like."

"Again." He took a step closer to her. "That is not your concern."

She took a step toward him. The tips of their shoes were now touching. "It is when I have discovered that Mrs. Jensen intends for Charlie and Lilly to take care of her children if she marries you."

Dr. Orton paused and a bit of his bluster died away. "Who told you such a thing?"

"Isaac Jensen."

"He is only a child."

"But why would he say something like that, if he hadn't heard it from his mother?"

Dr. Orton didn't have a quick response. He stepped away from Marjorie and went to the mantel where Anna's portrait sat. He stared at the picture.

"My children have already been through so much," Dr. Orton said, almost to himself. "I do not want them raising someone else's children, too. There has to be a better way to help Winnie."

A thrill of pleasure raced through Marjorie. Dr. Orton would not marry Mrs. Jensen, she just knew it.

But why the pleasure? Was it because Marjorie had succeeded in helping him see the truth about the situation? Or was it some other reason she couldn't identify?

Dr. Orton turned away from the photo and studied Marjorie for a moment.

She glanced down at her dress and found the waistline to be askew and blotches of drool on her shoulders. She touched her hair and discovered it was lopsided, with pins coming out on the side. "I must look a fright."

He didn't say a word but merely swallowed and walked around her to open the door.

She exited his office and went into the dining room.

Mrs. Jensen's mouth was pulled taut and her eyes were red, as if she had been crying. Petey had his airplane back in his hands, but Isaiah was now in tears. Charlie was chewing on a dinner roll, his face grim, and Lilly was lecturing Isaac. One of the twin girls was pulling the sideboard drawers open, digging inside, while the other was on her mother's lap playing with Mrs. Jensen's necklace. Miss Ernst still held Laura in her arms, looking as helpless and frightened as a cornered animal.

"Miss Maren." Dr. Orton touched her elbow to gain her attention and then quickly pulled his hand back. "Please help Miss Ernst bring in the children's supper, and as soon as they are finished, return them to the third-floor nursery." He went to Miss Ernst and took Laura out of her hands, his face as grim as Charlie's. "We will let Mrs. Jensen enjoy an evening to relax."

Marjorie righted her hair as she stepped out of the dining room and into the kitchen.

With one look at the distraught Mrs. Jensen, Marjorie didn't feel as triumphant as she had hoped.

Chapter Eight

Marjorie stood near the refreshment table in the Orton's front parlor and smiled while she watched Lilly. The young girl's eyes shone and her cheeks were filled with color as she went from guest to guest, talking like a grown-up and offering more finger sandwiches.

"The party is a success," Dora said as she came beside Marjorie.

"If Lilly is happy, then I call it a great success," Marjorie agreed.

Dora held a glass of punch in her gloved hand. "It does my heart good to see how much she admires you." She took a sip of her drink. "Anna would be so happy."

Marjorie couldn't deny the pleasure Dora's words brought to her heart. "I wish I had known Anna."

Dora's blue eyes softened even more, if that were possible. "You get a glimpse of her in each of the children. She lives on in Lilly's graciousness, in Charlie's giving heart, in Petey's quiet stubbornness and in Laura's gentle charm. I even see her in John's selfless commitment to medicine. Anna was the one who enabled him to build his practice and made his stellar reputation what it is today."

"I'll do whatever I can, in the short time I'm here, to make sure her legacy lives on in the things she loved and the people she cared about."

"That's why I like you, Miss Maren," Dora said. "I know that you truly care about Anna's children."

"Please, call me Marjorie."

Dora squeezed Marjorie's forearm. "Good. And you must call me Dora."

"I will."

Dora and Marjorie both looked toward the archway leading to the front hall where Dr. Orton had just entered.

A warm flutter rushed through Marjorie at his unexpected presence, taking her by surprise. When had her barely concealed tolerance turned to pleasure? "I thought Dr. Orton would be at the hospital all afternoon."

Dora took another sip of her punch and watched Dr. Orton over the rim of her cup. She set it down and wiped at her upper lip with her napkin. "It appears he has come home early."

Dr. Orton glanced inside the parlor, his eyes skimming the group, until his gaze landed first on Marjorie and then on Dora.

"If you'll excuse me." Dora set her cup on a nearby table and crossed the parlor with the ease of a gazelle. She met Dr. Orton in the hall and was greeted with a heartwarming smile.

Marjorie sipped her own punch, watching Dr. Orton and Dora exchange pleasantries. She wished she could hear what they were saying. Instead, the hum of chatter and the clinking of silverware on bone china filled her ears.

Dr. Orton motioned toward his office and Dora nod-

ded. She preceded him into the room. The door was
left open and Marjorie took a few steps to the left to
see inside.

Dora sat in the chair Marjorie usually occupied in
Dr. Orton's office. He sat on the edge of the desk, close
to Dora, his rapt attention on the young lady.

"Miss Maren, thank you for this wonderful tea
party." Miss Baker appeared at Marjorie's side.

Marjorie turned to the lady from the mercantile.
Miss Baker stood next to the fireplace, a plate of pas-
tries in her hand.

"Dr. Orton's home is as lovely as I had imagined."

Marjorie nodded as her eyes surveyed the room.
The front parlor was beautiful with oversize windows
looking out onto the covered porch, comfortable floral-
covered furniture and a large gilded mirror over the
mantel. Light poured in through the windows, warming the room and offering a pleasant glow on an otherwise dreary November day.

"I've always said you can tell a lot about a family
from their parlor." Miss Baker took a bite of pastry.
"This is delicious. My compliments to the cook."

"I'll let Mrs. Gohl know," Marjorie said. "What can
you tell about the Ortons from their parlor?"

"They are wealthy but practical. They have their
guests' comfort in mind, but their furniture is still styl-
ish and well made."

"Practical, you say?" Marjorie asked.

"Why, yes, I believe I did."

"Would you say you're a practical person?"

Miss Baker seemed to consider the question, a giggle
in her voice. "I can't say that I am. I spend far too much
money on sheet music, I eat far too many sweets, and
I enjoy spending my Saturdays at the Lowell Theater."

"You have no idea how happy that makes me." Marjorie thought of the list she had made for Dr. Orton's wife. Miss Baker appeared whimsical, yet bold. A good combination. She was also pretty and loved children—or at least, Marjorie assumed she did, since she taught Lilly's Sunday school. But best of all, she wasn't practical. "Lilly told me you teach Sunday school. Do you have any other jobs?"

"I am an assistant to our local photographer."

"What a fascinating job." It was good to hear that Miss Baker had a career. It showed Marjorie that she was a self-assured woman who didn't mind challenging the status quo—exactly what Dr. Orton needed. Marjorie wanted to believe Miss Baker would be a good candidate for Dr. Orton, but she couldn't be sure. Maybe the best way to find out would be for Miss Baker to come to dinner, just as Mrs. Jensen had. "Miss Baker—"

"It's Rachel."

"Rachel, would you care to join the Ortons for supper tomorrow night?" She quickly thought through the list of women she had already invited to supper. Three in all. But the other two were coming on Wednesday and Friday. "I'm sure Lilly and Charlie would enjoy hosting their Sunday school teacher…and I think Dr. Orton would enjoy getting to know you better."

Rachel's cheeks tinged with color. "Do you think so?"

"I do." Marjorie glanced across the room and past the hall to his office. What was he discussing with Dora? Was he even now speaking to her about marriage? Why did the thought bother Marjorie so much? Was it because Dora was too much like her sister and wouldn't stand up to Dr. Orton when she needed to?

"I would love to come to dinner."

Marjorie glanced back at Rachel. "Good. Six o'clock?"

"I'll be here."

"We look forward to having you. Now, if you'll excuse me."

"Of course."

Marjorie walked over to Lilly. "Is everything going well?"

Lilly grinned up at Marjorie. "I'm having ever so much fun!"

"Wonderful." Marjorie patted her shoulder. "Let me know if you need something. I'm going to the kitchen to see if Mrs. Gohl requires any help."

"All right."

The room was filled with fourteen single women, and Marjorie had spoken with all of them, but only three had seemed right for Dr. Orton.

Marjorie smiled at each guest as she walked nonchalantly through the room, toward the archway leading to the front hall. She would make the pretense of checking on Mrs. Gohl, but really she wanted to hear what Dora and Dr. Orton were discussing.

Ever so slowly, Marjorie moved past the office door, just out of view from the parlor.

"…I feel as if I'm betraying Anna's memory," Dr. Orton said.

"You're not. You're doing this *for* Anna."

There was a pause and Marjorie imagined Dr. Orton was looking at the photograph again.

"Don't worry," Dora said. "I'm happy to do it. I know Anna would want it this way."

"What about Miss Maren?"

"I think she'll be relieved."

Marjorie inhaled a breath and held it for several moments. Dr. Orton had proposed to Dora? But…she wasn't right for him, not right at all. She was a lovely person, but she was too passive. He needed a woman who wasn't afraid to speak her mind and tell him when he was wrong—which was more often than he realized.

"When will you tell the children?" Dora asked.

"I don't see any reason to tell them now. We can wait until closer to the date."

"And when will that be?"

"Right before Christmas."

Marjorie exhaled her breath. There was still time to change his mind. Maybe, if he liked one of the women Marjorie had invited over for supper better, he would call off his engagement to Dora. No one but Dora and Marjorie would need to know.

"My lips are sealed," Dora said. There was a pause and then she added gently, "John, you're doing the right thing—"

"Miss Maren." Lilly appeared at the parlor door holding an empty pitcher. "Could you please tell Miss Ernst to get us more punch?"

Marjorie took a step away from the office door and nodded. "Yes, of course."

"We're also running low on sandwiches."

"I'll tell her."

Dora suddenly appeared at the door with Dr. Orton just behind her.

Marjorie smiled and walked past them with the empty pitcher in hand.

She would pretend she hadn't heard a thing.

John entered the front parlor and found Lilly, Dora and Miss Maren sitting on the sofa, their faces glowing, but their postures exhausted.

"Papa." Lilly sat up. "There's leftover punch and cu-

cumber sandwiches if you'd like some. I can get them for you."

"Maybe in a little while."

Lilly stood and walked across the room. She put her arm around John's waist. "I'm tired. I think I'll go read for a while."

John squeezed her in a hug and then winked at her as she smiled and left the room.

"Was it a success?" he asked the two women who remained.

Miss Maren sat up a bit straighter. "It was a success. Lilly did a marvelous job. I believe everyone had a good time, too."

"She really did," Dora added. "She's turning into a fine young lady, right before my eyes. All the guests were quite impressed with her hospitality. We should applaud Marjorie for teaching her well."

It was the first time someone had called Miss Maren by her given name. It suited her.

"She's a natural," Marjorie said. "I taught her very little."

"Anna would be proud." John cleared the emotion from his voice. "Thank you—both of you—for doing this for Lilly. It's something Anna would have done if she were here."

Dora stood and approached John. She took his hand and squeezed it. "It was our pleasure, wasn't it, Marjorie?"

Marjorie also stood, stacking empty plates, but didn't look their way. "It was."

"Leave that for Miss Ernst," John said. "You deserve a break. Go and enjoy the rest of your day off."

She continued to clear the dishes, but still she didn't look at him. "Where would I go, and what would I do?"

Dora glanced at Marjorie. "Maybe next Sunday I can watch the children and John can take you out and show you more of the town." She smiled up at John. "It's been a while since you went driving. I think Marjorie would enjoy a day out. It would be good for you, too, I think. You used to enjoy it so much."

"I still do."

Marjorie studied them with a quizzical frown, but looked away when John met her eyes. She bent over and picked up a napkin lying on the floor.

Would she enjoy spending an afternoon with him? The idea of getting her alone for a few hours sounded more appealing than he would have thought. Was it decent to do something like this with the governess? On the other hand, who would show her around if it wasn't him? "Would you enjoy that, Miss Maren?"

She straightened, that same puzzled look on her face. "You wouldn't mind, Dora?"

Dora shook her head and offered a smile. "Mind? I would love to spend the day with my nieces and nephews."

"Then it's settled," John said, feeling a bit nervous, though he didn't know why. "Next Sunday, if the weather cooperates, I'll take Miss Maren out for a drive."

Marjorie stared at the two of them as if they had just said something preposterous.

Dora patted his arm, stealing his attention off Marjorie. "I should be going."

"I'll walk you home."

"All right."

They exited the parlor and John helped Dora put on her wraps.

Marjorie walked to the archway. "Goodbye, Dora."

"Goodbye, Marjorie, and thanks again for a lovely party."

John opened the door and Dora slipped out. He closed it behind him, but not before glancing at Marjorie one last time. Why did she look so confused?

The air was crisp and filled with the scents of fall. Decaying leaves, smoky bonfires and wet earth wafted past. Front porches were decorated with colorful pumpkins, gourds and cornstalks. Thanksgiving would soon be upon them.

The first Thanksgiving without Anna.

"I really do think you're making the right decision in going to the medical conference," Dora said to John. "I'm happy to stay at your home and help Marjorie with the children."

"If I'm not married by then."

"If you are married, I'll be happy to help your wife take care of the children—if she needs help," she quickly added.

"You don't think Anna would mind me talking about her death?"

"No. If it can help even one patient, I'm sure Anna would have wanted you to speak up."

"I've had some success using cinnamon oil as a treatment and preventative." He paused. "You and Mother Scott are still taking ten drops a day in a glass of water, aren't you?"

"Yes." She slipped her arm through his elbow as they shuffled through fallen leaves. "You need to stop worrying about us."

"How can I? You're the sister I never had. Anna would be angry if I didn't worry about you."

"I miss her."

John took several breaths before he answered, "I miss her, too."

"Then you must go. You said the conference is right before Christmas?"

"Yes—but what if one of the children becomes sick while I'm gone? I wasn't here with Anna when she became ill, and I regret my decision to leave town every day. Is it too much to risk leaving again?"

"John," Dora said in frustration. "It's an honor to speak at such a prestigious medical conference. The children will be fine—and you'll only be a few hours away by train in Minneapolis. If someone becomes sick, which they won't since they're taking their cinnamon oil, we'll call you home."

"Promise?"

She laughed and rested her head on his shoulder, just as she had done the day he met her when she was an eight-year-old girl.

"Ah." Mother Scott exited the Scott home and stood on the front porch, a grin on her face. "I knew, given time, you two would come to your senses. When is the wedding?"

Dora groaned beside John.

They were still far enough away that Mother Scott couldn't hear them, but he lowered his voice and spoke for Dora's ears alone. "When are you going to tell her about Jeremiah?"

"Don't breathe a word," Dora threatened under her breath. "I was going to tell her before Anna became sick, but since then, I haven't had the courage. She's been through so much, and now she has such high hopes for you and me."

"Jeremiah won't be patient forever."

Dora smiled up at John. "You may be surprised. He's the most patient man I know."

"Why the wait?"

"I don't have the heart to leave Mother alone in this big house—and it would be cruel to you to have her across the street with nothing to occupy her time. She would spend her days interfering in your life."

"And how would that be different than now?"

Dora laughed and pushed him playfully.

They drew closer to the Scott home and John fairly whispered, "Don't wait on our account. I want you to be happy. Life is too short to be without the one you love."

She squeezed his arm and then pulled away and joined her mother on the front porch. "Thank you for walking me home, John. I had a wonderful day."

Mother Scott displayed a triumphant smile. "I knew it. I just knew it."

Dora kissed her mother on the cheek. "Sorry, Mother. John and I are not getting married."

"Goodbye," John called, leaving Dora to her mother.

Mother Scott harrumphed and John only smiled.

He turned back toward his house and took it all in. Anna had loved this house since she was a child, growing up across the street. When it came up for sale, they had quickly purchased the home, thinking they would take care of Mother Scott in her old age.

Mature oak, elm and maple trees covered the corner lot and small bushes hugged the foundation. Nooks, crannies and eves gave the house character, while the large front porch and stained-glass windows gave it class. Smoke curled out of the chimney—and Marjorie stood at the parlor window.

Marjorie.

The woman had become a strange and wonderful addition to his home. A spark of life had been lit and the flame was fanning brighter and brighter. He saw it in Charlie's grin, and Lilly's joy. They still had moments of sadness, but now they had someone new to talk to about their mama, someone who wasn't part of the pain, but part of a brighter future, if only for a little while.

Marjorie slipped away from the window, and the lace curtain fell back into place.

John put his hands in his pockets and kicked at a pile of leaves in the street. He still didn't know much about her past and hadn't had a chance to ask her. He had written to his mother again, asking for more details, but hadn't received a reply.

Though Marjorie drove him crazy at times, the children loved her. And that was worth far more to him than a few mishaps and unanswered questions.

Chapter Nine

"Have you been giving the children their cinnamon oil every day?" Dr. Orton asked Marjorie.

She nodded as she followed him to the back hall, not minding that he asked her this question every time he left the house. She knew how important it was to him. "Yes. They take it every morning with breakfast, just as you asked. Charlie and Lilly had it before they left for school this morning."

"And what about you? Are you taking it?"

"Yes." A yawn threatened to escape Marjorie's mouth and she quickly put her hand up to hide it.

Dr. Orton took his coat off the hook and looked her over with a critical eye. "Aren't you getting adequate rest, Miss Maren?"

Another yawn claimed victory and her eyes watered. "I think you're right, Laura must be teething. She hasn't slept more than two hours in a row since I arrived."

"I've heard her." Dr. Orton buttoned his black overcoat. "Put her teething ring outside to freeze—that might soothe her gums. You can also try some of the Steedman's numbing powder, but I've found it to be only slightly helpful. Other than that, there's little you can do but wait it out."

"That's what I was afraid of." Marjorie took his hat off the hook and handed it to him.

He paused and took the fedora. "Thank you. I know it isn't always easy to care for the children, but you're doing a fine job."

His compliment brought warmth to her chest, but she couldn't find the words to thank him.

He studied her for a moment, as if trying to piece together a puzzle. "I would like to have a chat with you this evening. I have a few questions."

"When will you be home?" she asked.

"By suppertime, I hope."

So did Marjorie. Rachel Baker would be arriving at six o'clock and it was imperative that he was home. With the knowledge of Dr. Orton's marriage plans to Dora, Marjorie was racing against time.

Dr. Orton picked up his black medical bag and opened the back door. Cold air rushed into the hall as he took a step outside. He stopped and nodded at Marjorie. "See that you get a bit of rest this morning now that Petey and Laura are taking their naps."

The suggestion sounded too good to be true. "I will."

"I have a whole library of books at your disposal in my office," he said. "Feel free to browse among them and choose something you'd like."

She couldn't hide the surprise from her voice. "You wouldn't mind?"

"Not at all. What good are books if they aren't being read?" He touched the brim of his hat and then turned down the path leading to the carriage house and his waiting Model T.

Marjorie watched him for a few moments, admiring the cut of his wide shoulders under his black coat and the way he carried himself with determination and strength. Though he grieved Anna, he still found purpose in his work and in his family. He was not a man crippled under hardship, but had used his pain to reach outside himself and help others.

Was Marjorie doing the same with the hardships she had endured? Was she soaring toward new heights, accomplishing a job few women in her social circles had ever attempted? Or was she using the Orton family as a way to hide from the embarrassment of being turned out of her parents' home, and the fear of failing at her pursuit to be a film actress in California?

The jarring questions left her feeling unsettled.

It had been days since she thought of being in the movies. There had simply been no time to dwell on something that seemed so frivolous now that she had found purpose in caring for the lives of the Orton children. Did she still want to go to California?

Dr. Orton cranked his Ford and then jumped into the driver's seat. He glanced in her direction and she quickly closed the door, standing safely inside the warm hall, away from his serious gaze.

It didn't matter if she still wanted to go to California or not. Soon Dr. Orton would be married, and she would no longer be needed. If she didn't pursue a career in the movies, she would have nothing else. No other purpose. No other dreams. No home to go to. She would fail at yet another pursuit, just as her father said she would.

A shudder raced through her as she walked into the front hall.

The house was quiet with Petey and Laura in their beds. Miss Ernst was enjoying her morning off, and Mrs. Gohl had gone to the grocer's.

Marjorie walked toward Dr. Orton's office, her feet sluggish. Another yawn overtook her as she pushed the door open.

Without Dr. Orton's presence, the room felt like an uninhabited cave. Dark trim covered the room, with a wood-tiled ceiling and tall bookshelves along two walls.

Marjorie wandered over to the first shelf and lifted an eyebrow. *Little Women.* She hadn't expected to see that book in Dr. Orton's office, next to his large medical tomes. It had been one of Marjorie's favorites as a young girl.

She lifted it off the shelf and meandered to the leather sofa near the fireplace. The grate was empty, so she laid a fire and then curled up on the sofa, pulling an afghan over her legs.

A sigh escaped her lips as she nestled in for a good read.

Her eyes felt heavy, but she opened the book and read the first line: "'Christmas won't be Christmas without any presents,' grumbled Jo, lying on the rug…"

Marjorie sat up with a start. The fire had dwindled down to embers and *Little Women* lay on the floor in a haphazard tilt. She sat up straighter, blinking several times.

How long had she been asleep? And what had awakened her?

Laura's cry filtered into the office.

Marjorie pushed aside the afghan and stood from the sofa. The room was surprisingly cold.

She reached down and picked up the book—and stopped short. Little scraps of paper littered the office floor.

Marjorie quickly scanned the room, her pulse ticking hard against her throat. At least a dozen books were strewn about, some lying open, others closed, and some bent in strange positions—but every single one was cut to shreds.

"No." She shook her head as she raced to the first one. She picked up the thick book and turned it over to look at the cover. *Diseases of the Skin*. She dropped it on Dr. Orton's massive oak desk and picked up the next one, even thicker. *Gray's Anatomy, Descriptive and Surgical Guide*. "No, no, no."

A pair of large kitchen shears caught Marjorie's eye next. She grabbed them from near a book entitled *Prescriptive Medicine*. Dozens and dozens of book pages had been cut out of each of them, scattered all over the room.

There could only be one explanation: Petey. But where was he?

A new fear overtook Marjorie as she glanced out the office door. Petey could be anywhere.

She raced out of the office and into the front hall. The entry was even colder than the office, and the front door was propped open.

Marjorie gasped. "No!"

She ran onto the front porch, the cold air biting at her skin. She had to find Petey. But where would she look?

She rushed around the side of the house. "Petey!" She yelled his name over and over until her voice became hoarse. "Petey!" He was nowhere in the yard. She looked in the carriage house, under all the bushes and inside the toolshed.

"What's the matter?" A shrill voice filled Marjorie's ears. Mrs. Scott. She stood on her front porch, a shawl wrapped around her shoulders. "Is Petey missing?"

Marjorie's heart pounded so hard she felt it pushing against her breastbone, making her chest ache. She hated to admit to the lady that the boy was gone, but she swallowed her pride. She needed help. "Yes. I can't find him anywhere."

Mrs. Scott hurried off her porch, down the steps and crossed the street. "Did you look inside the house?"

"The front door was open." Marjorie wrung her hands, frantically searching the neighboring lawns. "He could be anywhere!"

"Just because the door is open doesn't mean he's outside." Mrs. Scott's voice was surprisingly calm. "Go look inside and I'll keep looking out here."

Marjorie raced back up the porch steps and into the front hall. "Petey!"

Laura's cries filled the house, but the baby would have to wait. At least she was safe inside her cradle.

Suddenly Laura's cries stopped, and Marjorie paused as she looked under the dining room table. She stood and raced up the stairway. "Petey!"

She ran across the upper hall. The night nursery door was cracked open—but Marjorie had left it closed. She pushed open the door, clutching the knob, and found Petey standing beside Laura's cradle, zooming his airplane high over Laura's head.

"Petey." Marjorie sank to her knees, breathing hard. "Thank You, God."

Petey turned to Marjorie, his head tilted as he stared at her on the floor.

Marjorie pulled herself to her feet, her whole body shaking. "Petey, you scared me. I thought you were missing."

He didn't say a word but turned back to Laura, flying his airplane for the baby's entertainment.

"Miss Maren?" Mrs. Scott called up the stairs.

"Petey's here," Marjorie called back, her voice weak. "He's safe."

Marjorie left the children in the nursery and descended to the hall where Mrs. Scott stood with her arms crossed. Gone was the levelheaded, concerned grandmother, and in her place was the mean old lady from across the street. She scowled at Marjorie. "Anything could have happened to that boy. What were you doing?"

Tears stung the back of Marjorie's eyes. "I fell asleep."

Mrs. Scott shook her head, her gaze roving Marjorie in disdain. "I looked inside John's office. It appears you were sleeping for a while. John bought those books while he was in medical school and just after he came to Little Falls and started his practice. He and Anna scrimped and saved for months to buy one volume. Do you realize what Peter has done? What you've done?"

Marjorie put her hands to her temples, her stomach starting to roll.

She had failed at her job. That was what she had done.

John set the book on the circulation desk of the Carnegie Library and smiled at Miss Faulkner, the librarian. "I've been waiting for this one to be published." When possible, he borrowed copies of new medical books from the library before investing in them for his home office.

The *People's Medical Adviser Book* had been published for laymen, but John liked to read books like this to know what his patients were reading, and whether or not it was sound advice. Inevitably he would get a patient that had followed some harebrained plan and needed more help in the end.

Miss Faulkner took the book from his hands and removed the index card from the front cover pocket. "How are the children? Will we be seeing them here for story time on Saturday morning? We miss them."

Anna used to take the children to story time every Saturday, but since her death, and with the widespread disease, John had not even told Marjorie about their usual activities. "Things have been a bit difficult—"

Miss Faulkner lifted her slender hand. "Say no more. It was insensitive of me to ask."

John studied her for a moment, struck with the realization that Miss Faulkner was considered an old maid by many people's standards, but she was probably only in her late twenties. She was tall and slim, with dark brown hair pulled back in a bun and a plain face. Her lips were pretty, if lips could be.

She lifted her eyebrows as she looked back at him. "Did I insult you? If I did, I'm so sorry."

John shook his head. "No. I'm fine."

She stamped the index card and put it in a long, narrow file drawer. "The book is due in three weeks." She handed it back to him, a pleasant smile on her face.

John scratched his chin for a moment.

He had told Winnie that though he cared about her and the children, it would not be a good idea to combine their two families. She had seemed to agree, after the fiasco in the dining room. John had offered to help financially, but Winnie had turned him down, saying she would find a way to survive.

John had given Mrs. Gohl extra grocery money and had told the cook to purchase supplies for the Jensens and leave them on her back stoop anonymously. It was the least he could do for an old friend.

But here stood Miss Faulkner, with no children and nothing to hinder her from marriage to a man with four of his own. She had always been nice and thoughtful, taking the time to get to know the children over the years.

Would she consider marriage?

"Miss Faulkner..." He paused. How did a man go about asking someone such an important question? Maybe the library wasn't the best place. "Would you care to join my family for supper this evening? I know the children would enjoy seeing you—and I would enjoy your company, as well."

Miss Faulkner's hand fumbled and she dropped the medical book on the counter. "Oh, I'm sorry."

He put his hand over the book. "That's all right."

She looked back at him, her blue eyes blinking rapidly. "You want me to come to supper at your house? With you?"

He offered her a smile. "Yes. Do you have other plans?"

Her eyebrows jumped and she pointed to her chest. "Me? No—I don't have any plans this evening."

"So you'll come?"

She swallowed and nodded. "I—I suppose."

"Good. Six o'clock?"

She nodded again—or maybe she hadn't stopped nodding.

"I'll see you then. Goodbye." He picked up the book, tipped his hat at her, and then strode down the steps and out the front door to his waiting Ford. He cranked the starter and drove the three blocks to his home.

Dr. McCall had come in early and told John to take

the rest of the day off to get some rest. It was a rare offer, and John was only too happy to agree. After he opened his home library to Marjorie, he had realized he hadn't read a book since before Anna's death. He would use his free afternoon to read.

He parked the automobile near the carriage house and then strode up the walk. Dark clouds filtered out the sun, and a nip in the air made him pull his collar up to his chin. A storm was probably on the way, and this one would more than likely produce snow that would stick.

With Thanksgiving only a week away, it wasn't uncommon to have measurable snow. He just wished it would hurry and put a halt to the influenza.

John pushed open the back door and walked into the hall. Lilly and Charlie would still be in school and Laura might be taking an afternoon nap. Petey and Marjorie would probably be in the day nursery playing or going over his colors and shapes.

It would be a quiet, peaceful afternoon.

He whistled as he hung up his hat and coat and set his medical bag on the table. He pushed open the door leading into the front hall and crossed the space to his office.

Marjorie was on her hands and knees, her backside toward him, and pieces of paper were lying about his office.

He pushed the door open wider and she turned at the sound, her blond head appearing over her shoulder. "Dr. Orton!"

He frowned as he took in the scene. What was the woman doing now?

She stood quickly, wiping the knees of her purple gown, her hand full of paper. "I didn't know—" Her face crumpled and tears appeared on her cheeks. "I fell asleep—Petey woke up—I woke up—there was paper everywhere—Petey was gone—the door was open—" She sputtered and cried, pointing at different places in the room with each cryptic statement. "Mrs. Scott yelled at me—Petey was with Laura—I found Mrs. Gohl's shears—and this." She held up the paper, a sob leaving her body. "I'm so sorry."

John set the borrowed medical book on his desk. "Miss Maren—I have no idea what you're talking about."

She wiped at her face, gulping large amounts of air. "Your books—Petey cut up your books."

"My books?" He glanced around the room and that was when he recognized all the paper. They were pages from his books, or what was left of them. He picked up *Diseases of the Skin* and flipped through the massacred pages. "My books," he said again, this time in disbelief. He put *Diseases of the Skin* down and picked up *Prescriptive Medicine*. It, too, was destroyed. Nine other books lay in a pile on John's desk, all of them victims of Petey's shears.

He looked at Marjorie. "These books meant a great deal to me—"

"I know!" she wailed. "Mrs. Scott told me."

"Mother Scott was here?"

Marjorie wiped at her nose in a very unladylike gesture. "She heard me yelling for Petey outside when he was missing and she came over to help—"

He dropped *Prescriptive Medicine* and grabbed her arms. "Petey is missing?"

She shook her head quickly, her tears all but forgotten for the moment. "No. He's here. H-he was fine the whole time."

John released her arms and put his hand over his heart, closing his eyes briefly. "Thank You, Lord."

"I tried to reprimand him, but it wasn't only his fault."

John lifted another book. "What were you doing when all this happened?"

Marjorie indicated the sofa, the tears starting all over again. "I fell asleep."

John sighed and set the book on the desk. "What's done is done."

She blinked at him, her green eyes glimmering with tears. "You're not going to fire me?"

He reached into his back pocket and removed a clean handkerchief. "I'm not going to fire you for falling asleep, especially when I was the one who told you to rest."

"But—" She took the handkerchief and wiped at her nose and cheeks. "This is my fault."

He lifted his brow. "You *want* me to fire you?"

"No." She put her hand on his forearm and the touch sent a familiar feeling through him—the same feeling he used to get when Anna touched him.

He pulled away from her hand, his skin on fire, and couldn't look her in the eye. No woman had ever had this effect on him, besides his wife. "You're only human. You're tired." He swallowed and toyed with the edge of a lacerated book. "See that it doesn't happen again."

Marjorie was quiet for so long that John finally looked up at her.

Her face was wiped dry and her tears had stopped. She looked at him with the strangest mixture of disbelief and sympathy. "I am sorry."

"I know. I'm just happy Petey is safe and that nothing worse happened."

"I'll replace your books."

He shook his head. "It isn't necessary—and many of these books are now out of date anyway." He smiled ruefully. "They're getting old, just like me."

"You're not old."

She didn't think he was old? She had to be at least twelve years younger than him.

If she didn't think he was too old... He stopped his thoughts before they could go any further. Miss Faulkner was coming to supper tonight. She was practical, sensible and levelheaded. Exactly what John needed in a wife.

He didn't need someone as unpredictable as Marjorie. Regardless of how much he enjoyed coming home to her—even when his home was torn apart.

Chapter Ten

It was tiresome, this search to find a wife. John straightened his tie as he looked at his weary reflection in the mirror. How many more times would he have to entertain a young lady before finding the right one? He would have much preferred to spend the evening with his children and Marjorie around the supper table, hearing about their day and enjoying their laughter. He had planned to finally talk to Marjorie about her past, but, instead, he would be talking to Miss Faulkner about the future.

The scent of chicken and dumplings wafted up the stairwell. It was Lilly's favorite meal. If John had known Mrs. Gohl was preparing it for tonight, he would have invited Miss Faulkner for another evening.

Instead of eating in the dining room, the children would stay in the day nursery on the third floor. He just needed to make his wishes clear with Marjorie this time around. Nothing but an emergency would interrupt his meal with Miss Faulkner.

He stepped out of his bedroom and strode through the hall to the third-floor stairwell.

The children's voices trailed down the stairs. It sounded like they were in the midst of a game.

He stepped through the door into the nursery and saw Marjorie standing in the middle of the room, a blind-fold over her eyes, her arms outstretched, her fingers wiggling in the air.

"I know you're over here somewhere, Lilly Belle." Marjorie used Lilly's middle name just as Anna used to.

John paused for a moment, surprised at how much he enjoyed hearing Marjorie say his daughter's full name. It somehow made her feel like family.

Lilly crouched in the corner, under a slant in the ceiling, her hands over her mouth, a silent giggle shaking her body. Charlie was in the opposite corner but came up behind Marjorie and touched her shoulder, then ran away.

Marjorie spun. "Who was that? Charlie?"

Petey sat cross-legged near the dormer, his airplane in hand, watching the other three play blindman's bluff, a gentle smile on his face.

"This isn't fair," Marjorie said as she walked over to the wall and felt around on the surface. "You should make some noise, or something."

Lilly's eyes shone with mirth as she glanced at John. She lifted her hand and silently pointed at Marjorie, indicating that he should also tease her.

John smiled at his daughter's merriment, and recalled all the fun he'd had playing parlor games as a young man. Blindman's bluff had been one of his favorites.

He tiptoed across the nursery floor, the boards creaking under his weight. He drew close to Marjorie and slowly lifted his hand to tap her shoulder.

She turned right at that moment and threw her arms around John's middle.

"I got you, Charlie!" she said in triumph.

John stood motionless for a split second, enjoying the feel of being in her arms and smelling the lilac scent she wore. He slipped her mask off and her dimples shone. But then her laughing eyes grew round and she jumped back. "Oh, my."

Lilly laughed so hard she lost her balance and tumbled to the floor.

Charlie bent over and slapped his knee. "She thought you were me, Papa."

Even Petey joined in the laughter—and his was the sweetest of all, because it was the most absent from the home.

Marjorie's cheeks turned a delicious shade of pink.

John tried hard not to laugh. "I wish you could see your cheeks." He reached up on instinct and touched her right cheek—and then became serious.

Marjorie stared at him, blinking her beautiful green eyes and took a step back.

He lowered his hand, unsure why he had done something so familiar. He cleared his throat while his children still reveled in the moment. "I came to tell you that you will dine with the children here in the nursery this evening."

She lifted her hand to the cheek he had touched, and she kept it there for a moment, not looking at him.

Lilly's laughter stopped. "Why, Papa?"

"I have a guest coming this evening."

"What time is it?" Marjorie asked suddenly, her hand dropping from her cheek.

"It's almost six o'clock now," John answered. "I need to get downstairs and wait for my guest."

Marjorie's cheeks drained of their previous color.

"What?" John asked.

"You have a guest coming? Tonight?"

"Yes. Miss Faulkner. She's the librarian at the Carnegie Library."

"Dr. Orton." Miss Ernst suddenly appeared at the top of the steps. "Miss Faulkner is here for supper."

"Please tell her I'll be right down."

"But I thought…" Marjorie paused. "What about Dora?"

"Dora?" John repositioned his suit coat. "What does Dora have to do with anything?"

Marjorie shook her head. "I don't know, apparently."

"Miss Ernst will bring your food up here." He began to cross the nursery but stopped and looked back at Marjorie. "Under no circumstances do I want to be bothered again."

"What if one of us gets sick, or hurt?" Lilly asked.

He tilted his head and looked at her. "Lilly, don't be silly. If you're hurt or sick, you can bother me. But nothing else."

"What if—"

John put up his hand. "Ask Miss Maren." He continued to cross the nursery and stepped through the door.

"Dr. Orton," Marjorie called out, and rushed across the room. "There's something you need to know."

He recalled how she had tried to persuade him regarding Mrs. Jensen and he shook his head. "It will have to wait. If you have something to tell me, please see me after my guest leaves." He descended the stairs and crossed the upstairs hall.

He shouldn't feel nervous, but he couldn't keep the jitters at bay. What if he and Miss Faulkner had nothing in common? It would be a long meal. He really knew nothing about her.

Miss Ernst met him just before he began his descent down the main staircase to the first floor.

"Dr. Orton, there's a woman here for supper."

John frowned at his maid. "Yes, I know. You already told me."

Miss Ernst clasped her hands, her eyes large. "There's a *second* woman here."

"A second woman? Who is she?"

"A Miss Baker."

John search his mind for a Miss Baker. "Is she the lady who goes to our church?"

"I believe she's the children's Sunday school teacher."

John scratched his head. "What is she doing here? You said she's here for supper?"

"That's what she told me."

"Where are they now?"

"I told both of them to wait in the parlor." Miss Ernst wrung her hands. "I didn't know what else to do."

"That's fine." John walked around her. "Please see that the children and Miss Maren get their supper."

"Yes, sir."

John quickly descended the stairs and walked across the front hall and into the parlor.

Two women sat in the room, on opposite sofas, looking very prim and proper—and very uncomfortable. They both rose when he entered the room.

"Good evening." He smiled at Miss Faulkner, and then Miss Baker—trying to discern why she was in his home.

"Good evening," Miss Baker said, extending her hand. "Thank you for the invitation to supper."

Miss Faulkner turned her blue eyes on John. She fidgeted with her reticule. "I'm sorry—did I come on the wrong night?"

"No." John clasped his hands behind his back. The awkward tension continued to rise with each breath he took. He looked at Miss Baker, unsure what to do with her. "I'm sorry, Miss Baker—have the children done something wrong at church?"

Miss Baker giggled. "Not at all. They're practically perfect."

John lifted an eyebrow. Practically perfect?

He cleared his throat, hating to embarrass her—but what else could he do? "I'm afraid I wasn't expecting you this evening."

"When were you expecting her?" Miss Faulkner asked John, her shoulders rising in indignation. "Do you have a woman planned for every night of the week?"

"Of course not."

Miss Baker's cheeks filled with color. "I'm terribly embarrassed. Miss Maren said you'd like for me to come to supper this evening."

"Miss Maren?" He glanced at the door leading to the hall, expecting her to be standing there, adding chaos to yet another situation. "I'm sorry, but she's dining with the children in the nursery this evening and she didn't tell me she was expecting a guest. You're free to join her there, if you'd like."

"No." Miss Baker laid her gloved hand on John's arm, glancing slyly at Miss Faulkner. "She intended for me to dine with you, Dr. Orton."

"Who is Miss Maren?" Miss Faulkner asked. "Do you have ladies dining on every level of your home this evening?"

"I'm afraid there's been a misunderstanding," John said.

"Apparently." Miss Faulkner put her reticule under her arm. "I will take my leave now."

Miss Baker fiddled with her gloves but didn't say a word.

"I wish you wouldn't leave," John said. "I had looked forward to our meal together."

Miss Faulkner stood straight, her back stiff. "Dr. Orton, I am not a young, inexperienced woman who will fawn at the feet of a man who shows interest in me." She pointedly looked at Miss Baker. "I have a bit of self-respect."

"I'm not suggesting—"

"I'll see myself out." Miss Faulkner strode from the room, never looking back.

The front door slammed shut and John cringed.

Miss Baker lifted her pretty brown eyes, her voice innocent. "I'm sorry for the trouble I've caused."

"No, I'm sorry. You had no idea." But Marjorie did! Why hadn't she told him she had invited a woman over for supper? She had no right to meddle in his affairs, yet she did constantly, and with little conscience.

He would tell his governess exactly what he thought about her matchmaking, if that was what this was.

Miss Baker made no move to leave. She swung her reticule in her hands and glanced up at John, a smile lighting her face.

Was he obligated to feed the lady? He hadn't extended the invitation—yet it would be rude to send her home hungry. "Would you care to join me for supper?"

"Yes. I would." She linked her arm through his and practically pulled him from the room.

As soon as supper was over, and Miss Baker was gone, he'd have another talk with Marjorie. This time he would tell her if she meddled again, he'd send her back to Chicago.

* * *

The meal couldn't end soon enough for John. Miss Baker had talked incessantly about herself, and though she said quite a lot, he really hadn't learned anything of value.

He closed the front door and watched Miss Baker walk down his sidewalk as the grandfather clock struck eight chimes.

It was time to confront Marjorie.

Frustration mounted as he climbed the stairs two at a time. The children should have been put to bed thirty minutes ago. He had hoped to say good-night to them, but it had been almost impossible to get Miss Baker to leave.

What had Marjorie been thinking? It wasn't her place to invite women over to his home for supper. The idea was preposterous, at best.

She had a lot of explaining to do.

After a string of mishaps and poor judgment on her part, he was wondering if she was the best person for the job of governess. She didn't dress appropriately for her position, she unnecessarily exposed the children to public places, she disrespected an important member of society, she fell asleep and almost lost his son and now she invited strangers to his home for supper—and she had only been in his house for ten days! What would happen next?

The upstairs hall was shrouded in shadows. He hated to bother her in her bedroom again, but this conversation could not wait.

No light seeped from the crack at the bottom of her bedroom door. Was she asleep?

Right now it didn't matter.

He knocked on her door and waited several minutes.

She didn't answer.

His gaze wandered down the hall to the next door. A faint light emanated from the night nursery. Maybe she was still putting the children to sleep.

He walked down the hall and slowly turned the handle, pushing the door open gently, and then paused on the threshold.

Marjorie stood in a nightgown with a robe cinched around her slender waist. A single lamp offered a soft glow from the corner of the room, illuminating her blond curls flowing freely. She held Laura against her shoulder, her back toward John, and swayed while she lovingly patted Laura's back. Brahms's "Lullaby" flowed beautifully from her lips.

"Lullaby, and good night,
With pink roses bedight,
With lilies o'erspread,
Is my baby's sweet head…"

John leaned against the doorframe, all anger slipping away as he took in the tender scene. Laura's downy head lay snuggled into the crook of Marjorie's shoulder, her cheeks pink with sleep, and her lips puckered from a recent feeding. She looked so content and natural in Marjorie's arms.

Marjorie gently lowered Laura into her cradle, the next verse filling the room with its sweet melody.

John glanced at Lilly, asleep on her bed, a soft smile on her lips. Could she hear the song as she slept?

Marjorie pulled a blanket up to Laura's chest and then held her curls back as she lowered her body to place a kiss on Laura's forehead. Her hand rested on Laura's cheek for a moment and then Marjorie stood straight, still singing the song.

She turned to exit the room and her gaze fell on John, standing in the doorway.

The song ended abruptly as she stared at him.

He looked at her for a few moments and then motioned for her to join him in the hall. He quickly stepped away from the door and stood in the dark passage, taking several deep breaths, trying to still the emotions stirring in his body.

It was natural to have affectionate feelings for a woman holding his child…wasn't it? There couldn't be any other explanation.

Marjorie was his children's governess. Though she was gentle and caring, and his children had come to love her, she was also outspoken, unorthodox and impractical. She challenged him constantly and he had a feeling she didn't follow all his rules.

Marjorie stepped through the door and closed it quietly behind her.

The hallway was now completely dark and he could only make out her soft silhouette from the faint moonlight filtering in through the windows over the stairwell.

His heart beat an irregular rhythm and he had to swallow several times.

This was ridiculous. She was his employee and he had to tell her he was disappointed in her. He stood straight and spoke. "Miss Baker came to supper tonight."

She wrapped her arms around her waist. "That's nice."

"That's nice?" He wished he could concentrate on reprimanding her. Instead, he could only think about her curls and her beautiful voice as she sang to Laura. "You had no right to invite a guest to my home to dine with me."

She was quiet for a moment and then she spoke softly. "I have a confession to make."

He put his hands behind his back, suddenly unsure what to do with them. "What?"

"She's not the only woman coming to supper this week."

"What?"

"Miss Addams and Miss Fletcher will also be coming."

"But—why?"

She took a step toward him, and he pulled back. He could smell the lilac scent she wore and it made his mind a jumbled mess. Why was he responding to her this way? She was the governess. He must keep that in mind. She was no different than Miss Ernst or Mrs. Gohl.

"You said you're looking for a wife," she said. "I thought each of them would be a good candidate."

He stared at her for several moments, speechless in the face of her confession. "Don't you think I'm capable of finding my own wife?"

She didn't answer.

"Miss Maren, you hardly know me, yet you assume someone like Miss Baker would be a good match?"

"Yes, I do."

"I just spent two hours in her company, and I can assure you she would not."

She lifted her shoulders. "Now you know. If she hadn't come, you might wonder."

"I could have told you before her arrival."

She put her hands on her hips. "Dr. Orton, may I be so bold to say you don't know what kind of wife to look for?"

He crossed his arms, indignation rising in his gut.

"No, you may not. I know exactly what I'm looking for. I wrote a list."

"I did, too, as a matter of fact."

"You wrote a list for my future wife?" He could hardly believe what she was saying. "What gives you the right to do that?"

"I care about your children—and you."

She cared about him? He swallowed the rush of surprise that surfaced at her statement. "I appreciate your concern—"

She took another step toward him and put her hand on his arm. "I want to know that once I leave this home, you and the children will be in good hands."

Her touch did strange things within him, and he had the urge to pull her into his arms and revel in more of her.

Guilt assailed him. Anna had been gone less than two months. How could he have these thoughts for another woman so soon? Surely these feelings were simply because he was tired and frustrated and lonely. Marjorie was a beautiful woman. Any man would notice.

He took a step back from the temptation she unknowingly presented. "We'll be fine."

"I need to be sure."

He ran his hand through his hair. "Trust me."

"Please give Miss Addams and Miss Fletcher a chance."

What were his other options? "I can't uninvite them—but I insist you and the children dine with us." If he was going to entertain two women he didn't want to entertain, then at least he'd have his children present and enjoy their company.

She sighed. "As you wish."

"And you are not allowed to invite anyone else to

this home unless you have my permission. Do you understand?"

Another sigh.

"Miss Maren?"

"Very well. But what about Dora?"

"Dora and Mrs. Scott are always welcome, but again, it's not your place to invite them."

"No, that's not what I mean." She was silent for a moment, and when she spoke, her voice was a bit hesitant. "I was surprised to hear you invited Miss Faulkner to supper after Sunday's talk with Dora."

Sunday's talk with Dora? What had he said to Dora that had anything to do with Miss Faulkner? "I don't understand."

"The conversation you had with her in your office."

"My office? How did you hear us?"

She glanced down and ran her slippered toes across the carpet. "I overheard while passing."

"We talked about a medical conference I'm invited to speak at before Christmas. What does that have to do with Miss Faulkner?"

She lifted her head. "You didn't propose to Dora?"

"Propose?" He couldn't hide the surprise from his voice. "Definitely not—and if you believed I had, why would you then invite another woman into my home?"

She opened her mouth, and then hesitated. "I thought maybe I could convince you to…keep your options open." She smiled and grasped his arms. "But I'm so glad you didn't propose."

Her touch was too much, and her joy at the revelation was too confusing. He pulled back and spoke in a harsh tone. "I hope we've come to an understanding. You will join me when the other two ladies come to supper—and you will not ask anyone else to come."

"Fine."

"Good night, Miss Maren."

"Good night, Dr. Orton."

John turned and strode down the hall to his bedroom. He almost slammed the door behind him, but caught it just in time.

He couldn't allow himself to dwell on Marjorie Maren, or his growing attraction to her.

The sooner he found a wife, the better.

Chapter Eleven

Three different dresses were strewn about Marjorie's bed as she buttoned up the fourth one she had tried on since church. Dr. Orton had told her to be ready to go for a drive at two o'clock, and it was now quarter to the hour.

Her hands shook as she readjusted the pins in her hair, once again. Why was she so nervous? She had been in the same home with the man for over two weeks now, and had just gone to church with him that morning. They had eaten lunch together with the children afterward. There was no reason for the anxiety she was experiencing.

A knock sounded at her bedroom door.

"Come in."

The door opened and Dora poked her head inside. "Hello, Marjorie."

The familiar face should have calmed her, but it had the opposite effect. Dora was here to take care of the children, which meant Marjorie was running out of time to prepare.

"A letter was accidentally delivered to our home yesterday." Dora stepped into the room and extended the envelope to Marjorie.

A letter? It was the first letter that had come for her since she left Chicago. With shaking hands she removed it from Dora's grasp and scanned the handwriting.

Preston.

Why would Preston write? The last time they had spoken was the night before their wedding date. She had hoped he would kiss her and speak of love. Instead, he had spent the evening going over household accounts, his expectations for their servants and their social calendar. It had felt as if they were embarking on a business deal, and not a marriage.

After he left her parents' home, Marjorie had gone to her room and sobbed. She didn't want a loveless relationship. She wanted passion and romance.

The desire to flee had overtaken her, and she had not appeared at the wedding the next day.

"I hope it's good news," Dora said. "You don't look very happy to see the letter."

Marjorie forced herself to smile. "I'm just a bit surprised."

"I'm going to tell the children I'm here now." Dora squeezed Marjorie's arm. "I hope you have fun this afternoon." With that, she left the room.

Marjorie's legs felt wobbly, so she sat on the edge of the bed and slowly lifted the flap of the envelope. What would Preston say? Would the letter be filled with scathing words—or would he plead for her to return?

She almost laughed at the second thought. Preston Chamberlain would not lower himself to beg.

That left only one possibility.

She lifted the letter from the envelope and unfolded

the paper. He did not address her, but simply started to write.

Where does one begin a letter such as this? I have felt every conceivable emotion in the two and a half weeks since you left me at the altar. I have asked myself a thousand questions, but the ones I cannot seem to find an answer to are: Why did you do it? And why did you wait until the very last second? I've thought through every conversation we had, and cannot fathom what went awry. Clearly I did nothing wrong, so that leaves me to believe it was a fault within you.

The newspapers have had a riot with this thing. Do you understand how embarrassed my family is? I am angry that you jilted me, but furious that you put them through so much pain. What about your own family? Have you no heart?

When I heard you went to Minnesota to be a governess, I couldn't believe my ears. What in the world would possess you to give up me for such a common life? You had a chance at being someone, Marjorie. I should have known you wouldn't follow through with your promise. You never do.

As far as I'm concerned, you had your chance at being a Chamberlain, and now you are simply a common laborer, lost in a sea of faceless strangers.

Marjorie lowered the letter, tears blurring her vision. She had expected him to be angry, but had not antici- pated how hurtful he could be. *I should have known you wouldn't follow through with your promise. You never do.* Was he right? Had she left him because she wasn't capable of sticking with something until the end?

No. She shook her head. She had left because it was the right thing to do. It was better to walk away than to be saddled in a marriage without love.

The hall clock struck the hour.

Marjorie shoved the letter back in the envelope and placed it under her mattress. The last thing she needed was for someone to discover why she had run away from Chicago. She wasn't prepared to answer all the questions that would arise.

With one last glance in the mirror, Marjorie grabbed her coat and left her bedroom.

She descended the stairs and found Dr. Orton pacing in the front hall. When he saw her, he stopped and watched her cross the room.

She started to put on her coat, but he took a step toward her.

"Let me help."

She handed the coat to him, her hands still trembling from Preston's letter. "Thank you."

His hand brushed her chin as he slipped the coat on over her shoulders, and their eyes met.

He quickly took a step back. "Dora has the children on the third floor. Are you ready?"

Marjorie swallowed and buttoned up her coat. Why was she acting so silly? Her nerves increased with each button she secured. "Yes."

He nodded and then strode to the back hall.

She followed behind, slipping on a pair of gloves to keep her hands warm during the cold automobile ride.

Dr. Orton held the door open for her and she passed into the backyard. A fine layer of snow covered the brown grass, but the warm sun shone overhead, keeping the streets clear.

They walked to the Ford on the stone path, Marjorie in front of Dr. Orton. When they arrived at the auto, he opened the passenger door for her and she sat on the cold leather seat.

He closed the door and then cranked the car to start. It rumbled to life, jostling Marjorie until she began to giggle.

Dr. Orton got into the Ford and glanced in her direction, a smile on his face. "What's so funny?"

Nothing, really, but her nerves were starting to get the better of her.

This was ridiculous! She stopped giggling and forced her face to become sober. "Nothing."

He gave her an odd look and then put the auto in Reverse. "I thought I would start by taking you to the falls in the river."

"All right."

They drove for several blocks in silence, past the courthouse and the library, past the downtown businesses, closed for the day, and past the stately post office with its large stone pillars. The Mississippi flowed sedately just ahead as Dr. Orton turned left and took the automobile down a small incline.

The falls were dammed behind a massive concrete structure, but water still flowed through the gates, crashing down on the bedrock below.

"This is one of my favorite places in town," Dr. Orton said as he parked the auto. "I often come here when I need to think or…pray."

Marjorie couldn't take her eyes off the powerful water. It mesmerized her as it danced over the spillway. It was so whimsical and yet—practical. The dam offered electricity to the entire town and powered dozens of industries along the river.

"Dora mentioned a letter arrived for you," Dr. Orton said. "I was wondering when you might hear from someone back home." He repositioned himself on the front seat and turned toward her. "I've been meaning to ask you about your family and life before you came to us. I really know very little about you."

What could she tell him, without giving away too much information? The newspapers had been very unkind to her, making up all sorts of tales about why she had jilted Preston. If Dr. Orton believed the lies, he would think her a terrible human being.

Maybe it was better if she didn't tell him anything about her engagement. He would have questions she wasn't prepared to answer, and he might go digging for more information. If he read some of the stories that had been reported, he might make her leave, and she couldn't have that. Not yet, not before she had found him a wife and completed her job.

"There's not much to tell. I grew up in Chicago. My father is a banker and my mother a socialite." She tried not to sound bitter. She loved her parents, and she supposed they loved her. They were simply the product of their social class, and she a disappointment to them. She had tried her whole life to please them, to fit into their world, but it went against her nature. Jilting Preston was simply the last disappointment in a long line of failings.

"How did I not know you before?" He studied her with his handsome brown eyes, and she had to look away. "You said you were my mother's neighbor?"

The water continued its fight for freedom around the dam gates, and then it tumbled southward on a path to the Gulf of Mexico, a course marked from the beginning of time.

"We moved to our home when I was ten years old, after you had left Chicago," she said. "Your mother became like an aunt to me and your younger brother, Paul, like a cousin." She smiled, thinking about Mrs. Orton.

Dr. Orton had her eyes.

"I'm not clear as to why you left Chicago," he said. "Do you truly want to go to California to be an actress?"

"Yes, I do."

"Why?" There was no censure in his voice, just curiosity.

Would he understand? "I want to become a movie actress so I can bring happiness into other people's lives."

He studied her, his eyebrows dipped low. "What do you mean?"

She sighed. "Sitting in a movie theater, you're transported to another time and place. You forget your troubles, even if for just a little while, and you get to experience a happily-ever-after—even if you will never have one of your own."

"Of course you will," he chided her, but his concern softened the lines on his face.

She didn't want to talk about matters of the heart with him. "Even so, I want to bring that type of joy into people's lives."

"Marjorie." Dr. Orton put his hand over hers. It was the first time he had said her name. "You don't need to be in the movies to bring that type of joy into people's lives. You've already done so in my children's lives."

His touch sent wonderful sensations flowing through her and caused her mind to wander down a path filled with romance—but he wasn't interested in romance.

He was only interested in practical things, just as Preston had been.

She pulled her hand away. "Thank you." She swallowed and looked back at the dam. "That's why I'm going to California. Just think how many more people I could impact."

He must have sensed her reluctance to continue their conversation, because he pulled away from the dam and didn't say another word about her past.

For over an hour, John drove Marjorie around Little Falls. He brought her past White Pine Lumber Company, home to the largest lumber mill in the world, and north to Belle Prairie, where the Belle Prairie Mission had once stood proudly on the banks of the Mississippi. He even drove her to the ruins of old Fort Ripley. He told her about the history of the area, and about the people who had shaped Little Falls into the thriving community he had joined ten years ago as a young man, just starting out on his journey.

She sat quietly, listening to what he said, but he felt as if she were miles away in California, or maybe Chicago. Her revelation had surprised him—but enabled him to see inside her heart, a place he didn't realize he longed to go until he was there.

"Would you like to see the hospital where I work?" he asked.

She tore her eyes from the scenery of the countryside. "Is it safe?"

"Safe?"

"Will I be exposed to influenza?"

"Are you taking your cinnamon oil?"

She scrutinized him. "Do you really think it works?"

"I do. I've had great success with the treatment.

That's why I've been asked to talk at the medical conference in Minneapolis."

"You're going to talk about cinnamon oil?"

He waved at a former patient outside a small home as they drove south toward St. Gabriel's Hospital. "Among other things, yes." He paused for a moment. "I've also been asked to talk about my own personal loss."

She was quiet for a moment. "Is there medical benefit to discussing Anna's death?"

His chest felt heavy with the reminder of his wife. As the days had progressed, and he had been preoccupied with his patients and with Marjorie's misadventures, he had kept the pain at bay. It was moments like this that it felt raw, like a fresh wound still bleeding. "At first I didn't think so, but then the conference director wrote a letter, explaining how my personal experience can help the other doctors feel more empathy toward their patients."

"Don't they have empathy now?" Marjorie asked. "I imagine all of them have been overwhelmed with loss. How could they not feel empathy?"

They drove through the downtown once again, this time going past the music hall and bank square. "Some have become desensitized to the loss. The director hopes my story will cause them to soften their hearts toward their patients' plight."

The sun sat low in the pale sky, illuminating Marjorie's curls. "Are you ready to talk about Anna's death?"

Was he? Did it matter if he wasn't? Life had forced him to move forward at a rapid pace. Three months ago, he would never have thought he'd be searching for a new wife—yet he was. He didn't think he'd be invited to speak at a prestigious medical conference, about a disease no one really understood—yet he was. He hadn't anticipated sitting in his Model T with a beautiful young woman, who set his pulse racing in a way that made him feel as if he was somehow being unfaithful to his marriage—yet he was.

"I don't think I'll ever be ready to talk about Anna's death, but I'll try." He stopped for a pedestrian to cross the street. "Dora has said she'll come to the house to help take care of the children while I'm away—if you want her to."

She didn't say anything for a moment. "You said the conference is right before Christmas—just a month away. Do you think you'll…?" Her words died away.

He glanced at her and found her fiddling with a button on her coat. "Do I think I'll what?"

"Do you think you'll be married by then?"

He directed his eyes toward the street once again, his palms suddenly sweating against the steering wheel. "Yes. I hope to be married by then, or at least planning a wedding," he said with little emotion. "Though it won't be a grand affair. After all, it will be a practical arrangement with no need for a big ceremony."

"Practical," she said quietly.

"Yes. Practical."

He turned left off Main Street and took the street leading to the yellow brick hospital on the southern end of town. The four-story building was one of the tallest in Little Falls. A matching building stood next door, housing the St. Otto's Orphanage. The sisters took care of the ill, the aged and the fatherless, and they did it with grace and humility. John was honored to be part of such a fine ministry.

He stepped out of the Model T and walked around to open the door for Marjorie.

She stood and put her hand on his arm, just before

he closed the door. Her eyes begged him, even before she uttered a word. "Please don't marry just for practicality's sake, John. Find someone who can take care of all your needs—but, at the same time, can make life an adventure for you every day. Find someone you want to grow old with—and not just because she'll make a good mother, but because..." She paused, her tone softening. "Because you love her."

He swallowed several times, unable to look into her penetrating gaze. "I've made up my mind. I will not marry for love."

Marjorie removed her hand from his arm and didn't say another word.

They walked into the hospital, side by side, and for a long time, he could still feel her touch on his skin.

Chapter Twelve

John crumpled yet another piece of paper and tossed it into the wastebasket near his desk at the hospital. It was the day after Thanksgiving, which meant he only had three weeks to prepare his keynote address for the medical conference.

He should be thinking about what he wanted to say, or at the very least, how his patients were faring on the floor above him—but all he could think about was Marjorie and their time together during their drive. At work, his thoughts often drifted to her. At home, he had become increasingly aware of her movements, listening for her voice, watching for a glimpse of her.

More reason to keep his focus on finding a wife. The sooner he was married, the sooner Marjorie could leave.

"Dr. Orton?" Nurse Hendricks lightly knocked on his open door. "I have the records you asked for."

John glanced up at his longtime nurse and took the folders she offered, thankful for a distraction from his thoughts. They were the records of patients who had survived influenza after getting his cinnamon oil treatment. He recommended ten drops in a glass of water to prevent influenza, but if a patient came to him already infected, he would prescribe ten drops in a glass of water every two hours until the fever subsided. If treatment began within a few hours of the onset, patients often showed signs of improvement within twelve hours. If treatment began later, it could be twenty-four to thirty-six hours before they were better—provided it wasn't too late.

If only he could get Dr. McCall to use cinnamon oil, perhaps others would be saved.

Nurse Hendricks studied him for a moment. She was close in age to John, but her youthful face showed no lines or wrinkles. Maybe because she had never married or had children.

"Are you feeling all right?" she asked. "You look terrible."

"Always ready to deliver the truth, aren't you?"

She smiled and folded her arms over her white uniform. "The bitter truth. It makes me a good nurse. Now tell me what's going on."

He waved aside her question. "I'm fine."

She took a seat across from his desk, her light brown eyes focusing on his face. "You might as well get it off your chest. I'm not going anywhere."

"Don't you have a job to do?" he teased. "I know for a fact that Mrs. Smith needs something."

"She always needs something." Nurse Hendricks leaned back in her chair. "Right now you have my undivided attention. Is this about the conference?"

John pushed away from his desk and stood. "No. This is a personal issue."

"Oh." Her one word was filled with a hint of discomfort.

"You asked." He crossed his arms and lifted his brow.

"I know." She laughed ruefully and braced her hands

on the armrests. "I can take it—no matter how personal it is. I'm a nurse, remember?"

John walked over to the window and looked out at the frozen earth. A snowstorm had finally passed by, layering the ground with a foot of pristine snow. It hung off the Norway pines just outside and insulated the roofs of the houses nearby. The bleak gray sky threatened more, which meant the disease was finally now under control—at least until spring.

He turned back and looked at her. "I need to find a wife, preferably before the end of the year."

She sat up straight. "A wife?"

"A mother for my children, actually."

"And that's what's bothering you?"

"Yes."

She looked down at her hands, her brisk voice now barely a whisper. "What's the trouble? Surely you, of all people, wouldn't have a hard time convincing someone to marry you."

He laughed. "I wish it was that easy."

Nurse Hendricks slowly stood from her chair. She was a tall woman and was eye level with him. Her face was serious. "It could be that easy."

John paused, but his pulse jumped. "You?"

"Don't look so surprised. I'm a woman, after all. I grew up with a houseful of siblings. I know my way around a nursery."

"Of course, but—" But he had never thought of her in that way. She was strong, independent and professional. She never spoke of her personal life, so he knew very little about her. He thought of her as a colleague, just as he did Dr. McCall. It never occurred to him to think of her any other way.

She lowered her gaze. "If you've run out of other options, you could consider me."

He rubbed his forehead, unsure how to proceed. He'd known her for years, and had always thought of her as the most competent nurse in the hospital. He had never considered that she might leave her work to marry and have a family. "Would you quit your position here at the hospital to do this for me?"

She glanced up at him and for the first time in the ten years he had known her, a shade of crimson filled her cheeks. "All you need to do is ask."

John couldn't have been more surprised by this turn of events. Had he ever addressed her by her first name? He was fairly certain it was Jacqueline—but he didn't know for sure.

Maybe this was the answer to his prayers—the answer that had been under his nose the whole time. He respected her and she fit every item on his list. She wasn't attractive, but she had a kind face, and when she smiled, her eyes twinkled with humor.

Best of all, he had never once had romantic thoughts toward her. He could honor his marriage vows to Anna and live with Nurse Hendricks in name only. Her skills as a nurse would prove invaluable as she took care of the children.

John couldn't help smiling. He would ask her out to a restaurant instead of have her at the house. Each time he had invited a female guest to dine with him had been a disaster. "Could I take you out for supper? I don't believe we've ever spent time together away from the hospital. It would give us a chance to talk."

She nodded. "I would like that."

"How about tomorrow night?"

"All right."

They stood for a moment in silence. Finally he took a step toward her and offered his hand. "It's Jacqueline, right?"

She took his hand and nodded.

"Tomorrow night," he said.

"What's tomorrow night?" Charlie suddenly appeared at John's door, his cheeks and nose pink from outside. He pushed into the office with Lilly and Petey close on his heels.

Marjorie was the last to arrive holding Laura on her hip. Her cheeks and nose were also pink, and her green eyes were shining—until her gaze fell on John holding Jacqueline's hand.

He let go instantly and took a step back.

"To what do I owe this surprise?" John asked his family.

"What's tomorrow night, Papa?" Charlie asked again.

"Children, do you remember Nurse Hendricks?" John asked.

"Hello, children," Jacqueline said.

The children greeted her, though Petey shied away.

"Nurse Hendricks, this is the children's governess, Miss Maren."

Jacqueline extended her hand to Marjorie. "It's a pleasure to meet you."

"Likewise." Marjorie shook her hand, her eyes scanning Jacqueline.

"We have a surprise for you," Lilly fairly sang. "You'll never guess."

"I'll leave you to your surprise." Jacqueline smiled at John and then left the office.

Charlie watched her leave, his perceptive gaze narrowed on John. "What's tomorrow night?"

They would learn about Jacqueline eventually. "I've

asked Nurse Hendricks to go out to supper with me."
He couldn't meet Marjorie's eyes.

"Supper?" Charlie asked. "Are you thinking about
marrying her, too?"

"Right now it isn't any of your concern."

"But it is," Charlie insisted.

"What's the surprise?" John asked Lilly instead.

Lilly's face lit up again. Apparently she forgot about
his supper plans with Jacqueline. "Miss Maren is bringing us Christmas shopping!"

John glanced at Marjorie, his brow raised.

"You said the threat of influenza has died down,"
Marjorie said. "I thought it would be good to get the
children out of the house and focused on something
joyful."

"The disease isn't gone completely."

"But they're taking their cinnamon oil."

"Miss Maren said we could go to a matinee at the
Lowell Theater, too!" Lilly said, jumping up and down.

"The matinee?" John asked.

"She said we'll love it!" Lilly grinned. "But best of
all, she said we're to invite you to come with us."

"Will you come, Papa?" Petey asked. "Please?"

"I don't think it's wise to go out in public quite yet,"
John said. "Miss Maren should have spoken to me
about these plans before she shared them with you."
He glanced at her—and instead of looking contrite, she
looked deceptively innocent.

Charlie's face darkened and he crossed his arms.

"Papa." Lilly's chin quivered, just as it had the day
he told her about Anna's death. His children had been
through so much these past few months, surely they
deserved one afternoon of fun.

He sighed. "All right. You may go."

Lilly's eyes cleared and she ran into his arms. "Thank you, Papa."

"Will you come with us?" Marjorie asked.

John glanced at the stack of reports on his desk, and the wads of crumpled paper in the wastebasket. "I really shouldn't take the day off—"

"It would mean a great deal to the children," she said.

John looked back at her, the desire to spend the day with her and the children a force he couldn't deny.

"It's just one day," Charlie said, his voice a bit grumpy. "Can't we enjoy one day together?"

John ruffled the boy's cap. "If it means that much, I'll see if I can get someone to cover for me."

The children jumped up and down, their cheers rising to the ceiling.

John looked over Charlie and Lilly's head to see Marjorie's face.

She smiled at the children and then met his gaze and offered him a victorious grin.

He couldn't help smiling in return.

Marjorie stole a glance at John as the screen flickered before them, making his face easy to see. He held Laura in his arms. She was fast asleep, allowing the rest of them to enjoy *Tarzan of the Apes*. Marjorie studied his handsome face, so full of love and compassion for his children and his work. She couldn't comprehend the great strain he was under to provide for his family and save a community of sick and dying. Marjorie had never met a more honorable man in her life.

Next to John, Charlie watched the movie wide-eyed, his mouth ajar as he was engrossed in the story taking place. Beside Charlie was Petey, who held his toy airplane, his face filled with a bit more reservation, though he watched avidly.

Beside Petey, next to Marjorie, Lilly sat primly in her wooden seat, her blue eyes darting around the screen. When captions appeared, Lilly bent over and read them aloud for Petey, who couldn't read yet.

A pianist sat at the front of the theater, playing the appropriate music for each scene.

Usually Marjorie was riveted to the story, watching the actors and actresses come to life with grand expressions and dramatic performances. But *Tarzan of the Apes* didn't hold her attention today. Instead, she couldn't stop looking at the Orton family. She pictured them in her mind, a couple years from now, sitting in this very row of chairs, watching Marjorie on the big screen.

What would each of them look like as they grew older? What would they do with their lives? Where would they go? Who would they marry?

Would they remember Marjorie and the few short months they'd had together?

John turned his head at that moment and met her gaze. His thoughts were imperceptible as he looked at her.

A delicious sensation coursed through her at his look, but she forced herself to return her gaze to the screen, reminding herself that John Orton was not meant for her. He could not offer her the kind of relationship she desired to have.

"Has anyone ever grown up in the jungle like that?" Lilly asked, not taking her eyes from the screen.

"There are many people who live in jungles," Marjorie answered quietly. "But I don't believe any of them have been raised by apes."

Lilly giggled and didn't say anything else.

Marjorie tried to follow the story, but she couldn't stop thinking about Nurse Hendricks. Was John considering her for a wife? The woman had appeared to be confident and straightforward. Maybe she would stand up to John and not allow him to sacrifice his family for his job.

Would Nurse Hendricks be sitting in the seat Marjorie currently occupied when the family watched Marjorie on the screen?

The thought left Marjorie feeling sad…and lonely.

Tarzan ended, much to the children's dismay.

They walked out of the theater, everyone bundled up with small packages in their hands from their earlier shopping.

"Must we go home?" Charlie asked, a yawn escaping his mouth.

"Mrs. Gohl will have supper ready for us," John answered as he handed Laura to Marjorie.

They piled into the Model T as John cranked it to start. He got into the front seat with Marjorie and Laura, while the three older children sat in the back. The children could not stop talking about the movie. They asked Marjorie and John all sorts of questions about jungles and apes, and movie projectors and cameras.

Their joy was the very thing Marjorie hoped to bring to others when she was in the movies.

The Orton home was only four blocks from downtown, so they made the trip quickly in the cold weather. John parked inside the carriage house and they all hurried into the warm back hall.

"I think I'll join Miss Maren in the movies one day," Charlie said as he took off his coat and hat.

"No, you won't," John said, unbuttoning Petey's coat.

"You'll get a good education and make something of your life." He looked up at Marjorie, an apology on his face. "I'm sorry, that didn't come out right."

Marjorie shook her head and hung up Lilly's wool sailor coat. "Come children, let's wash for supper."

"Marjorie—" John put his hand on her arm.

She stepped away from him and ushered Lilly out of the back hall, not wanting him to see how his words stung. "Don't bother to explain. It's fine." She swallowed the lie, knowing how some people felt about the movies. Many actresses had poor reputations—but she would be different. She would have nothing to do with the lifestyle they were known for. And even if people thought poorly of her, what did it matter? She had already lived through the worst scandal in Chicago's recent history. She could handle anything that came her way…well, almost anything. It surprised her how much it mattered what John thought.

Marjorie walked into the front hall, Laura in her arms, with all the other children following. John brought up the rear of the group, still trying to get her attention, but at the moment, she couldn't face him.

Miss Ernst appeared, her red hair sticking out of her maid's cap. "Mrs. Scott is in the parlor waiting to speak to you," she said to John. "She's been here for over an hour."

John sighed. "Miss Maren, can you see that the children are washed for supper?"

"She wants to see Miss Maren, as well," Miss Ernst said. "I'll tend to the children."

Why would Mrs. Scott want to see Marjorie? She mimicked John's sigh and handed Laura to Miss Ernst.

The children disappeared with the maid and Marjorie

couldn't help touching her hair to make sure every pin was in place. "What do you think she wants?"

John only shook his head.

They walked into the parlor and found Mrs. Scott standing near the window, looking out onto the front yard. She must have heard them, because she turned. "There you are."

"Hello, Mother Scott," John said. "What brings you here today?"

"Miss Marjorie Maren," Mrs. Scott said. "And this little piece of information." She held up a slip of newspaper. "It seems Miss Maren has been hiding some things from us."

John looked at Marjorie, a question in his eyes.

Marjorie took a step forward and spoke quickly. "Don't believe everything you read in the newspapers. Most of it was made up to sell more copies."

"Made up?" Mrs. Scott lifted the newspaper clipping and read. "'Miss Marjorie Maren, the daughter of prominent banker and business tycoon Joseph Maren, failed to appear at her wedding to railroad fortune heir Preston Chamberlain and has now gone missing. A grand wedding was planned, with a honeymoon to Europe. Mr. Chamberlain had even purchased an elaborate home for his bride-to-be, tailored to her specific demands and filled it with expensive furnishings and a full staff.

"'Where is the bride, we ask? And why would she run away from the most eligible bachelor in town? Sources have confirmed that Miss Maren was seen in the arms of a married man the night before her wedding. Did she run off with the man? Ladies, if your husband is missing, he could very well be in Miss Maren's arms this very moment—'"

"They lied," Marjorie said.

John frowned as Mrs. Scott handed him the clipping.

"See for yourself, John," Mrs. Scott said with a smug nod. "I told you she was no good."

John looked at Marjorie. "I don't understand. Is any of this true?"

She swallowed, ashamed that he had heard this from someone other than her. "Some of it—"

"And you let her spend time with your children?" Mrs. Scott asked. "She's a terrible influence. Dora would be so much better for all of you. Why don't you simply propose and get on with your lives?"

"Mother Scott, please." John spoke to his mother-in-law but didn't take his eyes off Marjorie. "Now is not the time to speak of Dora."

"But when is it time? I'm afraid she won't wait forever—"

John pointed to the newspaper article. "Miss Maren, can you please explain this?"

"She'll only tell you more lies," Mrs. Scott said.

"Mother Scott, maybe you should leave." John tore his eyes from Marjorie. "I would like to talk to Miss Maren alone."

Mrs. Scott took a step toward Marjorie and wagged her finger under Marjorie's nose. "You're a disgrace to the Orton and Scott families. I knew the moment I saw you that you were carrying a secret. You have that sly look about you—"

"Mother Scott." John's voice filled with warning. "No one deserves to be treated that way—especially in my home. You need to leave immediately."

Mrs. Scott's mouth fell open. "I can't believe you'd speak to me that—"

"Please leave." John walked out of the parlor and opened the front door.

Mrs. Scott looked from Marjorie to John, disbelief on her face. "Fine. I'll leave—and I won't return until this woman is safely out of your home."

Marjorie's back grew stiff as she watched the woman depart.

Mrs. Scott swept her dress away from John as she exited the house.

John closed the door firmly and reentered the parlor. "Now, tell me what all this is about."

Marjorie licked her dry lips, suddenly in need of something to drink.

John crossed his arms. "What part is true and what is made up?"

Marjorie had faced her parents and numerous friends after she jilted Preston—but none of them made her as nervous as John. Why did she care so much about what he thought of her? She would rather face Preston right now.

"It's true that I was engaged to Preston Chamberlain, and it's true that he purchased a home for us—though I had nothing to do with furnishing it or hiring the staff. That was part of the problem. It should have been fun to do those things together, shouldn't it? But with Preston, everything was so practical and matter-of-fact. He treated the whole thing like a business venture—and I suppose it was. He and my father had been working together for years—"

"Marjorie, you're rambling."

She took a deep breath. "It's also true that I stood him up at the altar. I didn't have the courage to face him and call off our engagement." Or, rather, she didn't have the courage to face her parents, knowing how disappointed they would be. "So I simply didn't show up at the wedding." She said the last few words barely above a whisper. Marrying Preston was yet another thing she had failed to complete.

"What about…?"

"The married man?"

He nodded, watching her carefully.

It was true that she was in the arms of a married man—but not for the reason John thought. She clasped her hands, trying to hide their sudden shaking. "That part is true, too. But nothing happened."

"Why were you in his arms?"

She bit her bottom lip for a moment. He was the last person she wanted to discuss this subject with. "I can't say."

"Why not?"

"I can't tell you why—I need to protect him."

"From me?"

"From gossip. I can't risk saying anything. You'll have to believe me that nothing was inappropriate about the hug."

"Why didn't you tell me the truth when we first met?"

"I was afraid you would believe the rumors."

"Then you don't know me very well."

"You're right. I *didn't* know you well—but now that I do…" She paused. "Well, I'm almost sure I can trust you to believe me."

John was quiet for a moment as he stood across from her. "You'll have to trust me to believe you, just as I'll have to trust that you're telling me the truth."

She needed him to trust her, especially if the whole truth was ever revealed.

Chapter Thirteen

John pulled up to the curb and looked at the address Jacqueline had given him. Before him stood a large boardinghouse only two blocks from the hospital. White trim and black shutters hung against red clapboard. Smoke spiraled from the chimney while an evergreen wreath hung on the front door, its ribbon blowing in the cold wind.

He should have been excited to pick her up and spend the evening with her—after all, he could potentially be spending the rest of his life with her.

So why was he dreading their meal together?

Before the thought fully formed, he knew the answer. It was because he'd rather be at home with his family. He had left them sitting in the parlor with plans to make popcorn over the fireplace and read *Little Women* together after supper. Charlie had been sitting in a wing-back chair, one leg draped over the armrest, while Lilly had sat on the floor, playing with Laura, and Petey had been running through the room, flying his toy airplane over tables and sofas and around the lamp.

But it was Marjorie who had captured his full attention. She had sat on the sofa, opposite Charlie, engaging him in a conversation about something that had happened at school. The two of them hardly noticed as he had said goodbye.

Despite his promise, John couldn't forget the conversation he'd had with her after Mother Scott left the day before. He trusted her that nothing inappropriate had happened in Chicago, but it didn't stop him from wondering what part of the story was true, and what part had been made up by the newspaper. Why had she been in another man's arms? Who was the man, and why was she trying so hard to protect him?

He sighed as he walked up the sidewalk to the boardinghouse. Before he could knock, Jacqueline was standing there with a smile on her face. He had never seen her in anything other than her white nurse's uniform, and it took him a moment to recognize her.

"Hello, Doctor," she said.

"Hello..." He paused, just about to call her Nurse Hendricks. Instead, he said, "You can call me John."

She offered him a shy smile. "I don't think I can."

He extended his arm. "May I call you Jacqueline?"

She stepped over the threshold and closed the door, and then tentatively wrapped her arm through his. "Of course."

"Then I hope you can call me John."

She laughed nervously. "I'll try, but forgive me if I slip up. Ten years is a long time to call someone a name and then call them something different."

He brought her to the Ford and opened the passenger-side door. "Are you nervous?"

Jacqueline let out a quick breath. "Terribly."

"Then that makes two of us." But he wasn't nervous to be with her—he was nervous that this was all a big mistake and he should have stayed home.

A smile of relief lit her face. "Thank you for understanding."

John cranked the car to start and then jumped into the driver's seat. "I hope you like the Sand's Café."

She looked at him with a grin. "I don't care where we go tonight."

They drove to the Sand's Café in downtown and found a booth near a large plate-glass window. Automobiles and buggies drove down Main Street, and pedestrians strolled on the sidewalks. The lights from the Lowell Theater blinked, drawing his attention as people entered the building to see *Little Orphan Annie*.

The restaurant was cozy, with a balcony nestled high in the wall across the room. A couple sat there, noses practically touching as they gazed into each other's eyes. The woman smiled at the man and offered him a kiss before she giggled and pulled away.

John couldn't help picturing Marjorie in that little balcony. She would be talking and laughing and full of life. He would probably spend the entire meal with his chin in his hand, just watching her and laughing at her uncanny ability to get into trouble. He had a feeling she would be affectionate and playful, just like she was with the children.

"John." Jacqueline fluttered her hand in front of his face. "Eugenia is here to take our order."

John blinked several times and then smiled as one of the Sand sisters stood before him, a pad and pencil in her hand.

"Do you want what they're having up there?" Eugenia asked with a little wiggle in her brow. "I'm not serving kisses here tonight. Meat loaf, yes, hugs and kisses, no."

Jacqueline's cheeks filled with color and John cleared his throat. "I'll have the meat loaf."

"I will, too," Jacqueline said as she lifted the menu.

Eugenia winked at them. "Coming right up."

John finally met Jacqueline's gaze and he offered her an embarrassed smile. "Sorry. I was lost in thought."

"I've been like that since yesterday when you asked me to supper." She glanced at his head and nudged her chin in his direction.

"My hat!" He quickly removed it from his head. "Forgive me. I'm preoccupied tonight."

"So it seems."

He looked her over. "I've never seen you in your everyday clothes. You look different without a nurse's uniform." Instead of a white dress, she had on a plum-colored affair. It was a bit old-fashioned, especially compared to Marjorie's extravagant clothing.

"I feel like my nursing uniform has become my everyday clothes, especially since the influenza outbreak." She crossed her arms, looking every bit the competent nurse he knew. "Let's stop stalling and start talking about the reason we're here tonight."

"That's what I like about you—"

"No nonsense."

"Exactly." He pushed aside his silverware and put his clasped hands on the table. With a deep breath he plunged forward. "I've been looking for a wife for several weeks now."

"I've been looking for a husband for about ten years."

"My children need a mother."

"I'd love to have children."

John paused. "Would you really consider this?"

Jacqueline reached across the table and put her hands over his. It was the first intimate touch they had ever shared and it sent a strange and unpleasant feeling through John.

"I've admired you for years," Jacqueline said. "The way you handle patients, the devotion you had for your wife, the love you have for your children. You're the most amazing man I've ever met. When Anna died, I mourned with you—but a part of me hoped that maybe, once you stopped mourning, you might look my way." She shook her head in disbelief. "I never actually thought you would. I know I'm not much to look at—"

"Jacqueline." He wanted to remove her hands from his, but he didn't want to embarrass her. "I'm still mourning and I'm flattered that you think so highly of me, but—"

"I think I've always been in love with you, but I was content to watch you from a distance." She lowered her eyes until her lashes brushed her cheeks. "Could it be that I might share your life? It seems like a dream come—"

"Nurse Hendricks." This time he did remove his hands. "I'm afraid you've misunderstood me."

Jacqueline pulled her hands into her lap, her eyes filled with mortification. "What?"

"I have no interest in love or romance." Heat gathered under his collar and he pulled it away from his sticky neck. "I need a mother for my children, and that is all. If you marry me, you will sleep in the governess's room and will be expected to care for Charlie, Lilly, Petey and Laura. I mean no disrespect, but I will marry in name only—nothing else."

Jacqueline swallowed. "Is it because I'm too plain?"

"What?" He was struck speechless for a moment. "No, of course not. Looks have nothing to do with this." He swallowed the lump of discomfort in his throat.

"No. You're a fine-looking woman. Any man would be proud—"

"Is it because of my age? I know I'm over thirty years old and no longer a desirable age to bear children—"

"No," John said again, wishing he could get up and leave this conversation. "Age has nothing to do with this, either. I simply do not want a traditional marriage. I am still grieving Anna and I would not dishonor my vows to her and marry again for love."

"But with time…"

John shook his head. "I am content to remain in separate rooms permanently."

Eugenia brought their plates of meat loaf and mashed potatoes. She glanced at both of them with curiosity in her gaze. "Is there anything else I can get for you?"

John and Jacqueline shook their heads.

When Eugenia was gone, neither one touched their food.

"I had hoped to have children," Jacqueline said quietly, pushing aside her plate of food. "I would not be content to raise Anna's children without a few of my own."

Anna's children.

John absently turned his plate until the corn was facing him. When Marjorie was with the children, she treated them as if they were her own. She loved them unconditionally, and he had a feeling, if he married her, she would be content even if she never had any of her own.

His head came up at the thought.

Jacqueline studied him with an odd look.

"I'm sorry," John said, bringing his thoughts back to the present—back to Jacqueline. "But I can never offer you love or children of your own. I only have my home, my name and my children to offer."

She studied him for a moment. "You've always respected me for telling you the truth, haven't you?"

"Yes, I have."

"Well, here's the truth, Dr. Orton. It would never be enough to be married in name on—"

He opened his mouth to defend his position, but she put up her hand and continued.

"Yes, legally I would have your name and be entitled to everything you own, but I would be no different than a hired governess. If I'm to be hired by anyone, then I will stay on at the hospital where I can have the freedom to come and go, and where I can continue to look for a man who will love me and offer me everything my heart desires."

She was right. What he was offering her wasn't fair. "You deserve nothing less than true love, Jacqueline."

She reached across the table and squeezed his hand, this time for just a moment. "You do, too, John."

"I can't ask God for true love twice in a lifetime." He lifted his fork and sank it into his mashed potatoes. "Besides, I have no desire to love again."

"May I add one more thing?" she asked.

He offered her a nod.

"Your children also deserve to have a mother who loves them like they need to be loved—not one who simply agrees to marry you just to raise them. Even if she's willing to settle for a loveless marriage, make sure she's not willing to settle for loveless parenting."

Her words were filled with truth. His children deserved unconditional love, but who would love them like a mother?

Marjorie filled his thoughts once again. After watching her with his children, he could no longer picture someone else filling the role of mother to Charlie, Lilly, Petey and Laura. When he closed his eyes at night, it was Marjorie he saw sitting at his table, and playing with his children, and rocking Laura to sleep. It was Marjorie he pictured when he came home from work. She would be ideal.

He might not be able to give her everything she desired in a marriage, but unlike Jacqueline, Marjorie loved his children and they loved her. Maybe that would be enough of an incentive for her to stay.

But could he marry her, and keep her at a safe distance?

He took a bite of his meat loaf and swallowed it down with a drink of water. It would be hard, but if it meant his children were receiving the love and attention they needed, he would do whatever needed to be done.

Maybe the answer to his prayers was already living in his home.

Snow fell softly against Marjorie's bedroom window as she sat curled up in an overstuffed chair. A lamp glowed over her shoulder, and the fireplace crackled beside her, sending smoke and embers up the chimney. The book in her hand remained open, but she could not concentrate on the words. Her gaze and her thoughts were focused outside, away from her room, and somewhere in town where John was dining with his nurse.

Marjorie sighed and put her bookmark in place.

It was no use. She could not focus until John was safe at home.

The children had been in bed for thirty minutes, which meant she should try to get some rest, but she knew sleep would elude her. Her mind was wide-awake.

The door leading to the night nursery creaked open and Lilly entered Marjorie's bedroom. "May I come in?"

Marjorie smiled, thankful for a diversion on this cold, snowy night. She held her arms open. "Please come in, Lilly Belle."

Lilly rushed across the room and climbed into Marjorie's lap. She laid her head on Marjorie's shoulder. "I couldn't sleep."

"Neither could I."

"What do you do when you can't sleep?"

Marjorie ran her hand over a strand of Lilly's golden hair. "I try to pray or read my Bible. Sometimes I write in my journal. But if none of that works, I drink warm milk and eat a cookie."

Lilly lifted her head. "I think milk and cookies would make me very sleepy."

Marjorie giggled. "I had a feeling that might work. Shall we go to the kitchen?"

Lilly nodded and climbed off Marjorie's lap.

They tiptoed out of Marjorie's room and used the servants' stairs to go to the kitchen.

The room was dark and chilly. Marjorie flipped on a light switch and walked over to the gas stove. She hadn't spent much time in Mrs. Gohl's kitchen—or any kitchen for that matter—but she did know where the milk and kettles were, since she often prepared the special formula John recommended for Laura.

Lilly went to a small pantry and opened the oak icebox. She pulled out the milk while Marjorie stood on tiptoe to get the copper kettle from the top shelf, making sure she didn't bang the kettles together and cause the whole house to rise. "You're such a good helper, Lilly. What would I do without you?"

Lilly giggled as Marjorie set the kettle on the stove and Lilly poured the milk inside.

"Now, don't let it scorch," Lilly warned. "Keep the heat low and stir it constantly with a whisk."

Marjorie smiled as she turned on the gas burner. She might not know her way around a kitchen, but she could warm milk—even if that was almost all she knew how to make. What would she do on her own in California before she earned enough money to hire servants? She might very well starve.

Marjorie glanced at the kitchen clock. It was ten minutes after eight. When would John return home?

"I was thinking about Papa and Nurse Hendricks," Lilly said as she stood beside Marjorie, watching her stir the milk.

"What were you thinking?"

"I don't want my papa to marry her."

"No?"

Lilly put her arm around Marjorie's waist. "I want you to stay here forever."

Marjorie put her free hand around Lilly's shoulder. "I wish I could stay forever."

Lilly looked up at Marjorie, her innocent face filled with questions. "Then why don't you? I can talk to Papa and ask him to let you stay."

"I wish it was that easy." Marjorie watched the white liquid spin around the kettle. "Your papa wants to get married again so you can have a mother. It's very important for children to have one, you know. A mother can do more for you than a governess."

"Why don't you marry my papa?" Lilly asked.

"Oh, sweetheart." Marjorie stopped stirring the milk and squatted down until she was eye level with Lilly. "I would love to be your mother, but I am going to Cali-

fornia. Your father will find someone who would make
a far better mother than me." She offered Lilly a smile.
"I'm still trying to help him find the perfect one."

"I think I already have."

Lilly and Marjorie both turned their heads at the
sound of John's voice.

"Papa!" Lilly raced across the kitchen and jumped
into her father's arms.

He hadn't removed his hat or coat, and snow clung to
his clothing. He watched Marjorie with his dark brown
eyes. She stood and turned back to the stove, blindly
stirring the milk, wishing her stomach didn't feel so
strange every time he appeared unexpectedly.

"What are you still doing awake, Lilly?" John asked.

"Miss Maren and I couldn't sleep, so we came downstairs for warm milk and cookies."

John's heavy footsteps crossed the kitchen floor until
he stopped just beside Marjorie. "It looks like the milk
won't be ready for a little while. Go and grab a couple
cookies." John set Lilly on her feet. "And then get to
bed. We have church in the morning."

"May I bring my cookies to my room?" Lilly asked
hopefully.

"Just this once." John took his hat off and set it on
the table next to the stove. "I need to speak with Miss
Maren. Alone."

Marjorie looked down at her robe and slippers, all
too conscious of her unbound hair.

Lilly ran to the pantry and pulled a cookie jar off
the shelf.

John continued to stand beside Marjorie.

Steam began to rise from the milk as her mind
swirled with what he had just said. Had he asked Jacqueline to marry him? He said he found the perfect

mother for his children... Then why this stab of pain? Wasn't that what she wanted? To be replaced?

She licked her dry lips but didn't look at him, not trusting her emotions at the moment. "Maybe I should bring Lilly up to her room." Marjorie started to move away from the stove, but John gently held her arm.

"I'd like for you to stay."

His touch sent warmth through her body, but it was the tickle of his breath upon her cheek that caused gooseflesh to race up the back of her arms. He smelled of a spicy cologne that made her head swim and her pulse beat against her wrist and neck.

They stood that way until Lilly hurriedly left the room with a handful of cookies, as if she was afraid her father would change his mind. "Good night," she mumbled over her shoulder, a cookie already in her mouth.

As soon as she was gone, John reached around Marjorie and turned off the gas. The flame under the kettle sputtered and died.

Marjorie swallowed and waited, unsure what she should do or say. His earlier comment still echoed in her mind and heart. Would Marjorie be forced to leave much sooner than she had planned...than she was ready?

"Would you like me to pour you a glass?" he asked close to her ear.

The last thing she wanted at the moment was a glass of warm milk, but she nodded. "Yes, please."

John moved away from her and took two glasses out of a cupboard. His movements were slow and steady as he poured milk into each one. When he was done, he offered her a glass. "Be careful. It's hot."

She took the glass of milk but didn't take a sip. The liquid heated the glass and warmed her hand.

"Would you please sit with me?" John asked.

Marjorie's breath was unsteady and her hands shook. "All right."

He indicated the table in the corner of the room, near the floor-to-ceiling window, where the light didn't quite reach.

John pulled out a chair for Marjorie and she took the seat.

Snow continued to fall outside, gently brushing the window and falling on the white ground. It was a steady snow with little wind to move it about.

"How long do you think the storm will last?" she asked, unable to look him in the eye.

He took off his hat and coat, and then sat across from her at the small table causing their knees to touch.

She repositioned herself.

"Marjorie."

"Yes?"

"Will you please look at me?"

She tore her gaze off the snow and looked into his warm brown eyes.

"Did you hear what I said earlier?" he asked. "When I first entered the kitchen."

She nodded, but she couldn't bring herself to repeat his statement. She couldn't bear to think of what it meant.

How had she allowed herself to get so entwined in this family?

"I said I have finally found the perfect mother for my children."

Nurse Hendricks. It made sense. He had known her for years. They worked well together. Marjorie hated to admit the truth, but she was almost certain John had found a woman who would fulfill many of the items on *both* of their lists. "When will you get married?"

"As soon as she says yes."

"You haven't asked her yet?"

He shook his head slowly, his gaze intense. "These things take time."

She played with the rim of her glass. Almost relieved that he hadn't asked her yet. It meant she'd have more time with the children before she was forced to leave—yet he didn't have much time left. "Remember, I'm leaving the first of the year."

"I know, and I'll be gone for a few days before Christmas."

She frowned as she studied his handsome face. "I don't understand why you need more time to ask her— isn't she agreeable to the idea?"

It was his turn to study her. "I don't know."

"Then why not ask her? Even if she says no, you may still have time to convince her."

He swallowed. "All right." He cleared his throat, his face very serious. "Will you marry me, Marjorie?"

Marjorie stood so quickly she bumped the table and the two glasses of milk tipped. White liquid spilled across the table and splashed her nightgown. *"Me?"*

He rose, milk dripping from his trousers. "It's not the worst idea."

"But—what about Jacqueline?"

"She would never love my children the way you do."

Marjorie pointed to her chest. "*I* can't marry you."

"Why not?"

"There are so many reasons." The most important was that he didn't love her—and she could never marry a man who didn't love her.

Unexpected moisture gathered in her eyes. She

turned away so he wouldn't see her silly tears and crossed to the sink to grab a dish towel. She was able to get herself under control before she came back to the table and wiped the warm mess.

John grabbed another towel and bent down to clean the floor. He looked up at her, his voice soft, entreating. "I'm sorry I upset you. I thought, since the children love you…maybe you'd consider staying."

"The children?" Pain sliced through her. Yes, the children loved her—but that would not be enough to sustain a marriage. She needed the love only a husband could give. She refused to settle for anything less—refused to sleep in the governess's room for the rest of her life.

"I know what happens when a man and a woman marry each other without love." She set down the damp rag, her voice quivering with emotion. "Bitterness grows where love should reside, and they become angry and cold toward each other, and toward the world. I could never enter a loveless marriage."

He slowly stood. "Marjorie, I cannot—"

She shook her head. "I know." She couldn't bear to hear his words—not now, not when he had just proposed. She knew what he would say, but hearing him say it would be too much. "I should go to bed."

She walked around him and he didn't try to stop her.

The back stairs were dark as she climbed them. One of the treads creaked, making her jump and causing the tears to start up all over again.

She stopped and leaned against the wall. What did it matter if John proposed to her without loving her? He needed a mother for his children; she knew that from their very first conversation. Hadn't she even tried to find someone for him to marry? His proposal should

mean nothing to her—another business proposition—
no different than him asking her to be the children's
governess.

Yet it did matter.

He was the second man to propose marriage without offering her love.

Was it too much to ask for someone to love her?

Chapter Fourteen

John rested his hands against the top of the kitchen table, staring at the falling snow just outside the window. A gust of wind whipped around the house, swirling the flakes in a dizzying dance, much like the thoughts and emotions raging inside him.

He'd made a mess of things. What had he been thinking to just blurt out his question? He had planned to lay out all the reasons why she would be the perfect mother for his children. He knew it might take some convincing, but he didn't expect her to get so upset.

Milk still clung to the crack in the table and dripped off the edge and onto the floor. John set both glasses upright and stared at the dirty towels. He sat at the table and put his head in his hands. He had been a fool to even think she'd agree to give up her dreams to help him. She deserved more than what he could offer.

Yet he wanted her to stay. The idea of her leaving left an empty void in the pit of his stomach.

The faint sound of crying met his ears and he lifted his head.

Marjorie?

He stood and walked over to the stairs, flipping the

kitchen light off as he went. He would apologize to Mrs. Gohl in the morning for the mess—but right now he had something far more important to tend to.

The stairway was dark, but as he turned the corner, he saw Marjorie's outline on the landing. She leaned against the wall, her face in her hands, and she was crying.

Empathy filled John's chest and he longed to put his arms around her. He hated seeing her upset, especially if he had caused her tears.

But why had he caused them? Was the thought of marrying him so terrible?

"Marjorie," he said gently as he stopped on the landing.

She looked up at him. The glow of a hall lamp reached down the stairs and he could faintly make out the lines of her beautiful face, tears streaking her cheeks. She really would make a stunning actress on the movie screen. And if she looked half as heartbroken on film as she did in this moment, men and women all over America would cry with her.

He touched her cheek and moved a tear off her delicate skin. "What's wrong?"

She didn't move away from his touch. Instead, she studied him, her face filled with uncertainty. She looked so soft and vulnerable in her nightgown and robe, with her hair trailing down her back. It curled around her face, making her look even more unguarded at the moment.

She slowly lifted her hand and placed it on top of his.

"I can't marry a man who doesn't love me." Her voice was filled with sorrow. "It's the reason I left Preston."

John removed his hand from her cheek and put a little space between them on the landing. "My children's love is not enough?" He felt foolish even asking. Of course it wasn't enough. And the look in her eyes confirmed his foolishness.

"A child's love is not enough to sustain a marriage. My birth didn't help my parents' marriage—if anything, it complicated everything."

"I'm sorry, Marjorie." He leaned against the opposite wall. "I wish I could offer my heart—but I'm afraid I buried it with Anna. I can never allow myself to love again or betray her in that way."

She shook her head and a lock of her blond hair fell over her shoulder. "I wouldn't ask you to. But someday, you will remarry, and I'm worried—" Her voice caught and she began to cry again. He felt helpless to stop her.

He took a step toward her again and moved a curl away from her cheek, reveling in the silkiness. "What's wrong now?"

She bit her trembling lip. "It's silly." She tried to laugh. "I'm just being silly."

"What?"

"I'm suddenly…afraid of the woman who will some-day replace me."

"Afraid?"

"I'm afraid to leave the children in the hands of someone else." Emotions warred within her gaze. "Maybe *j-jealous* is a better word, though I despise it." She stood straight, as if she was ready to face the truth. "I do love your children and I don't like the thought of someone else stepping in and taking my place."

A bit of hope took root in his heart. He was desperate to convince her, and hoped it wouldn't take much. "Then don't go. Stay…for the children."

She looked at him through her watery eyes, probing him. "Only for the children?"

For one brief, irrational moment, he let down his guard and put his hand back on her cheek.

She looked up at him, her eyes inviting.

Before he could think about the repercussions, he dropped his lips to hers and captured her mouth in a kiss.

Her lips parted in surprise and he deepened the kiss, pleased when she melted under his touch. It felt strange to kiss someone other than Anna—but it also felt wonderful.

All too soon, he realized what he was doing, and he pulled away, ashamed of his rash behavior. "I'm sorry— I shouldn't have done that."

She put her fingers to her lips, her eyes bright with uncertainty.

He wanted to tell her to stay for him, too—but he couldn't. It wouldn't be fair, to either of them. Shame assailed him, and panic raced up his legs. He needed to get away from her. She posed too much of a threat to his heart. What had he been thinking? He couldn't be married to Marjorie in name only. Eventually he wouldn't be able to keep his distance. Wasn't this stolen moment proof? "I was wrong to ask you to marry me. Please forgive me—for everything tonight."

He couldn't stay there with her. Embarrassment and shame coursed through him. He took the stairs two at a time and crossed the hall. He entered his bedroom and quickly closed the door, locking it on instinct, his breath coming hard.

He ran his hands through his hair, frustrated by how he had handled the whole situation. He wouldn't blame her if she left tomorrow. He had asked her to stay—and for what? For a broken man who offered her nothing in return. And what of that kiss? What had he been thinking? What must *she* be thinking? He had been a heartless cad. Asking her to marry him, kissing her the way he did and then telling her he would never love her.

Anger at himself burst inside his chest and he wanted to growl at his stupidity. He paced the room, reliving all the moments that had just passed—but he paused when he heard her bedroom door click down the hall.

John sank to the floor and dropped his face into his hands.

Anna's lavender sachet filled the bedroom with her scent, bringing back a lifetime of memories. Guilt washed over him just thinking about his wife, and how he had dishonored her by kissing another woman in their home.

He had wept the night Anna died, and he wept the night of her funeral. Tonight, he wept again, because for the first time he realized he had lost more than his beloved wife the day she died.

He had lost a lifetime of love, affection and companionship. Never to be had again. He had to let Marjorie go. She was a woman any man would be proud to have as a wife—and she would make a wonderful mother. Yet he was not free to pursue her, to open his heart to loving her like she needed to be loved.

He wiped at his face, resolve hardening his heart. He had been wrong to ask Marjorie to marry him. It had been a foolish decision that both of them would regret.

He would turn his efforts back to his list to find a mother for his children before the end of the year—one he wouldn't be tempted to kiss...or love.

Marjorie stood in her bedroom, leaning against the door, tears streaming down her face. Her poor heart had been pummeled and left tender and bruised.

John had asked her to marry him but told her he could never love her.

Then he had kissed her like she had never been kissed before. Oh, why had he gone and done something so terribly wonderful? A kiss changed everything. Made her feel things she never dreamed of feeling.

How would she face him in the morning?

Her corner lamp was still on, and the book she had been reading before Lilly came in was sitting on the chair. The fire had died down to embers and the snow continued to fall, though now it wasn't soft but had turned into hard pellets of ice.

She flipped off the lamp, removed her robe and slippers and crawled between the cold sheets, shivering for a long time.

It was true, she loved the children, but how could he think that would be enough? She wanted to be angry at him, but she couldn't. He was grieving and only wanted what was best for his family.

Marjorie rolled onto her back and stared up at the dark ceiling. She admired John more than any other man she had ever known. She enjoyed the times she spent with him and looked forward to him coming home from work. She adored his laughter and the way he cared for his children with discipline and love. She respected his work and marveled at the way he was revered in the community.

But what did any of it matter, if she did not have his love?

Marjorie looked over at the window and watched the snow. It gathered in the corners and sounded like sand hitting the glass.

She thought back to the conversation with John in

the kitchen, and the myriad emotions that had flooded her being. But one emotion stuck out above the overs.

Jealousy.

Marjorie groaned. "Jealousy?"

Saying the word out loud the second time made it sound even more horrible. She had told him she was jealous of someone coming in to replace her with his family, but that was only half the truth. She was even more jealous of someone becoming his wife, which could only mean one thing. She cared for John much more than she had realized, or was willing to admit.

But when he had pulled her into his arms and kissed her on the stair, the jealousy had melted away, and other emotions had taken her by surprise—the most powerful was fear.

Fear that she would fall in love with him if she didn't guard her heart—and fear that he would never return that love—which was the greatest fear of all.

If she was smart, she would leave immediately and not risk falling in love. But she couldn't leave, not yet. She didn't have enough money to get to California. If she continued to work for John for three weeks, she'd have just enough saved up to buy a train ticket.

She hadn't completed her other goal, either. John needed a wife. The children needed a mother.

Her list no longer mattered like it had in the beginning. She was less concerned about finding a woman who would stand up to John, and more concerned that she find someone who would love him and the children like Marjorie would love them.

She knew right where to go.

The afternoon sun was hidden behind gray clouds as Marjorie knocked on the Scott's front door. The cold wind continued to blow, swirling the snow into large drifts around the side of the house. Automobiles had been put away, and the town had come alive with horse and sleigh. That very morning, John had brought his horse from the livery and had attached it to the sleigh to bring them all to church.

It had been a cold ride—and not just because of the weather. She and John had barely spoken all morning. The tension between them was as awkward as she had expected.

The uncomfortable morning had turned into an uncomfortable afternoon and Marjorie had left as soon as lunch finished. She would take advantage of her afternoon off and see to her plans.

The door opened and Mrs. Scott stood in her black mourning gown. Her lips were pursed and her nose was red as she stared at Marjorie. "What do you want?"

"I'd like to talk to Dora, please."

Mrs. Scott harrumphed. "You're not welcome in this house."

"Oh, Mother." Dora appeared behind her mother. "Marjorie is freezing. Let her in." She opened the door wider. "Come in, Marjorie."

Mrs. Scott narrowed her eyes but didn't try to stop Marjorie as she stepped over the threshold.

The house was warm and smelled of pumpkin pie. A large stand-up radiator emanated heat from the corner of the foyer.

"Let me take your hat and coat." Dora held up her hand and took the items from Marjorie after they were removed.

"Thank you for seeing me," Marjorie said, touching up her curls.

"Of course." Dora motioned toward the back of the foyer. "Come into the parlor."

The Scott home was less extravagant than the Ortons', but still elegant. The foyer held an open staircase and a tall coat tree with an oval mirror. Oak floors extended from the front door, into a parlor and all the way to the dining room beyond.

Mrs. Scott followed Marjorie, her arms crossed.

"I was afraid something was wrong when neither of you came to church today," Marjorie said.

"Mother has a cold and we haven't had a chance to bring out the sleigh," Dora explained.

"We don't have a man about the place to see to such things." Mrs. Scott sent a pointed look toward Dora. "We have to hire a man to do it for us, or wait until John has a spare moment."

Dora lifted her eyes toward the ceiling and then smiled at Marjorie. "Please have a seat."

Marjorie sat in a wingback chair, near the crackling fireplace. She had hoped to speak to Dora alone, but there was no way to ask Mrs. Scott to leave her own parlor.

"Would you like tea?" Dora asked, sitting on the sofa across from Marjorie.

"No, thank you. I won't keep you long." She glanced at Mrs. Scott, who still stood watching her.

"Be about your business and then skedaddle," Mrs. Scott said.

"Mother." Dora lifted her brow. "Be kind, or I'll have to ask you to leave."

Mrs. Scott harrumphed again and then turned. "I'm going to go lie down. I don't feel well."

"I'm sorry," Dora said the moment Mrs. Scott was

out of sight. "She's always been a bit outspoken, but she has become worse since Anna's death."

"Everyone grieves differently."

Dora placed her hands in her lap, a smile on her face. "I'm so happy you've come to visit. To what do I owe this surprise?"

Marjorie took a deep breath and leaned forward— but nothing came out of her mouth.

Dora looked at her expectantly, but Marjorie couldn't bring herself to say what she had come to say. Pain and disappointment waged within her chest, threatening to dislodge the tears she had held at bay since deciding to do this last night.

It was the right thing to do. It made sense. It was necessary.

"I've come to ask you to marry John."

Dora's hand fluttered over her chest. "Pardon me?"

"He's looking for a wife, a mother for his children. Who would be better suited to love him and the children? You're the closest relation to Anna they'll ever have."

Dora blinked several times. "Marjorie—I don't know what to say."

"Say you'll marry John. It would be a great relief for me, knowing you were caring for them after I left."

"I can't marry John."

"Don't you love him?"

"Of course I do. He's my brother. I was eight years old when he married Anna. I've looked up to John practically all my life."

"What prevents you from marrying him?"

Dora made a funny face. "Marjorie. He's my brother."

"Not really."

"In every way that matters—besides…" She paused,

her face taking on a shine. "I'm in love with someone else."

Marjorie had not anticipated that response. "I had no idea."

Dora glanced toward the foyer to where Mrs. Scott had just disappeared. "I don't speak of him often, because I don't want to upset Mother."

"Why would it upset your mother if you spoke of him?"

"She has such hopes that John and I will marry." Dora fiddled with a fold in her skirt. "But, more than that, Jeremiah lives in Minneapolis and if we married, I would have to leave her."

"I see." Marjorie couldn't help feeling deflated. If Dora would not marry John, then who would? She was running out of options.

"May I speak candidly?" Dora asked.

"Of course."

"I think you should marry John."

Marjorie's back stiffened. "I cannot."

"Why?"

"It's complicated." Marjorie glanced at the clock. She really should be going.

"For what it's worth," Dora smiled, "marriage is always complicated, and life is too short to let the complications stop you from true happiness."

Marjorie stood. "I should go."

"I hope I didn't offend you."

"Of course not." Marjorie went to the foyer and picked up her wet hat and coat. If she was going to find a wife for John, she would need to use the rest of her day to keep looking. She put on her outerwear and turned to Dora. "Goodbye."

Dora opened the door. "Goodbye, Marjorie."

Marjorie stopped and put her hand over Dora's. "Take your own advice and tell your mother about your beau soon rather than later."

Marjorie stepped out into the cold and braced herself against the blowing snow. It would be a long walk to the music hall where there was a performance for the Little Falls Musical Club.

Surely there would be a woman there who would marry John.

Chapter Fifteen

She had finally done it. Marjorie Maren had gone too far.

John could hardly see straight as he pulled the horse and sleigh into the carriage house three weeks after the ill-fated night he had kissed Marjorie.

He wished he could simply park the horse and storm the house to tell Marjorie exactly what he thought of her latest shenanigans. Instead, he unhitched the mare, rubbed her down and fed her oats. Then he wiped the sleigh and closed up the carriage house.

The time and energy it took to accomplish his tasks did not lessen his anger—it only fueled the irritation more.

By the time he trudged up the path in the snow from the recent storm, his body was slick with perspiration and his heart pounded with exertion.

What in the world had Marjorie been thinking? Was she truly that desperate to marry him off?

He slammed the back door and tore his hat and coat off his body. He detested yelling in his home, but right now he didn't care if the house fell down around him. "Marjorie!" His voice boomed in the back hall. He threw open the door leading to the front hall. "Marjorie!" he yelled again.

Petey sat on the bottom step, his airplane in hand, and looked at John with the widest blue eyes John had ever seen.

"Where is Miss Maren?" John asked.

If Petey's face was any indication, John must look like a monster right about now.

Instead of answering John, Petey stood and ran up the stairs as if a bear were on his tail.

"Marjorie!" John yelled again.

"Where's the fire?" Mrs. Gohl rushed into the front hall with a dish towel in her hand.

"Where is Miss Maren?"

"Last I heard she had taken the children up to the day nursery—but I don't think she'd want you up there—"

John was already taking the stairs three at a time.

"They're planning a surprise for you, sir," Mrs. Gohl called after him. "They'll be so disappointed if you see."

John rounded the corner landing and continued up the stairs. He passed Petey in the upper hall and threw open the third-floor stairway door. "Marjorie!"

There was a flurry of scraping and foot rustling just above his head on the third floor. John raced up the steps, and just as he opened the door, Marjorie was there.

She pushed the door back with all her weight. "You can't come up here."

Their faces were mere inches apart, and she smelled wonderful.

It only made him angrier. "What were you thinking?"

Lilly appeared under Marjorie's elbow. "Papa, don't look. We're planning a Christmas surprise for you."

"They've been working on it since Thanksgiving," Marjorie said. "Don't ruin the last three weeks of preparation by barging in here."

John clamped his jaw closed and took several deep breaths. He finally spoke through his tight lips. "Come down to my office immediately."

Marjorie's face revealed her apprehension.

Good. She should be very concerned right about now.

"I'll be back soon, children," Marjorie said, looking over her shoulder. "Lilly, can you please put everything back in place? And, Charlie, please find Petey. He needs to help you..." She paused and quickly glanced at John. "You know what he needs to do."

"Petey is cowering in the hallway," John said as evenly as he could manage.

"Cowering?" Marjorie's eyes filled with alarm.

John turned and started down the stairs. "Now, Miss Maren."

Her light footsteps followed him down the stairs and into the hall.

"Petey." Marjorie stopped and bent down to Petey's level. He was sitting on the floor with his knees up to his chest and his airplane clutched in his hand. "What's the matter, sweetheart?"

"He'll be fine," John said.

"But he's trembling." Marjorie looked at John like he was a cad. And maybe he was, but right now he only wanted to talk to Marjorie.

John pointed toward the stairs. "In my office. Now."

"What did you do to Petey?"

"Nothing." John tapped his foot. "Now, Miss Maren."

She put her hand on Petey's head, sympathy filling her voice. "I'll be back as soon as I can. I'll read *Peter Pan* to you, all right?"

Petey just stared at John without answering.

Marjorie stood and brushed past John with an air of disdain.

Excellent. Now she was mad, too.

They marched down the stairs, past a startled Mrs. Gohl and into John's office.

He barely had the door closed when he turned on her. "What were you thinking?"

She crossed her arms, her eyes accusing him. "How rude and heartless you are. Petey is terrified of you right now, and frankly, so am I. Have you looked in the mirror? Your hair is standing on end and the scowl on your face—"

"You know what I'm talking about. There is yet another young woman in this town who will never look me in the eye again. And it's all because of you."

She stared at him, her mouth clamped shut.

"It was completely inappropriate to send Miss Olson to the hospital. I was mortified—and so was she."

Marjorie's arms slowly lowered to her side, a bit of her anger dissipating. "Mortified? Why would both of you be mortified?"

"Miss Olson didn't bother to tell me why she had come to my office until *after* I gave her an examination."

Marjorie's hand flew up to her mouth and she blinked at him with her green eyes. *"What?"*

"Imagine the embarrassing conversation that ensued."

"I didn't tell her to go to you for an examination. I just said to go there and meet you. You said I couldn't invite women over to the house anymore—"

"So instead you send them to the hospital where I would assume they need medical attention?"

"Why didn't she tell you the purpose of her visit before?"

"Apparently she was nervous." He had never met Miss Olson before she had stepped into his office. Her symptoms had been vague and she had stammered as she talked to John.

Nurse Hendricks had been in the examination room with him, but neither one could pinpoint what was wrong with the young lady. The only experiences he had with unmarried women who acted so upset were with unmarried *pregnant* women.

Thankfully the exam had not gone much further than listening to her heart and lungs and palpating her stomach. But it had been enough. "When I asked her if she might be pregnant, her face turned white and she looked like she would pass out. The poor woman was finally able to stutter out why she had come between sobs and hiccups—and then she fled my office."

Marjorie swallowed and looked properly contrite—but it wasn't enough for John.

"Why, Marjorie? Why would you send a stranger to me like that? I've rarely been so humiliated and I cannot imagine how she is feeling at this very moment."

"I thought…" She paused and turned away from him.

He wouldn't let her go so easily. He put his hand on her shoulder and turned her to face him again. He couldn't hide the hurt in his voice. "Do you truly think I'm that desperate to find a wife?"

"Aren't you desperate? You're leaving for Minneapolis tomorrow and you won't return until the day before Christmas Eve. I'll be gone a week after that." She implored him with her voice. "Who will take care of the children after I leave?"

He put his hand on the back of his neck and tried

to rub away the tension. Who would take care of the children? He had been diligently looking for a wife for weeks now, but no one had satisfied him. "Maybe you could stay until I find someone."

"You know I can't."

How odd that the first day she had arrived she was the one begging to stay, and he wanted her to go.

"Then I will have to find another governess."

Marjorie took a step toward him. "You can't."

"Why not?"

Her eyes looked a bit panicked. "You have to get married before I leave."

"Why?"

"Because I made a promise to myself that I'd find you a wife and I can't leave the job unfinished."

"Marjorie, that's ridiculous. You are not responsible to find me a wife."

"But I have to." She paced across the floor to his desk, her thumbnail between her teeth. "Maybe, if I have your cooperation, and we do this together, I could find someone for you while you're gone."

He shook his head. "You're talking nonsense now."

"The only reason none of the other women have worked is because you didn't cooperate—"

"That's absurd. None of them were fit to raise my children—"

"John." She put her hands on her hips. "You can't be so particular."

He couldn't believe he was having this conversation with Marjorie, of all people. He still couldn't be in the same room with her, or the same house for that matter, and not think about her constantly. The only place he had a reprieve was at the hospital, but even there thoughts of her snuck up on him—especially when she sent young, unsuspecting women to him. "I'm not being particular. This is a very serious decision and I won't make it lightly."

"Your standards are too high. You must lower them, or you'll never find someone."

"Don't be ridiculous. We're talking about a mother for my children. My standards should be exceedingly high." The truth was, every woman he had interviewed in the past few weeks had not measured up to Marjorie. If he was going to find a wife, he would have to stop comparing them to her—which had proven almost impossible.

"There has to be someone," she said softly.

"There's not."

She crossed her arms about her, almost like a hug, but didn't say a word. What could she say?

"Will you stay until I find someone?" he asked.

"What choice do I have? The job will not be complete until you're married."

He let out an inward sigh.

She planted her feet and squared her shoulders. "I will stay until you find a wife—but you'll have to allow me to help you find her."

"What would that entail?"

"I can invite women over for supper—"

"With a proper warning—"

"And you must give them your undivided attention."

"Then I insist—"

"No." She shook her head. "If I'm going to stay until you find a wife, then *I* insist on having full authority to find her for you."

"Full authority?" He laughed. "I would never leave this completely in your hands."

"Clearly I cannot leave it in your hands, either. I plan

to go to California after the first of the year, and I will find a wife for you before I leave."

"In a week and a half?"

"Yes."

"That's impossible."

"Not if we work together."

John took a deep breath. What did it matter? If he couldn't have Marjorie, then he would have to settle for second best. "Fine."

She nodded once, but a hint of sadness edged her eyes.

Not for the first time, John wished his circumstances were different and he could offer her the type of marriage she longed for.

Marjorie had finally found her. She could feel it deep in the marrow of her bones. Mrs. Worthington would be John's new wife.

Marjorie stood outside the modest two-story home just a few houses down from the Ortons' front door and knocked. The day was bright and clear, and the sun gave surprising heat. Drops of water fell from the eaves of the home and gathered in puddles. The streets were sloshy and impossible to pass by automobile, but there wasn't enough snow left for horse and sleigh, either, so many people were out walking on this Sunday afternoon.

A maid answered the door, her black-and-white uniform clean and crisp. "May I help you?"

Marjorie presented her calling card. "Is Mrs. Worthington at home?"

The maid accepted Marjorie's card and nodded, taking a step back. "Please come in. Mrs. Worthington is in the parlor with her parents. May I take your hat and coat?"

Marjorie slipped her outerwear off and handed them to the smiling maid, who motioned toward the rear of the house. "This way, please."

Nerves fluttered inside Marjorie as she glanced at her surroundings. No matter how many times she had approached a woman in regards to John, it had not gotten easier. In fact, it had only become harder. She was running out of time and options. John had already been gone for two days at the conference, and Christmas was fast approaching. When he returned, there would be little time to keep looking. The children had a special program arranged for him, and it took much of Marjorie's spare time to prepare.

Hopefully this time Marjorie had found the perfect woman for John. From everything she'd heard, Mrs. Worthington would be an ideal match.

But would the young widow agree?

And, more important, would John?

"Miss Marjorie Maren to see you, Mrs. Worthington."

Three people sat in the spacious parlor. An older gentleman and lady, and a younger woman about thirty years old. All three stood when Marjorie entered.

The room was appointed with lovely furnishings, if a bit gaudy. A large fireplace dominated the space and potted plants filled every corner.

Three sets of curious eyes followed Marjorie across the room.

She hadn't anticipated an audience for this meeting. The very thought made her palms sweat.

"It's nice to meet you, Miss Maren," the younger woman said. She was beautiful, with dark brown hair and stunning blue eyes, and she carried herself with a confident ease. "I'm Mrs. Worthington and these are my parents, Mr. and Mrs. McCumsey. Won't you have a seat?"

"I do hate to be rude," Marjorie said. "But I was hoping to have a private conversation."

Mrs. Worthington shared a questioning glance with her parents. "I suppose we could step out onto the porch…"

"We were just about to go for a walk," Mr. McCumsey said. "Please feel free to have a conversation here in the parlor."

As the older couple left the room, Marjorie offered them a grateful smile.

Mrs. Worthington studied Marjorie as she waved her hand toward one of the chairs her parents had left. "Please have a seat." Mrs. Worthington sat in the chair she had been occupying earlier and began to pour Marjorie a cup of tea. "I must confess I'm intrigued by your visit. Have we met before? Your name sounds familiar."

"We have not, but I've heard a great deal about you. I'm sorry to hear about your late husband."

Mrs. Worthington paused in serving the tea and looked down at the large diamond ring on her left hand. "Thank you. It was all so terribly sudden. I'm still a bit surprised to find myself back here in my hometown after being in Chicago for the last decade. I've only just arrived yesterday."

"Yes, I know." Marjorie nodded. "I've been told you know my employer, Dr. Orton."

Mrs. Worthington's lovely blue eyes brightened and she leaned forward. "How is John?"

Marjorie swallowed a stab of jealousy at the familiar way she referred to him. "He's—". She took a deep breath. "He's fine, though he's mourning his own loss."

"It's awful, isn't it?" Mrs. Worthington shook her head and handed Marjorie the cup of tea. "Anna and I were best friends as children. I was the one who introduced the two of them—had you heard that?"

Marjorie nodded. Dora had told her the whole story.

"I went to Northwestern University in Chicago," Mrs. Worthington said, settling back into her chair. "My mother had so hoped I'd choose Smith, but I wanted to stay in the Midwest. New England can be so stuffy." She took a sip of her tea and then lowered the cup, her cheeks filling with color. "That's where I met John." She looked down and toyed with the teacup in her hand. "I suppose I fancied myself in love with him. And for a time, I thought he might love me, too. But Anna came to visit me, and once they met, I gave up all hope." She lifted the teacup to her lips and took another sip.

Just as Marjorie had suspected. Mrs. Worthington had been in love with John. "Will you stay in Little Falls?"

Mrs. Worthington set down her cup and lifted a shoulder. "I don't know what I'll do. My husband and I had no children, so I have little to worry about in that regard. Of course, my parents have offered to let me stay here, but I don't know if I could settle back into small-town life. Thankfully my husband thought of the future, and I'll be comfortable for the rest of my life, so my options are endless."

If Dora's information was correct, Mrs. Worthington's late husband had left her more than comfortable. He had left her a millionaire.

"Do you—" Marjorie licked her lips. "Do you suppose you'll marry again?"

Mrs. Worthington squinted at Marjorie. "I'm sorry, but who exactly are you?"

Marjorie smiled and tried to look innocent. "I'm Dr. Orton's governess."

"Governess…" Mrs. Worthington's gaze drifted over Marjorie's attire, as if she didn't think Marjorie looked like a governess. "Your name sounded familiar. Do I know you from somewhere else?"

"I am from Chicago. Maybe you've heard of my father, Joseph Ma—"

"Of course! My husband spoke of Mr. Maren all the time. I can't recall your mother's name, though."

"Her name is Esther."

"Yes, that's it—and—" Her eyes grew round and she put her hand in front of her mouth. "No." She shook her head. "You're not *the* Marjorie Maren, are you? Weren't you engaged to Preston Chamberlain?"

Marjorie adjusted her position and set her teacup down. "Yes."

Mrs. Worthington leaned forward, as if to receive a bit of gossip. "Why ever did you leave him? Wasn't he the beau to catch last year?"

This conversation was not going how Marjorie had intended.

"What else do I recall?" Mrs. Worthington asked, touching her long fingernail to her chin. "Wasn't there a scandal about a married man? I seem to remember something about it in the newspaper."

"All rumors." Marjorie smiled, waving her hand aside in nonchalance.

"Maybe," Mrs. Worthington said, lifting an interested eyebrow. "And maybe not."

Marjorie cleared her throat. "I was wondering if I could ask you a question—about Dr. Orton."

Mrs. Worthington didn't appear to want to change the subject. "However did you come to be John's governess? I had assumed you'd run away to be with the gentleman they mentioned in the papers."

"One should never believe everything one reads in the newspapers." Marjorie tried to laugh but didn't feel the humor. "About Dr. Orton…"

"Of course." Mrs. Worthington smiled. "What did you have to ask?"

Marjorie took a sip of her tea to wet her dry mouth and then straightened her back. "Dr. Orton has four children."

"Yes, I'd heard."

"And—well, this is very awkward for me to say— but he's in need of a wife."

"A wife?"

"I will be leaving after the first of the year, and Dr. Orton needs someone to help with the children."

"A wife, you say?" Mrs. Worthington stood, her elegant black mourning gown flowing as she walked to the window. She crossed her arms and stared outside, but her gaze looked much farther away. "I never imagined John and I would be single at the same time."

Marjorie also stood. "I heard from Anna's sister, Dora, that you were back in town, and I just thought—" She swallowed. "I thought maybe you and Dr. Orton could become reacquainted."

"Reacquainted? Now, there's an interesting thought." Mrs. Worthington turned, her gaze suddenly shrewd. "Why did you come here and tell me this, Miss Maren? What do you gain?"

"Gain?" Marjorie said the word as if it were tainted. "I gain nothing by coming here."

"Surely you have some motive."

"I simply care about Dr. Orton and his children, and hoped to reconnect old friends."

Mrs. Worthington approached Marjorie. "All this is very interesting, but I hesitate to believe you. I've met very few people who don't have a selfish motive behind their acts of charity, which I suppose this is in some way. John is probably devastated at losing Anna, and his poor children are heartbroken. Someone needs to rescue all of them."

"Marrying John would not be an act of charity."

"John? Are you that familiar with the handsome doctor?"

Marjorie decided in that moment that she did not like Mrs. Worthington. "I believe I should take my leave."

Mrs. Worthington studied her for a moment longer. "I still don't know what you gain from all this—but I really don't care. Now that I know John is in the market for a wife, I have a new direction in life." She offered Marjorie a self-satisfied smile. "Thank you, Miss Maren."

Marjorie's insides curled up, just like Petey did when he was upset. Something about the way Mrs. Worthington spoke told Marjorie that once she set her mind to something, she wasn't easily deterred. Nor did her prey often escape.

Maybe this wasn't such a good idea, after all.

Chapter Sixteen

Marjorie stood near the parlor window, her eyes on the street.

"You're worse than the children, Miss Maren," Miss Ernst said as she set a tray of hot apple cider on the table.

Marjorie looked at Lilly and Charlie, who also stood by the window, and the three of them giggled.

"Grandmother is coming," Lilly said to Miss Ernst. "And it's almost Christmas."

"Two reasons I'm also excited," Marjorie added with a wink.

A beautiful evergreen tree stood proudly in the southwest corner of the room, waiting to be trimmed. Fresh pine boughs hung over the fireplace and doorways, red and gold ribbons dangling down. Clumps of mistletoe were placed in strategic spots all over the house, and elegant Christmas decorations adorned shelves and tables. The house looked perfect for a holiday celebration and everyone inside eagerly awaited their first guest.

"I wish Papa was here," Charlie said, a bit forlorn.

"He'll be home in two days," Marjorie promised.

"Tomorrow he'll give his keynote address. Everyone must pray for him. It will be a difficult speech to give."

"Because he's talking about Mama?" Lilly asked.

Marjorie placed her hand under Lilly's chin and nodded. "Yes, and also because he's speaking to a crowd of his peers. It's hard to—"

"She's here! She's here!" Charlie called, jumping up and down. "I see the taxicab."

Marjorie and Lilly pushed aside the lace curtains and watched the cab stop in front of the house. The warm weather had continued, enabling the use of automobiles once again.

"Charlie, go out and help the cabdriver," Marjorie said. "Lilly, take Petey's hand and bring him to the porch. I'll get Laura."

The children did as they were told, and Marjorie ran up to the nursery and lifted the sleeping baby out of her crib.

Laura instantly awoke with a smile and Marjorie nuzzled her nose to the baby's. "Your grandmother is here to meet you."

Laura cooed and gurgled in response.

Marjorie took the baby down the stairs and went to the front porch just as Mrs. Orton was coming up the sidewalk, a grin on her face.

"Grandmother!" Lilly raced down the steps and threw her arms around Mrs. Orton. "I've missed you."

Mrs. Orton's kind brown eyes sparkled with mischief and joy as she hugged Lilly and Petey in her wide embrace. "I can't believe how much all of you have grown." She put her hand on her chin as she surveyed Lilly and shook her head. "You look more and more like your mother every day."

Charlie came from the cab, lugging a large suitcase

and holding a hatbox in his other hand. A young man followed him up the walk. Marjorie didn't pay him any attention, thinking him the cabdriver—but then she took a double look. John?

But it couldn't be John, he was in Minneapolis.

"Paul?" Marjorie said the name out loud and drew both his and Mrs. Orton's attention.

"Surprise," Paul said, grinning at Marjorie.

"Is that my newest granddaughter?" Mrs. Orton asked.

Marjorie held up the baby and Mrs. Orton was rewarded with a wet smile. "This is Laura."

Mrs. Orton took Laura in her hands, tears coming to her eyes. "Why, hello, little one. I'm your grandmother."

Not wanting to intrude on this tender scene, Marjorie turned her attention on their surprise guest. "I didn't know you were coming."

Paul stood just as tall as John and had the exact same eye and hair coloring, but their facial features were unmistakably different, though equally handsome.

"Are you happy to see me?" Paul asked. "I'm thinking after what happened last time—"

Marjorie put her finger up to her lips to quiet him.

Mrs. Orton continued to fawn over the baby while the other children spoke all around her. Hopefully no one heard his statement.

"I am happy to see you." She glanced at the cab as it pulled away. "Your wife isn't here?"

Paul shook his head, his countenance troubled.

Marjorie's lips grew tight as she put her hand on his arm. "I'm sorry."

"I'll tell you all about it later."

"Now, Marjorie." Mrs. Orton turned away from the children and Marjorie dropped her hand off Paul's arm.

"I want a hug from you, too, dear. And I want to hear all about your experiences as a governess."

Marjorie gave her longtime friend a hug, reveling in the familiar faces from back home.

"Papa won't be here for two more days," Lilly said. "But we'll have plenty of fun until he gets here. We've been waiting for you to help us trim the tree."

"My favorite thing to do," Paul said. "Are there gingerbread men to hang on the boughs and popcorn to string?"

"Yes!" Lilly said. "And we even have candy canes."

Paul rubbed his belly. "Keep them away from me."

Charlie lagged behind just a bit, his smile not reaching the magnitude Marjorie had expected. She reached out and took the hatbox out of his hand. "Are you happy to see your grandmother and uncle?"

Charlie nodded. "I just wish Papa was here, too."

Marjorie put her arm around his shoulders. "He'll be here soon."

Marjorie and Charlie followed the others into the house. Though there were only two more people inside, the noise level increased until Marjorie could no longer hear herself think.

The luggage was brought upstairs where Mrs. Orton would sleep in the guest room and Paul would sleep in John's room, for now. After they were settled, Lilly insisted they decorate the tree.

Hours of fun and laughter passed, and eventually the children were all too sleepy to stay awake. Mrs. Orton insisted on helping Marjorie bathe them and put them to bed. It was a treat to have a bit of help. Charlie was the first to lie down, complaining of a headache, and the others soon followed.

Paul also went to bed, promising to have a nice long

talk with Marjorie in the morning, but Mrs. Orton did not appear tired in the least. When Laura was finally asleep, Mrs. Orton touched Marjorie's sleeve. "Let's have a bit of tea before bed, shall we?"

The house was quiet as Marjorie brought the tea tray into the parlor where Mrs. Orton was sitting, watching the fireplace crackle. "John has made a wonderful home here."

Marjorie set down the tray. "I see so much of Anna in the little details."

Mrs. Orton nodded. "This is the first time I've been here without her. I had wanted to come to the funeral, but John had been so busy with the pandemic that they had been forced to bury her quickly and there wasn't any time for me to travel." She sighed as she looked about the room. "It feels real now, her being gone."

Marjorie sat on the wingback chair next to Mrs. Orton, the table between them, and began to pour the steaming tea.

"I'm proud of you, Marjorie," Mrs. Orton said. "Even though Anna isn't here, there is no oppression hanging over the house. The children are happy and content, and the place feels vibrant and alive." She smiled at Marjorie. "There's only one person to thank for all that. It's the reason I recommended you to John."

Marjorie dipped her head at the compliment. "They are the most wonderful children in the world—truly. I'm amazed at their fortitude. But I cannot take all the credit. John has been a wonderful father through all this. I'm…" She paused, hoping to find just the right words. "I'm amazed at his strength and love. Though he's been grieving, he's truly looked beyond himself to see the needs of his children and the community." She dropped a lump of sugar in Mrs. Orton's tea, and had to swallow the emotion clogging her throat. "He's a very special man."

Mrs. Orton placed her hand over Marjorie's. "You're in love with him."

Marjorie lifted her gaze and looked into Mrs. Orton's gentle face, ready to admit the truth to her friend. "I think I am."

The older woman smiled. "I had hoped."

"I never intended for it to happen," Marjorie said quickly. "But I couldn't help myself. I've never known a man like him before in my life."

"It does a mother's heart good to hear someone speak so highly of their child."

"It's just—" Marjorie let out a sigh.

"It's just what?"

"It's so complicated. I only planned to stay until the first of the year."

"Yes, I remember." She took the tea from Marjorie's hand. "You're going to California to pursue acting."

"You're the only person I told before I left."

"Does John know?"

Marjorie nodded as she poured her own cup of tea. The delicious peppermint aroma filled her nose.

"Are you still going?" Mrs. Orton asked.

"Yes."

"Even though you love him?"

"Yes."

"Why? Doesn't he care for you?"

Marjorie put two lumps of sugar in her teacup. "He—" She had always shared everything with Mrs. Orton, but somehow it was different talking about her son. "He asked me to stay."

"Marjorie." Mrs. Orton's voice filled with hope.

"But he doesn't love me."

"Surely, with time…"

"No." Marjorie shook her head. "I couldn't marry him, unless I knew he loved me with all his heart and was willing to have a marriage, in every sense. I couldn't take the risk that I would end up like my parents." She stirred her tea, trying to sound stoic. "Besides, I can't give up now. My bedroom in Chicago is full of half-written manuscripts from when I wanted to be an author, and half-completed paintings from when I wanted to be an artist. I always quit when it gets hard—I'm not quitting this time. I want to bring joy to people who are hurting, or lonely, or afraid."

Mrs. Orton was quiet for a moment. "There are a great number of hurting people in the world—and five of them live in this very home. In your quest to help thousands, you may miss the opportunity to help the five who matter the most to you."

Marjorie looked down at her teacup, watching the steam spiral into the air. "I know what would happen if I stayed and married John. We would grow bitter and resentful toward each other. It would be horrible."

Mrs. Orton touched Marjorie's chin, and Marjorie lifted her eyes.

"Marjorie, please don't give up on the love you have for John. It might be the very thing he needs to heal. There are many people who enter into a marriage for convenience, and grow to love each other later."

What she said was true, but Marjorie wasn't willing to take the risk.

"Miss Maren?" Charlie stood at the parlor door, his cheeks bright red and his eyes glossy. "I don't feel well."

Marjorie set down her teacup and hurried over to Charlie. She put her hand on his forehead. "You're burning up."

"My throat hurts and my head hurts." He swayed and Marjorie put her arms around him. "I want my papa."

"Let's get you to bed," Marjorie said.

Mrs. Orton joined her as she walked Charlie into the hall and up the stairs.

"What do you think it is?" Mrs. Orton asked.

Marjorie shook her head. "I don't know."

"Do you think it's influenza?"

"It couldn't be. They've been getting their cinnamon oil every morning…" Marjorie paused. When was the last time she had given the children their cinnamon oil? It had been three days since John left—could it be three days since they'd had it?

"Should we call John?" Mrs. Orton asked.

"He gives his keynote address at the conference tomorrow evening. We can't call him home now."

"What if Charlie has influenza?"

"We'll treat him here and if it gets worse, we'll send for Dr. McCall. He's as capable as John to see to Charlie's needs." They couldn't call John home. It wouldn't be fair to the conferees or to John. "Charlie will be fine. We've got it all under control."

She helped him to his bed and immediately brought him his cinnamon oil, hoping it wasn't too late.

John handed the cabdriver a generous tip. "Merry Christmas."

"The same to you, Doc."

The cab pulled away and John turned toward his house. The unseasonably warm December day invigorated his already good mood. The keynote address had gone well—very well. It had done him good to talk about Anna's death. In some ways, it was the closure he needed to move on. After sharing their story, and after John saw how it impacted other doctors, a part of him felt her death was not in vain.

His research into cinnamon oil had also been well received, and he'd talked to other physicians who had been using the same method. So little was known about the Spanish flu, but scientists across the planet were working hard to discover a cure. Until they had one, it would be doctors like John, and the others, who faced the battlefront with whatever weapons they could find—and for John, cinnamon oil was his weapon of choice.

He eagerly looked toward the house, excited to walk through his front door. It was the day before Christmas Eve, his mother should have arrived, there would be games and good food to eat, his children would be eagerly anticipating Christmas morning…and Marjorie would be with them.

The house looked strangely quiet as he strode up the front walk. A large wreath hung on the front door, and garland was strung on the porch railings. He had expected his children to be waiting at the windows, ready to search for the gifts he had brought them.

John opened the front door, a smile on his face. "Hello."

No one greeted him at the door.

He stepped into the hall and closed the door. He set his satchel on the floor and took off his overcoat and hat. "Merry Christmas."

Feet appeared on the stairway, and by the look of the hem of the elaborate gown, John knew it was Marjorie.

His heart stirred with joy. "Marjorie." He started toward her.

Her face finally appeared, and he stopped his approach. She looked as if she hadn't slept in days, and fear lined her eyes and mouth. A white mask hung around her neck.

"What's wrong?" he asked.

Marjorie stopped at the foot of the stairs and swallowed. "It's Charlie."

John's whole body responded as dread washed over him. He didn't wait for her to say more. He took the stairs three at a time.

Marjorie raced to keep up. "He became ill two nights ago with a sore throat, a headache and a fever."

"No."

"Dr. McCall was here to see him—"

"Why didn't you send for me?"

"I didn't want to bother you—"

"Bother me?" John stopped in the middle of the upstairs hall. "He's my son. I would move heaven and earth to be by his side." Panic raced up John's legs. This was exactly what had happened when Anna became ill. He hadn't been home to save her. It had been his fault. He should have been with Anna—should have been with Charlie—but Marjorie had made the choice for him. "You had no right to keep this information from me."

Tears spilled down her cheeks. "I'm sorry. I thought he'd be fine—"

He grabbed her upper arms, unable to see straight. "Am I too late?"

She shook her head violently. "No—he's still alive, but he's not doing well."

He abruptly let her go and turned—but he didn't know where they had put his son. "Where is he?" he yelled.

She pointed. "He's in my room."

John raced down the hall to Marjorie's bedroom and

pushed open the door. His mother and brother sat in the room, white masks over their faces, their eyes filled with sadness and fear.

John's legs went weak as he saw the telltale dark spots on Charlie's cheeks, indicating his son was running out of air. "God, no." It was the only prayer he could mutter.

He put his hand to Charlie's forehead, and the moment he felt his fever, his medical training took over. He threw off his coat, unbuttoned the wrists on his shirt and rolled his sleeves up to his elbows. He found a mask on the bureau and put it over his nose and mouth. There was no time to lose. He hadn't been home for Anna, but he was home for Charlie—and he would do whatever it took to make sure his son lived.

Just as quickly as resolve set in, doubt assailed him. What would it matter what he did? No one had determined exactly how to treat this disease. People either lived or died. Hadn't he just been with a hundred other doctors and researchers, all of them at a loss for how to cure influenza? Everyone had a different opinion on what the disease was and how to treat it. Some used wet cupping as a way to cleanse the blood, some used medicines they could get at a pharmacy and others would sweat the patients, raising their temperature so high it would cleanse the body from all impurities.

John took a deep breath.

This was his son. He would try anything to keep him alive.

For over an hour, John worked on Charlie. He asked Paul for help, but kept everyone else out of the room and out of his way. Thankfully Dora had the other children across the street, away from the sickroom.

First, he gave Charlie cinnamon oil; then he wrapped

his son in layers of blankets to promote extra body heat. They stoked the fireplace and brought in bricks to warm the bed. As Charlie lay sweating, John tried to get the boy to drink as much chicken broth as possible, but Charlie slipped in and out of consciousness, and it was almost impossible.

After a while, Paul put his hand on John's shoulder. "I'm not a physician, but I can see there's little left to do but pray."

"We can keep giving him the cinnamon oil every two hours." He raked his hand through his hair. "But I don't understand. The daily cinnamon oil regimen should have prevented this from happening."

"I suppose there are some things we'll never understand," Paul said quietly.

John strode into the hallway. "Miss Maren."

Mother and Marjorie were sitting on chairs beside each other, their heads bowed in prayer.

Marjorie immediately stood. "Yes?"

"Did Charlie have his cinnamon oil today?"

She nodded. "I gave it to him right away this morning."

"Did he get all of it down?"

Again, she nodded. "It was difficult, and it took us over an hour, but he swallowed every drop."

"And what about the other days, while I was gone? Did he drink the whole glass of water with the ten drops inside?"

She clasped her hands in front of her waist and looked as if she might become ill herself.

John strode toward her. "Tell me he took it, Marjorie."

She wrung her hands together and couldn't look at him.

He grasped her arms for the second time that day. "Please tell me you didn't forget."

Tears pooled in her eyes and slipped down her cheeks. "I forgot—"

"You forgot?" He wanted to shake her. "Why did you quit giving him the oil, Marjorie?"

"Quit?" She looked at him with red eyes. "I didn't quit—I forgot."

"It's the same thing." He dropped his hands and strode down the hall and back, his mind turning with the implications. "I trusted you with my children's lives. How could you let this happen?"

"I'm sorry." Her voice was so forlorn it hurt his ears. "I don't know how I let it slip my mind."

"You knew how important the cinnamon oil was." He stopped his pacing. "What about the other children?"

She put her hand up to her mouth. "I forgot to give it to them, too, but now they're taking it again."

He closed his eyes and let out a breath. "How could you do this to me?" He strode back to her. "I lost my wife to this horrible disease, and all I asked is for you to make sure my children received ten drops of cinnamon oil in a glass of water every morning, and you forgot. How am I to trust you with other things, if you could not do this simple task?"

She blinked several times, her green eyes rimmed with tears. "You can't."

Maybe she was right. "Then it's a good thing you're leaving."

John didn't wait to see her response. He hardened his heart and forced himself not to think about Marjorie and all that he could be losing in one horrible day.

Chapter Seventeen

The dark afternoon turned to an even darker night, followed by a bleak morning. Gray light filtered into the upstairs hall as Marjorie paced. The weather had turned bitterly cold overnight, bringing with it a horrible snowstorm that had started to blast the house sometime in the middle of the night.

John had only come out of Charlie's room twice through the long hours, and he had not spoken to her either time. His words from the previous day had clung to her, like a leech, sucking out what little life and hope she had left in her. All of this was her fault. If she had been diligent to give Charlie his oil, none of this would have happened. She had failed to complete yet another task, and this one had life-threatening consequences.

The echo of the grandfather clock chimed seven times. It was the morning of Christmas Eve, a day of anticipation and celebration. Charlie should be just waking up after a night of Christmas dreams. He should be eagerly waiting for the special time he would enjoy with the people who loved him most—not lying on the bed, close to death.

Mrs. Orton had gone to bed just a few hours ago,

making Marjorie promise to get her if something changed. She had encouraged Marjorie to get some rest, but Marjorie could not force herself to fall asleep. She had tried, sitting in the chair near the sickroom, but her body refused to obey what her mind knew she needed.

Though she was no longer caring for Charlie, she could not allow herself the simple pleasure of rest—not until Charlie was sleeping peacefully.

John had sent Mrs. Gohl and Miss Ernst away, to prevent them from getting sick. He had wanted Marjorie and Mrs. Orton to leave as well, but neither woman would budge. Mrs. Orton said they were needed to cook and clean, when necessary, and John had reluctantly agreed to let them stay.

Marjorie stopped near the window and looked out at the white-and-gray world. The sun hid behind the clouds, and would not be warming the earth today.

Despite her resolve to stay near Charlie's room, Marjorie's stomach growled, and she imagined John and Paul were also hungry. No one had eaten since lunch yesterday, and even that had been hardly touched.

Marjorie walked down the back stairs to the kitchen and flipped on the lights. The only breakfast foods she knew how to make were oatmeal and coffee, so that was what they would have for breakfast. It wouldn't be fancy, but it would be nourishing.

She had just placed the kettle of water and coffeepot on the stovetop when she heard the stairs creak. She turned and found Paul entering the room.

His face needed a shave and his hair was mussed. Dark circles marred his eyes and deep lines edged the corners of his mouth. So far, he was the only person John would allow in the sickroom with Charlie, and he hadn't slept, either.

Paul walked over to the cookie jar Mrs. Gohl had filled before she left, and took out two oatmeal cookies.

"There will be coffee ready shortly," Marjorie said.

Paul turned to her, as if noticing her for the first time. "That sounds wonderful."

"How is he this morning?"

Paul's jaw hardened and he took a seat at the kitchen table. "Not much different than last night."

Marjorie joined him at the table. She could not see past the falling snow, but she knew a world existed somewhere out there. Would it always look this dreary and forsaken?

"How are you holding up?" Paul asked her.

"Me?" She lifted a shoulder.

"You haven't slept and you've barely eaten since he took ill."

"I'll be fine."

Paul reached across the table and put his hand over hers. "You need to take care of yourself so you don't get sick."

Paul had always been a good friend, just as Mrs. Orton had been.

"What about you?" she asked. "You didn't look the best when you arrived, and now this." Marjorie studied him carefully. "How are things between you and Josephine?"

Paul's countenance became heavier and he set down his cookies. "She left me."

Marjorie's mind became fully alert. "What do you mean?"

Paul stood and paced across the room. "She's gone. That's why I came here with Mother. I couldn't stay in Chicago and face all the rumors."

Marjorie stood and joined him near the stove. "Where did she go? Is she alone?"

Paul shook his head, his lips set in a grim line. "She went west somewhere, and no, she's not alone."

"What does that mean for your marriage?"

He rubbed his whiskers. "She sent me a letter, right before I left, asking for a divorce."

"Paul." Marjorie took a step closer to him. "I'm so sorry."

He swallowed and his eyes filled with moisture. "I still can't believe she left me."

"What does your mother think?"

"I haven't told her." He finally looked at Marjorie. "She'd be devastated. Please don't tell her. I'll find the courage to say something on the way back to Chicago, but with all that's going on, neither she nor John needs to know."

"I understand." The first Marjorie had heard of Josephine's infidelity was the night before Marjorie's wedding to Preston. Paul had come to her upset, asking Marjorie if she knew where Josephine had gone. When she said she didn't, he confessed his fears, and Marjorie had offered him an embrace—the same embrace a maid had seen and reported to the newspapers. It had started all the ugly rumors.

Paul's shoulders fell and he wiped at his eyes. "I never imagined she was capable of hurting me this way."

Marjorie hated to see anyone cry, but a grown man was one of the hardest to watch. Just as she did the night before her wedding, she put her arms around her friend. "I'm sorry."

He dropped his head onto her shoulder.

They stayed that way for several minutes, until he

pulled away, his face now dry. "I feel like a fool, crying on your shoulder."

She smiled up at him. "You're not a fool. You're a man in pain."

He lightly touched her cheek. "Thank you, Marjorie. You've always been a good friend."

"And you've been a good brother and uncle. I don't know what we would have done without you these past few days." She hugged him this time, appreciating his steady support.

"What's going on?" John's voice met Marjorie's ears.

Marjorie jerked away from Paul, guilt flooding her cheeks with heat, though there was nothing to feel ashamed about.

"Nothing," Paul said to his older brother.

"Nothing?" John looked between them, his face just as scruffy as Paul's, and his eyes glazed over with fear and exhaustion.

"Marjorie and I are old friends." Paul walked away from Marjorie and approached his brother.

"That looked more than friendly." John's face revealed his revulsion. "You're a married man—yet I find another woman in your arms." His eyes filled with revelation and shock as he looked at Marjorie. "Was Paul the man you were caught embracing the night before your wedding to Chamberlain?"

"There wasn't anything to that, either," Paul said quickly. "The newspapers were looking for a story, and they were ready to trounce on anything they heard."

John crossed his arms, his face set in a scowl. "And why are you and Marjorie spending so much time in each other's arms?"

Marjorie left the stove and approached John. "It's really not what it appears."

"Then what's going on?"

Mrs. Orton appeared at the foot of the stairs, and it didn't look as if she had gotten much rest, either. "What's wrong? I heard your voices upstairs."

John and Paul stared at each other, and Marjorie could almost read their minds. Neither one wanted to upset their mother, especially now, while Charlie was so sick.

"It's nothing," Marjorie said. "Tempers are a bit high, and understandably so with everything that's going on. We all need to give each other space and try to rest." She motioned to the stove. "I'll have coffee and oatmeal ready soon. I'll bring some trays up when it's done."

"Mother, you should go back to bed." Paul walked toward his mother. He looked back at Marjorie, and pleaded with his eyes. He didn't want Mrs. Orton or John to know about Josephine—not yet.

She gave a slight nod.

Paul and Mrs. Orton walked back upstairs, but John stood in his spot, his arms still crossed, staring at Marjorie.

She swallowed. "I'll get Charlie's cinnamon oil ready, and I'll heat some of the broth Mrs. Gohl left for him."

"I want to know why you were in my brother's arms—my *married* brother's arms, both today and in Chicago."

What could she say? "He's upset. We're all upset. I was simply offering him some comfort." It was true, even if it was misleading.

"Comfort?" John took a step closer to Marjorie. "A married man does not seek comfort in the arms of another woman."

She turned back to the stove and took the Quaker oats from the shelf. "Grief knows no boundaries, John."

"Don't tell me about grief." He stood directly behind her and she could almost feel his steely gaze on the back of her head.

She trembled as she measured out the oats. "Everyone grieves differently."

"Again," he said slowly. "It is never appropriate for a married man to grieve in the arms of another woman."

He was right, of course, but what could she say? She turned back to face him, and found him even closer than she had thought. With the hot stove behind her, there was nowhere for her to move. His very presence, though angered, filled her with nerves and revived memories of the kiss they shared on the dark stairwell. "You'll have to trust me," she whispered.

She could sense that he was just as conscious of her presence, and he swallowed several times before he spoke. "I've tried to trust you in the past—and—"

He didn't need to complete his thought. She knew what he was thinking. All of this was her fault.

Tears welled up in her eyes. What he hinted at was true. "I'm sorr—"

The doorbell rang.

"Who would be here at this hour of the morning?" John stepped away and left the room.

Marjorie bent over in tears the moment he walked out of the kitchen, and she stayed that way for several moments, until she heard Mrs. Worthington's voice in the front hall.

John stared at Camilla Worthington as if seeing an apparition from a dream.

She stood on his front porch, the snow falling in a

sheet of white ice behind her. "I came over as soon as I heard about your son." She wore a long black coat over a black gown. A black hat sat at a slant over her forehead, and a black net covered her face. Snowflakes clung to her hat and shoulders. She looked as if she had come for an afternoon call, yet it was only seven in the morning. Where had she come from?

"You look surprised to see me, John."

"Surprised?" He'd never been more stunned in his life. "The last I heard, you were still in Chicago. Are you home for Christmas?" It seemed preposterous. She had not returned to Little Falls once in all the years he and Anna had lived in town.

"Aren't you going to invite an old friend in?"

He opened the door wider, but then stopped. "I can't let you inside. This home is quarantined."

"I already had the flu," she said. "And I survived."

Clearly. She had never looked lovelier, or more alive, with her dark hair and crystal-blue eyes. Twelve years had not diminished her appearance. If anything, age had enhanced her beauty, and wealth had given her an air of sophistication she had lacked when he first met her as a college student, fresh from Central Minnesota.

He slowly opened the door, still a bit in shock that she was standing on his front porch so early in the morning. "Come in."

She stepped across the threshold, running her gaze over his home, as if running a white glove over a mantel to test for dust. He couldn't help thinking she'd find his house lacking. After all, she lived in one of the grandest mansions on Chicago's Gold Coast.

"You have a very quaint home." She stepped into the front parlor and he followed.

He ran his hand over his hair, trying to put it into

some semblance of order. He rubbed his jaw, wishing he'd shaved and cleaned up. "Thank you."

"It's so like Anna. Gentle, modest and unassuming." She turned and looked at him. "When I first met you, I had thought you'd strive for so much more than this." She waved her hand about the room. "But after you met Anna, you settled in to please her."

"Why are you here, Camilla?"

"I heard your son is sick, and I wanted to offer my help."

He should be with Charlie right now, but his son seemed to be sleeping peacefully for the first time since John had entered the house fifteen hours ago. "There's nothing you can do. There's nothing anyone can do."

"Not even you?" Camilla asked, feigning disbelief.

"What brings you to town?"

"Haven't you heard?" She lifted the veil off her face, revealing smooth skin and calculating eyes.

"Heard what?"

"Mr. Worthington died very suddenly a few weeks ago. I'm home at the invitation of my parents." She examined her black gloves. "I'm deciding what to do with myself."

"I'm sorry. I hadn't heard you lost your husband. I've been a bit preoccupied lately."

"Yes, I imagine you have been."

"How did he die?"

She lifted a shoulder. "They think it was his heart. He was nearing seventy years old."

Forty years older than Camilla. When she married Mr. Worthington, John had wondered if she truly loved him, or if she had married for his money. He still wondered. "Won't you have a seat?"

She studied him closely and took a step toward him.

On instinct, he took a step back.

"You look horrible, John."

He lifted his hand to his whiskers, and then lowered it again, not ashamed of his appearance. Instead, he straightened his spine. "I lost my wife almost three months ago and my son is lying upstairs fighting the same disease that took Anna. How should I look?"

She lifted an eyebrow and looked away.

He sighed. "Why are you really here, Camilla? I never expected to see you again—not after—"

"The way we parted?" She finally looked back at him, the lines of her face hard. "Not after the way you rejected and humiliated me?"

John rubbed the back of his neck, wishing he had not answered the door. He had treated her unfairly twelve years ago when he met Anna. He had been young and stupid. But he didn't want to deal with his past mistakes now.

His head began to pound and his vision blurred. He should check on Charlie—and there was still the matter of Marjorie and Paul. He needed to have a talk with his brother and get to the bottom of their relationship. Why had Paul come to Little Falls in the first place? Was it to reconnect with Marjorie?

Camilla cleared her throat and he focused on her once again.

"Are you here for an apology?" he asked.

She shook her head. "No. I'm here for you to honor your promise to me."

"What promise?"

"The promise you made a week before you met Anna."

"I don't remember making you a promise."

She took a step closer to him and he could smell the

scent of gardenias. "I'll help you remember. We were standing on the shores of Lake Michigan. We were there with friends and there was a bonfire burning. It was nighttime and a full moon reflected on the lake. You held my hand and you said that as soon as you graduated from medical school you would ask me to be your wife. I remember every single detail of that night—and yet you can't remember one."

John searched his memory for the event and it started to come back to him in vivid detail—starting with the smell of her perfume. She had worn the same scent the night of the bonfire. He even recalled each of the friends who had been there that night.

She watched him closely. "Ah, I see it's starting to come back."

"That's why you're here? Is that why you came back to Little Falls?"

She lifted her shoulder again. "You finished medical school, and neither of us is married any longer, so I'm ready for you to propose."

John took another step back and bumped into a table. A lamp crashed to the floor, breaking into dozens of pieces.

"I see my suggestion is a bit of a surprise," she said.

"Everything about your visit is a surprise." There was no way he would honor his promise to Camilla Worthington. He'd had enough life experiences to realize he'd avoided the biggest mistake of his life when he left her to pursue Anna. Camilla was a shrewd woman, and she would be miserable to live with. She epitomized selfishness in all its many facets.

"Don't you want to marry me? I heard from a reliable source that you're looking for a wife."

John leaned forward. "What?"

Camilla's dark eyebrows rose. "You didn't send her?"

"I have no idea what you're talking about."

"Your governess visited me just the other day and told me you're looking for a wife and a mother for your children. She came to my house to suggest we get re-acquainted."

Marjorie had done this? The pressure in his head increased. How had she learned about Camilla?

"I have to admit, I was surprised to learn that the most scandalous socialite in Chicago was living under your roof, as a governess, no less. I had thought she'd run off with the man she'd rendezvoused with the night before her wedding to Mr. Chamberlain."

Paul.

Could it be true? He'd suspected it earlier, but they had both adamantly opposed the accusation. How could Marjorie have come to John's home after doing such a thing with his brother?

Camilla crossed her arms loosely. "I wondered what she would gain from telling me about you, and to be honest, I'm still wondering. You truly didn't send her?"

"I had no idea you were back in town, and even if I did, I would not send her to you."

"I see."

John had to take control of this situation. "I regret my actions twelve years ago, Camilla. I wish I would have handled things with more sensitivity. I apologize for hurting you, but I'm in no position to honor a promise I made as a young man. My life is much different now, and I have four children to take into consideration."

"Three, if fate has anything to say about it."

She spoke with such disregard that John's hair rose on the back of his neck. He didn't say another word but strode out of the parlor and opened the front door.

Camilla stood in the parlor for a moment and then slowly lowered the veil over her face. She walked toward John and stopped directly in front of him.

After a moment, she stood on tiptoe and planted a kiss on his cheek, close to his mouth.

John stood stiff and did not respond.

She pulled away. "Goodbye, John."

She walked out the door and down the steps, disappearing into the swirl of snow.

Chapter Eighteen

Marjorie slowly closed the kitchen door and set her forehead against the hard trim, exhausted and heartbroken.

John and Mrs. Worthington had reconnected, and if the kiss she'd just witnessed was any indication, it had been a pleasant reunion. With their past, it would be no surprise if they had already come to an agreement.

Which meant Marjorie's work with the Ortons had come to an end, once and for all.

It was for the best. After what happened with Charlie, John would probably never forgive her, and she didn't blame him.

Marjorie took the oatmeal off the stove and set three bowls on the counter.

The kitchen door opened and John entered.

Marjorie didn't acknowledge his presence. She couldn't. If she looked at him, she would weep.

He took a coffee cup down from the cupboard and poured the steaming brew. "I want you to be honest with me, Marjorie."

She swallowed the lump in her throat. "I've never been anything but honest."

She scooped oatmeal into the bowls, her movements stiff. She felt as if she were watching herself from a distance. Everything felt odd, but she was so tired she didn't care anymore.

"What do I need to know about your relationship with Paul?"

She put the bowls on a tray and walked into the pantry to get a pitcher of cream out of the icebox. "There is nothing inappropriate about our relationship."

"Then why were you embracing him now and in Chicago?"

She put a small bowl of brown sugar on the tray and added three spoons. She finally looked at him, and wished she hadn't. His face revealed the heavy burdens he carried, yet it was the look of mistrust in his eyes that gave her pain. "I cannot tell you. Only Paul can, and if he's unwilling to share, then I will not."

Frustration and confusion warred within his gaze. "What is that supposed to mean?"

"It means I will not tell you."

He swallowed and crossed his arms, watching her silently for a few moments before he spoke. "If you cannot tell me why, then I believe your work here is done."

Marjorie squared her shoulders with the last bit of energy she possessed. "I've already come to the same conclusion."

She lifted the tray in her trembling hands and moved around him.

He put his hand on her arm and she looked at him.

"Please, Marjorie." There was desperation in his voice. "Just tell me."

She wished she could—but what would it matter? She would need to leave regardless.

She moved beyond him and went up the servants'

stairs, balancing the tray and trying to see past the mist in her eyes. She would deliver the food, say her goodbyes to Charlie, pack a few essential items and go to the train station. She could be in California within a few days and they could send the rest of her things out to her later.

The hall was silent as she walked toward her old room.

She set the tray down on a hall table, secured the white mask she wore around her neck and pushed open the bedroom door.

No one was in the room with Charlie. He lay in the bed, wrapped in dozens of blankets, and slept quietly. He looked so peaceful. Maybe the worst had passed.

Marjorie sat on the edge of the bed and laid her hand against his forehead. He still burned with fever but seemed to respond to her touch. His eyelids fluttered and he nudged her hand.

She smiled. "Goodbye, Charlie."

He moaned but didn't open his eyes.

"Shh." She touched his cheek with the back of her fingers. "Sleep and get well." She knew she was risking a great deal, but she bent down, moved the mask below her lips and kissed his forehead. "I love you and I'll be praying for you, every day, for as long as I live."

Marjorie rose and went to her bureau. The rosebud Charlie had given her the first day was sitting on top, where she had admired it dozens of times. She picked it up and put it in a little jewelry box she'd brought from home. She put the box, along with a few other important items, in her satchel and then slipped out of the room.

The hall was still quiet, for which she was deeply grateful. She was about to go down the servants' stairs when she noticed Petey's airplane, stuck in the corner of the hall, where he often sat and played. In the rush to get the children out of the house, he must have forgotten to grab it.

Marjorie lifted the airplane and held it close. She would stop at the Scotts' to say goodbye to the children and give Petey back his airplane.

She walked down the steps and into the back hall, where she put on her hat and coat. She pushed open the back door and was instantly hit with a blast of cold air and snow. It felt like pellets of ice against her bare face, so she tilted her chin down and trudged through the storm, around the house and across the street to the Scott's.

Marjorie knocked on the front door and was met by Angie, the Scotts' maid.

"Come in," Angie cried, taking Marjorie's arm and practically hauling her over the threshold. "You'll catch your death out there."

"May I please see the children?"

"Of course. They're in the dining room eating their breakfast."

Marjorie didn't bother to remove her coat and hat. She wouldn't be staying long. She set her bag near the door and entered the dining room.

"Miss Maren!" Lilly was the first to see Marjorie. She jumped up from the table and ran around the room until she was in Marjorie's arms. "I missed you."

Marjorie hugged the girl tight. "I missed you, too. How are you getting along?"

"Fine."

Dora rose from the table. "How is Charlie? Any change?"

"His fever is still raging."

Dora pressed her hand to her lips and shook her head.

"We haven't stopped praying. Mother was awake all night praying. She's sleeping now."

"I haven't stopped praying, either." Marjorie went to the basket near the fireplace and looked in to find Laura playing contentedly with her feet. Marjorie smiled at the sweet baby and reached in to pick her up. "How is Laura?"

"She's doing fine, but I think she's been missing you," Dora said.

Marjorie nuzzled the little girl, and Laura cuddled up in her favorite spot against Marjorie's shoulder. "That's silly. How would you know if she's missing me?"

Dora smiled. "I can tell right now."

Marjorie turned away from Dora to hide the moisture that had gathered in her eyes. She kissed Laura's cheek and placed the baby back in the basket. Laura smiled up at Marjorie, her blue eyes twinkling. What would she look like as she aged? Would she look like Lilly? Would she be a silly little girl, or serious, like Petey?

"Petey." She turned to the little boy and extended the airplane. "You forgot this at home."

Home. The word felt just as lonely as it had after she left Chicago. Would she ever find a real home again?

Petey's face lit with excitement and he jumped off his chair. "My airplane!" He took it from her and before she knew what he was about, he wrapped his arms around her legs.

This time Marjorie couldn't hide the tears. They sprang to her eyes and clogged her throat.

"Thank you, Miss Maren." His sweet little voice was muffled against her skirt.

Marjorie wanted so desperately to pick him up and hold him in her arms, but she knew this connection was tenuous and if she asked for more, he'd pull back again. She would be content to accept whatever he was willing to give her.

"I shouldn't stay long," Marjorie said.

"Thank you for coming by to give us an update and to bring Petey's plane," Dora said. "Please let us know if anything else changes."

Marjorie couldn't bring herself to tell Dora she was leaving.

"Thank you for taking such good care of the children," Marjorie said, wiping her cheek.

Dora crossed the room and put her arms around Marjorie. "You need to get some rest. Things will look better once you've had some sleep."

Marjorie hugged her back. "I'll try." She would have plenty of time to sleep on the train.

"Goodbye," Petey said, holding his airplane close to his chest.

"Goodbye, Petey. Goodbye, Lilly."

Lilly gave Marjorie another hug and pulled her shoulders down until Marjorie's ear was near Lilly's mouth. "I'm praying for Charlie, too."

"Don't ever stop." Marjorie took one last glance at Laura, and then at Petey, Lilly and Dora, and walked out of the dining room.

She grabbed her bag and opened the door, ready for the cold this time.

It would be a long walk to the train depot, but she couldn't afford to hire a cab, and even if she could, they probably weren't out driving in this weather.

Marjorie trudged through the snowstorm for hours. She became so cold she was forced to stop in several businesses along the way to warm up, before heading back into the snow. Thankfully many stores were open on the last day before Christmas, even if business was slow.

She faced the hardest leg of her journey when she was forced to cross the bridge spanning the Mississippi River. The wind whipped across the frozen water, swirling the snow until it blinded her and she had to hold on to the railing to guide her steps.

The depot sat on the banks of the river, just beyond the bridge. She pushed the door open and stepped inside, breathing heavily. Half a dozen people sat about on the wooden benches, some sleeping and others playing cards or reading newspapers.

Marjorie stepped up to the ticket counter, her hands and feet feeling clumsy and frozen.

"Well, look-see what the storm blew in," the ticket agent said, chewing a wad of tobacco. "What can I do for you?"

"I'd like a one-way ticket to Los Angeles, California, please."

He lifted bushy eyebrows over spectacles. "That's a mighty long journey."

Marjorie nodded, reaching for her reticule.

"I'm afraid the trains have been stopped because of this storm. We have word that it's going to get worse before it gets better."

Marjorie's hands stilled. "The trains have stopped?"

"Until further notice."

"Do you have any idea when they'll start again?"

He took a slow breath, as if he had all the time in the world. "It could be a day, or two, or even three. There's no way of knowing. Once the storm passes, it'll take some time to clear the tracks."

"Three days?"

"You're more than welcome to wait here, or there's a hotel just two blocks from here. They still have a few rooms left."

A hotel? She asked the ticket agent how much her fare would be to California, and then how much he thought the hotel room would cost per night. She had just enough money for two nights, and a little to spare for food, but once she reached California, she'd have nothing.

Fear niggled into her conscience and she had to purposefully push it away. This was what she had planned to do all along. Surely God knew of her plans and would provide for her…wouldn't He?

She could always go back to the Ortons', but now that she had left, her pride hurt too much to return. Besides, John didn't want her there.

"Could you please get word to me at the hotel once the trains begin to move again?"

The ticket agent nodded slowly. "Will do."

Marjorie took a deep breath and then opened the door, ready to face the storm once again. At least she only had two blocks to walk this time.

She could make it two more blocks.

"Have you seen Marjorie?" John asked his mother.

Mother sat in a chair near the fireplace, her knitting needles in hand. Now that he had done all he could for his son, he had allowed her into Charlie's room. She looked up at John, her dark eyes looking tired above her mask. "Not since the three of you were fighting in the kitchen."

"But that was hours ago." John paced across the floor, one eye on his son and one on the clock over the mantel. His face mask scratched his whiskers, making his skin itch. "It's almost noon."

"Maybe she finally took my advice and went to bed," Mother said.

"Will you go check?"

"Are you worried about her?"

"Of course I'm worried about her," John said. "I'm worried about all of us."

Mother studied him carefully behind her spectacles. "When all this is done, you two need to sit down and have a nice long talk about the future."

"Not now, Mother." John ran his hand through his hair. He should clean up, but he hated to leave Charlie for any amount of time.

"You're both being ridiculous," she said.

"Please go and check on her."

Mother set aside her yellow yarn and rose from the chair, stretching her back and neck.

John took Charlie's temperature once again. Still a hundred and four degrees. Very little had changed since John came home. Charlie's face was bright red and his hair was slick with sweat.

Mother finally returned. "She isn't in the guest room—or any of the other bedrooms for that matter. Maybe she went to the Scotts'. Would you like me to go look there?"

"It's still snowing. I'll go." John glanced at Charlie. "He should be fine for now. If you need me, send Paul."

Mother put her hand on John's arm. "Do you think everything is all right with Marjorie?"

"I hope so." He walked out of the room and went downstairs to the back hall. He put on his outerwear and left the house. The storm had not let up. If anything, it blew harder and colder than before.

He had been too harsh on Marjorie and he regretted his angry words. In his fear and frustration he had lashed out at her. Had she gone to the Scotts' to sleep?

Maybe, when they were both rested, they could talk rationally about Paul.

John knocked on the Scotts' front door and was greeted by their maid. "Hello, Dr. Orton."

"Is Miss Maren here?"

"No, sir." She opened the door wider. "Please come in out of the cold."

Dora appeared in the foyer, her face filled with worry. "Charlie?"

"Still unchanged." John stepped over the threshold.

The maid closed the door and then disappeared into the house.

Dora approached. "How are you doing?"

"I'm fine—I'm here to find Marjorie. Is she here?"

Dora shook her head, her face filling with more concern. "She came over during breakfast to give Petey his airplane, but then she left."

"Did she say where she might have gone?"

"No, but I'll ask Angie." Dora disappeared and came back a few moments later with the maid.

"Do you know where Miss Maren went?" John asked.

Angie looked between Dora and John. "No, but she had a satchel with her."

"A satchel?" Dora turned her startled eyes on John. "Why would she have a bag? Did she say she was going somewhere?"

John rubbed the back of his neck. "She didn't say a word to me." But then he recalled the conversation in the kitchen when he had said it was time for her to leave. He hadn't meant right away—hadn't really meant what he said at all.

"Do you think she's out in this storm?" Dora asked. "Would she do something so foolish?"

"She was upset and exhausted. She wasn't thinking straight," John said. "I need to look for her."

"You can't go out in this storm."

"What if she's lost in the snow? She'll freeze to death."

"She's a grown adult, and there are enough places for her to get warm. Anyone would take her in during this storm. Besides, you need to stay with Charlie."

Yes. Charlie. But maybe he could leave Charlie in Paul and Mother's hands for a little while.

"This is my fault. I was angry with her—"

The door burst open and Paul stood on the porch, his coat thrown over his body in haste. "It's Charlie. Something's wrong."

John pushed past Paul and raced across the street. The ground was slippery and the snow was deep. He almost lost his footing more than once.

Finally he ran up the front steps and burst through the door. His feet fairly flew across the hall and up the stairs to Charlie's room.

Mother stood over Charlie's bed, her hands over her face.

Charlie convulsed on the bed, his body seizing.

His temperature was too high. The sweating wasn't helping, only hurting.

John pulled all the covers off his son, speaking quickly to his mother. "Get cool water and cloths."

"Where's your mask?" Mother asked.

"Forget the mask and get me the water!"

Mother disappeared just as Paul entered.

"We need to cool him down," John said frantically. "His temperature is too high."

"Tell me what to do."

"Draw a bath with lukewarm water."

"Right away."

Paul left the room and John began to remove Charlie's pajamas, praying with every breath he took.

Thankfully Charlie stopped seizing, but it took two hours of hard work to get his body temperature down. Every time the bathwater became too warm, Paul brought in another bucket full of snow. When John felt his temperature was in a safer zone, they brought him to his bed and Mother bathed his forehead with the cloths. When her arms became tired, John took over, and then Paul.

Finally Charlie's temperature lowered, and he was sleeping peacefully once again.

Paul had gone to the kitchen to rustle up something for them to eat, but Mother continued to sit next to John, fatigue lining her face, even as a sense of peace hovered around her countenance. He sensed she was praying, even if he couldn't hear the words.

John leaned forward, put his elbows on his knees and clutched his hands together. "Why is God doing this? Wasn't Anna enough? Now He wants Charlie, too?"

"God wants all of us, John. He desires our heart and soul."

"That's not what I mean."

Mother placed her wrinkled hand over John's, her gentle touch softening his tight grasp. "One of the hardest things in the world is to be a parent," she said. "It's even harder to watch your own child struggle through times like this. I had to learn the hard way how to trust God and His perfect plan—now it's your turn. There's really nothing I can say to help you trust Him. It's a choice you have to make on your own."

John dropped his chin to his chest. Who was he to question God's authority and will?

"I can tell you Charlie's life is a gift," Mother said softly. "And even if God chose to take him now, one day you'll see him again, just as you'll see Anna. Death is not the end, my son. It is simply the beginning for those who pass away, and a pause for those who remain behind."

Mother squeezed John's hands. "Unclench your grasp and let Charlie go into God's loving hands. He's much safer there."

Tears gathered in John's eyes and he did as his mother suggested. He dropped his hands and wept. He'd reached the end of his abilities and control. He would trust God, no matter what He decided to do with Charlie's life.

They sat in silence until John composed himself. Finally he rose and checked Charlie's temperature once again. A hundred and one. Much better than before.

He sighed as he touched his son's warm cheek.

"Why don't you see if Paul needs some help in the kitchen?" Mother asked. "I'll be here with Charlie."

John nodded and left the room.

Paul stood near the counter, slicing a loaf of bread. He glanced up when John entered the kitchen. "There's some jam on the table."

John's stomach growled. He went to the icebox, removed a jar of milk and then took two glasses off a shelf. He brought them to the table and sat.

The snow continued to fall, though it was now coming down in large flakes. Where was Marjorie? Had she gone out in the storm?

Paul set the bread on the table and took a seat across from John. They said a prayer and then devoured their bread in silence.

"Thank you for all your help," John said.

"I'm happy I arrived when I did."

John glanced at his younger brother, unable to hold his tongue. "Why did you come? I thought you'd be spending the first Christmas with your new wife in Chicago."

"It's a long story."

John swallowed hard. "Does it have something to do with Marjorie?"

Paul's face was serious. "It has nothing to do with her."

"Something happened and I need to know."

Paul sighed and set down his glass of milk. "I wanted to wait until Charlie was better before I had to tell you."

John sat up straighter in his chair. Was it as he had suspected?

"Josephine left me for another man."

John stared across the table. "What?"

"That's why Marjorie was consoling me in Chicago and now here. She's the only person who knows the whole story, and frankly I'm sorry I had to share my burden with her. She's already had to deal with so much."

"So you and Marjorie are not—?"

"No."

Yet John had accused her. "Why wouldn't she tell me the truth?"

"I asked her not to."

"So she was only protecting you?"

"She was also protecting you and Mother. I didn't want to bother you with all this right now."

They sat in silence for a moment and then John pushed back his chair and stood. "I should check on Charlie."

"I'm sorry, John. I wish things were different between me and Josephine."

John put his hand on his brother's shoulder. "I know you do."

John slowly walked up the stairs, Marjorie heavy on his heart. He had asked her to leave, simply because she could not betray Paul's trust. What kind of man was he?

He only hoped she was somewhere safe, because he couldn't leave Charlie's side to go looking for her.

But Paul could.

John checked on Charlie and then went back to the kitchen where Paul was cleaning up after their simple meal. "Will you go look for Marjorie?"

"Of course—but I don't know my way around Little Falls. I wouldn't know where to look."

"Maybe Dora will go with you. Mrs. Scott can stay with the children."

"I'll go immediately."

"Use the horse and sleigh."

A small measure of relief filled John's chest—until he realized Marjorie could have already boarded a train for the West.

What would he do if he never saw her again?

Chapter Nineteen

Marjorie stood near the window, watching the large flakes fall from the dark sky. Her room on the second floor of the Antler's Hotel gave her a clear view of the industries dotting the western banks of the Mississippi. Just beyond the hotel, a group of hearty carolers had gathered near a lamppost, filling the air with the joyful songs of Christmas. The glow from the light circled around the singers, giving them an ethereal appearance.

Marjorie lifted her window just an inch to allow the sound to enter in, though with it came a chill.

She wrapped her arms around her waist, tasted the bittersweet flavor of the orange she'd had for supper and sighed. There was no Christmas tree in her little room, no presents to hide for the morning and no one to share the beauty of the evening.

Who did she have to blame but herself? She had made the choices that had led her to this point.

She yawned, wishing she had slept longer. The moment she checked into her room, she had fallen on the bed in complete exhaustion. Hunger pangs had pulled her from her sleep half an hour ago, but she was ready to go back to bed.

A knock sounded at the door.

Marjorie frowned and closed the window. Who would be knocking at her door at this hour of the night?

The room she was renting was a simple affair with a single bed, a desk and a chair. Though the walls were papered in a creamy floral covering, there were no other decorations in the room.

She slowly opened the door.

A bellhop stood on the other side in a red-and-gold uniform.

"Yes?"

"You have guests in the south parlor, Miss Maren."

"Guests?"

"A Miss Scott and Mr. Orton."

Dora and John? No. If it had been John, he would have said Dr. Orton. It must be Dora and Paul. But why had they come? Was it to tell her Charlie had died?

Fear clawed at her chest and she didn't hesitate a moment longer. She stepped out of her room and followed the bellhop down the long hall, toward the grand staircase into the lobby and down another hall to the south parlor.

The bellhop opened the door and Marjorie entered.

"Marjorie!" Dora stood and walked across the room. She threw her arms around Marjorie. "We've been looking for you for hours. We finally went to the depot to see if you had left town, and the ticket agent sent us here to the hotel. Why did you leave?"

"How is Charlie?" It was the only question Marjorie wanted answered at the moment. The rest could wait.

"His fever rose dangerously high this afternoon," Paul said. "He had a seizure, but we were able to bring it back down. Other than that, nothing has changed."

Marjorie clutched her hands, feeling worse than before.

"Let's sit." Dora pointed to a sofa and two chairs on either side of a roaring fireplace.

Why had they come? It couldn't be to ask her back. John had made his feelings clear about wanting her to leave. If they hadn't come to tell her about Charlie, then what could it be?

Marjorie sat, her back rigid, as Dora sat beside her. Paul took one of the wingback chairs. For a moment, they all looked at one another.

Finally Dora spoke. "Why did you leave without telling anyone?"

"I thought it would be easier for everyone if I didn't make a big scene."

"But we were worried sick," Dora said. "We had no idea if you'd gone out in the storm and frozen to death."

"Is that why you're here? To make sure I made it to safety?"

"Yes, of course," Paul said. "John asked us to come. He would have come if he didn't need to stay with Charlie."

"But why?" Marjorie looked between them. "John was the one who told me it was time to leave."

Paul and Dora exchanged a confused glance. "John was just as surprised as us that you left."

He was?

"Why did you leave?" Paul asked.

Why? There were so many reasons. "It was time. My job is done."

"Your job is not done." Dora put her hand over Marjorie's. "It's only just begun."

"John will be married soon and I told him I was only staying until the first of the year."

"John is getting married?" Dora's eyebrows rose. "To whom?"

"To Mrs. Worthington."

"Mrs. Worthing—Camilla Worthington?" Paul's face revealed his feelings—clearly he did not care for the woman. "When did all this happen? I knew he and Camilla were serious at one time, but John realized his mistake in that regard. He would never marry her."

"But—" Marjorie swallowed. She didn't want to tell them she saw Mrs. Worthington and John kissing. It was painful enough for her to recall the event, let alone talk about it. "I have it on good authority that they are."

Paul stood. "John must be out of his mind. I can't stand by and allow him to make such a foolish decision."

"That still doesn't explain why you left a week early," Dora said. "Please come back with us and stay through the New Year. We all want you there."

"John wants you there, too," Paul said.

"He told you?"

"He didn't have to. I could see how upset he was that you were gone."

"Charlie needs you, too." Dora squeezed Marjorie's hand. "All the children are missing you. With Charlie sick, we won't be celebrating Christmas, but it still wouldn't be right for you to be here alone."

Marjorie removed her hand and stood. "The trains could start running at any time, and I want to be on the first one heading west."

"Why go now?" Dora asked.

"Why wait?" Marjorie countered. "I'm just prolonging a departure that will take place sooner rather than later. I've already said my goodbyes. It would be too painful to go back."

"I wish John could be here," Dora said. "He would talk some sense into you."

"I appreciate your concern," Marjorie said to her

friends. "But I'm really quite content to stay here and wait for the train."

"Even on Christmas?"

Marjorie lifted a shoulder. "How is one day different than another?"

Dora and Paul shared another glance and then Dora stood. "I wish we could change your mind."

"Please tell the children I love them and I'll be praying for them." Marjorie hugged Dora.

Dora hugged her back and then she stepped over to the door. "If you change your mind, come home. We'll welcome you back with open arms."

The Orton home was not hers. It belonged to John and his children, and one day to Mrs. Worthington. Marjorie wasn't needed right now. Not with Mrs. Orton's arrival. She could see to the children's needs.

"Thank you, but I'll be fine here."

Paul approached Marjorie. "Come back with us, Marjorie. It's not right for you to be alone right now. I explained everything to John. He knows the truth."

Marjorie took Paul's hand in hers. "Thank you. But this is where I'm supposed to be." Even if John knew the truth, she still needed to leave. There was no future for them.

He shook his head. "Goodbye, Marjorie."

"Goodbye."

Paul followed Dora out of the parlor and they both turned back to look at Marjorie. She waved them off, a smile on her face, when all she wished was to cry.

She didn't want to be at the hotel alone. She wanted to return with them, but everything she said was true. John would soon marry Mrs. Worthington and she would have to say goodbye. Why prolong the agony? John had said it was time for her to leave. With all that had happened, it was for the best. He couldn't trust her, and she didn't blame him.

Marjorie walked back to her room and closed the door. She flipped off the lights and curled up in a ball on her bed. The carolers were still singing. "Joy to the World" lifted to her room and Marjorie drifted off to sleep, feeling no joy at the moment.

John woke with a start. Sunshine poured in the window, revealing a glistening world covered in icicles and over a foot of fresh snow. A bright blue sky glowed overhead with not a cloud in sight.

It was Christmas morning.

John sat up straighter and stretched his aching neck. He tilted his head back and forth and rubbed the knots out of his shoulders.

Charlie.

He looked toward the bed and was met with a weak smile and the blinking blue eyes of his son. "Good morning, Papa."

"Charlie." John fell to his knees and tore off his mask. He grasped Charlie's hand and kissed his knuckles. "Charlie."

"Did I miss Christmas?" His son's raspy voice was the most wonderful sound in the world.

John put his hand on Charlie's forehead. Cool. Blessedly cool.

John laughed. "You didn't miss Christmas, son. Today is Christmas."

"Are there presents?"

John studied Charlie's face and smiled. "Right here, in your smile."

"I'm thirsty."

John took a glass of water off the table and helped his son take a drink.

"Am I going to die, Papa?"

John shook his head, tears gathering in his eyes. "No. God spared your life for something great, Charlie. You're going to be fine. It will be some time before you're back to normal, but you're past the worst of it."

Charlie nodded, as if he understood, but did he? "Where's Miss Maren?"

John paused. "She's not here."

"I heard her voice and felt her cool hand on my face." He took several deep breaths. "She made me want to get better." His voice faded as he fell asleep.

John grasped his son's hand and bowed his head. "Thank you, Lord. Thank You for sparing Charlie's life."

John stood, feeling like a new man. He wanted to throw open the windows and shout to the world. There was so much to celebrate and so much to be thankful for. His son would live. Today was Christmas, the day they celebrated the arrival of their Savior. The day God sent His one and only son. How much more John understood the great sacrifice God made to allow His son to come to earth as a man.

It was the greatest gift of all time.

John left Charlie's side. He would get cleaned up and go to his children. They would want to know that Charlie would be all right. They should spend the day at the Scotts', to let Charlie rest, but they could come home for supper and presents.

After he told them the good news, he would tell Marjorie and ask her to come back to celebrate with them.

Last night, when Paul had come home, he told John all about his visit with Marjorie at the Antler's Hotel.

Paul had been angry that John was marrying Camilla, and John had told him Marjorie was mistaken.

Marjorie needed to know the truth, and she needed to know that he was sorry. He had said things he regretted, but he had been scared and exhausted. Surely she would understand.

John knocked on the guest room door. "Mother."

It took a few moments, but she finally opened the door, wiping sleep from her eyes. "What's wrong?"

"It's Charlie."

Her eyes were wide-awake now. "No."

John grinned. "He's going to be fine. His fever broke."

"Praise God!" Mother threw her hands in the air and then around John.

"I'm going to get dressed and go tell the children. Will you sit with Charlie while I'm gone?"

"Of course."

John walked down the hall and into his room. Paul was sleeping with his arm over his head. John shook his leg. "Wake up! Charlie's fever has broken. He's going to be fine."

Paul lifted his arm and looked at John. A smile spread across his sleepy face. "That's good news to wake up to."

John pulled clean clothes out of his bureau. "I'm going to get dressed and tell the children."

Paul yawned. "It will be the best Christmas ever."

"Mother is sitting with Charlie. I may be gone awhile."

"Will you go tell Marjorie?"

John smiled. "I can't wait for her to hear the good news."

"Are you going to ask her to marry you?"

John paused. "I already have."

Paul pulled himself up, fully awake. "And?"

Suddenly John felt exhausted again. He sat at the foot of his bed. "She won't have me."

"Why not?"

"I told her it would be a marriage in name only."

Paul frowned. "Why would you say that?"

"It's complicated."

Paul rested against the headboard. "If you don't love her, let her go."

John looked out the window at the promise of a new day—a new beginning.

Paul leaned forward. "Do you love her?"

"I made a vow to Anna—"

"If I remember correctly, the vow says 'Until death do we part.'" Paul's voice was surprisingly gentle. "You would not dishonor Anna by falling in love again. You would be honoring God, who created love and marriage and family. I think Anna would want you to move on with your life. I don't think she'd wish you to be lonely and unhappy forever."

John studied his brother for a long time. What he said was true. Knowing Anna, she would want John to continuing loving and living—even if it was with someone other than her.

He glanced over at her Bible. It hadn't moved an inch since the last time she touched it, and it was now gathering dust. No matter how much he had loved her, she would not be coming back—yet John remained. He had fulfilled his vows to God and to Anna, and now…now it was time to move on.

"You're right."

Paul shrugged. "I usually am."

John grinned at his brother. "Sometimes you are."

Paul tossed a pillow at John's head. "You'd better hurry. Marjorie will probably be on the first train out of town."

John jumped off the bed and glanced at the clock. It was already eight. "Did she say when the train would leave?"

"I believe the ticket agent said it would leave just as soon as the tracks were clear."

John looked outside, again. The snow was piled in high drifts, and it would take time to clear the tracks, but he didn't want to risk missing her. He raced to the water closet and tried to make himself presentable, though it was no use. His hair was disheveled and his face in need of a shave, but it hardly mattered. He wanted to be the one to tell his children that Charlie would recover before going to the depot.

He rushed downstairs and pulled on his coat and hat. He was about to exit the house when a voice stopped him.

"John?" Mother stood in the front hall in her robe and slippers.

John closed the door. "Is it Charlie? Does he need something?"

She walked into the back hall, took his hand and then gently placed a small velvet box on his palm. "Paul told me where you're going." She closed his fingers around the box.

"What—?"

"When you married Anna, your father was alive, so I still needed this." She looked up at him, her eyes misting over. "Now I want you and Marjorie to have it."

John was quiet for a long time. "Are you sure?"

She nodded, a smile gracing her dear face. "Nothing would make me happier."

John opened the lid on the box. It was the first time he'd ever seen Mother's wedding ring anywhere but on her finger. She had been wearing it that very morning. Now the diamond glinted up at him, nestled in black silk. At one time, it was brand-new, but now the band was a bit worn around the edges, smoothed and softened by age and love.

"Your father and I were not perfect, but over time, and through many trials, we became one in marriage. I only hope and pray you and Marjorie will be as happy as we were."

John didn't know if he'd catch Marjorie in time—but if he did, he would be honored to offer her his mother's ring—if she'd have him. "Thank you, Mother."

She stood on tiptoe and kissed his cheek. "Now go."

He had no time to lose. If he didn't go now, he might never get a chance to tell Marjorie he was sorry about all the horrible things he'd said to her—or tell her that he loved her.

He slipped the box into his pocket, raced across the street and knocked on the door. Dora answered, her face filled with fear—but the moment she saw the grin on John's lips, she smiled.

"He's much better this morning," John said quickly. "He's going to make it."

Dora opened the door wider and pulled John into the foyer. "It's a merry Christmas indeed."

"Papa!" Lilly raced into the foyer and jumped into his arms. "Did God answer our prayers? Is Charlie all better?"

"He's much better."

"But he won't die, like Mama?"

John shook his head. "No."

Lilly threw her arms around John's neck and squeezed hard. "I'm so happy."

"Me, too."

Petey walked into the foyer, followed by Mother Scott. John shared the news with her.

Petey held his toy airplane and lifted his arms to John.

John set Lilly on her feet and then picked up his son.

"Where's Miss Maren?" Petey asked.

"She's gone and good riddance," Mother Scott said. "I'm happy to be done with the woman."

"Is she gone, Papa?" Petey asked, hugging his plane to his chest. "Like Mama?"

"She's not gone like Mama," Lilly said. "She's coming back. Don't worry, Petey. Miss Maren wouldn't leave us like Mama left us."

John squatted down to be eye level with Lilly. "Mama didn't have a choice, Lilly. You know that, don't you?"

Lilly nodded. "God took her home with Him."

John nodded.

"But God isn't taking Miss Maren home, is He?"

John swallowed. "I hope not."

"Can we keep her?" Petey asked. "I like Miss Maren."

It was the second best thing John had heard that Christmas morning. "I like her, too."

"John!" Mother Scott scolded. "Leave well enough alone. The woman is gone and she should stay gone." She crossed her arms over her bosom. "Now maybe you'll see the person standing right in front of you." She indicated Dora.

John stood with Petey in his arms. "Mother Scott—"

Dora put her hand on his arm. "Let me tell her, John."

"Tell me what?" Mother Scott asked. "Have you two finally come to your senses?"

"For the last time, Mother, John and I are not getting married."

Mother Scott looked at both of them and then turned and left the foyer.

"Can we come home now, Papa?" Lilly asked. "I want to see Charlie and Miss Maren. We have a surprise for you. We've been practicing since Thanksgiving."

"You can come home for supper tonight, but until then we'll let Charlie get some rest." John looked up at Dora. "Is that all right?"

"Of course." Dora smiled and put her hand on Lilly's shoulder. "We'll bake cookies and treats for tonight."

"Thank you."

"Will you go to Marjorie?" Dora asked quietly.

John nodded. "I need to hurry."

Petey lifted his airplane toward John. "Give her my plane and tell her to bring it back to me like before."

John took the peace offering from his son and patted his head. "I will."

"Tell her to come home," Lilly said. "We miss her."

Dora offered John a beautiful smile. "Tell her all of us want her to come home."

"I'll tell her." John stepped out of the house and crossed the street. The snow came up to his knees and he had to struggle to take each step. With Petey's airplane in hand, he went into his carriage house and hooked the mare up to the sleigh, moving as quickly as he could.

Just as he was pulling out of the carriage house, he heard the shrill whistle of the train traveling through the clear winter air and his heart sped up at the sound.

He prayed he wasn't too late.

Chapter Twenty

Marjorie had been told the westbound train would leave the Little Falls Depot at nine o'clock in the morning. As the train pulled out of the station, she couldn't help thinking she was making a mistake.

The whistle blew and steam poured out from under the carriage, blasting the cold air with a thick cloud. It billowed out, growing wider and wider until it eventually dissipated into nothing.

She had slept fitfully the night before, rising before dawn, and had sat in the hotel room staring out the window at the beautiful Christmas morning. Her thoughts were with the Ortons, but especially Charlie and John. Had Charlie made it through the night? She ached at the thought, and longed to be there beside him as he fought for his life, but knew it wasn't her place. John was more than capable of fighting for his son—but who would fight for John? Camilla? Was she there even now?

The train rounded the bend, on its way toward places West, and disappeared from sight.

Marjorie hugged her arms around her body and patted them furiously against her back to get the blood flowing again. She had stood on the platform and watched all the other passengers board, but hadn't had the courage to get on herself. She wasn't ready to leave—or rather, she wasn't ready to face the next chapter of her life.

Her dream to go to California no longer held the same appeal. A new dream had wiggled its way into her heart, planting itself firmly while she had been with the Ortons.

She longed to be a wife and a mother like never before, to bring joy into the lives of people she loved—and people who loved her in return. But that dream seemed even more far-fetched than going to California to be in the movies. Life had shown her that having a happy marriage and family was a very rare blessing.

She went back into the station to stay warm and wait for the next train.

Maybe she'd have enough nerve to get on that one.

"Looks like you missed the train," the ticket agent said from his perch behind the counter. He glanced at the large clock at the end of the depot. "No worries. Next one heading west should be along any minute. They were so backed up in the Twin Cities it should be easy enough to get on another one soon."

Marjorie found a spot to sit on a hard bench and put her satchel on her lap. "Thank you."

The ticket agent scratched his head. "Doesn't seem right, a young lady like you all alone on Christmas. Don't you have a home?"

Marjorie looked away from the well-meaning man and shook her head. "Not yet."

"Pity." He cleared his throat. "You're more than welcome to come home with me and have lunch with the missus. Would you like that?"

"Thank you for your offer, but I think I'll get on the

next train." She had another orange in her bag. It wasn't much, but it was all she could afford to eat.

"Suit yourself."

Marjorie glanced around the large depot. A handful of people were waiting for the next train. Most were talking among themselves, but one man sat alone on the opposite end of Marjorie's bench, and when she glanced at him, he looked up and smiled.

"Merry Christmas," he said.

"Merry Christmas." She looked away, not feeling like conversation.

"Have we met before?"

She looked back but didn't recognize him. He was an aging gentleman with a white mustache and sparkling brown eyes.

"Me name is Sam Turner." He spoke with a bit of an Irish accent. "I believe I met you at church. You're the Ortons' governess. Miss…" He held up his hand. "Don't tell me. Miss Maren?"

"That's right."

The sparkle in his eyes turned to amazement. "God answered me prayer when he sent you to the Orton family."

"I beg your pardon?"

Mr. Turner smiled and looked a bit sheepish. "Dr. Orton is a friend of mine. After his wife died, I asked God to bring someone into his home to be a mother to his children and a companion to him." He studied her for a moment, as if weighing the wisdom in his next statement. "Maybe me old eyes deceived me, but I saw how happy the children were with you—and how much John had grown to love you."

A dam broke within Marjorie and she turned into a sobbing mess before Mr. Turner.

He slid down the bench toward her and patted her hand in a fatherly gesture. "There, there. Don't cry, lass. Things aren't so bad." He handed her a clean handkerchief. "Ach, now, I've made a mess of things, haven't I?"

She wiped at her face, her cheeks growing warm. "I'm sorry for carrying on so."

"No need to apologize for tears, especially ones from so deep within. Is there anything I can do to help?"

She shook her head. "No, thank you."

He squinted, as if bracing himself for a blow. "Was it something I said?"

"Yes." She offered a little laugh.

He put his hand over his heart, his face revealing his distress. "It's sorry I am."

"No. What you said was wonderful."

He looked straight, confusion on his brow. "I wish I could remember what it was, then."

She laughed again, but then turned serious. "You said you saw how much John loved me—I wish it was so."

"Ah." He nodded. "I think I understand. Maybe these tears are because you don't think he loves you?"

She nodded and wiped at her nose once again.

"Then I think these tears are for naught."

She looked down at her hands and fiddled with the cotton handkerchief. "I wish I could agree with you—but he's engaged to another woman."

There was a long pause and then he said softly, "Are you so sure?"

She glanced at Mr. Turner with a question on her face.

But Mr. Turner was looking over her shoulder toward the door.

Marjorie turned her head.

John had just entered the depot, frantically searching the interior until his gaze landed on Marjorie.

"Merry Christmas," Mr. Turner said, sliding back to his end of the bench.

John strode across the wooden floor, his long coat flapping as he walked.

Marjorie stood on shaking legs. What was he doing here?

His gaze roamed all over her, as if he was looking for an injury. "How are you?"

"I'm fine. How's Charlie?"

He smiled and Marjorie clutched Mr. Turner's handkerchief to her chest.

"He's doing well," John said. "His fever broke and I expect him to make a full recovery."

The news was too good to be true. Marjorie sank to the bench, the tears starting all over again. The past few days had been the longest days of her life and she had never known fear as she'd known it while Charlie was sick.

John sat close beside her, his voice low. "I thought you had already gone."

"I couldn't get on the train."

"Why not?"

"I was afraid."

"That doesn't sound like the Marjorie I've come to know."

"Then maybe you haven't known the real me."

He took her gloved hand in his and she bit her bottom lip. It felt so wonderful to be held by him.

"I know the real Marjorie Maren," he said. "She's the young lady who walked into my home two months ago and turned everything upside down. She broke my rules, defied my orders and tried to marry me off to half the women in this town. Not once did I see fear in her eyes."

"Maybe you weren't looking hard enough."

"Or maybe…" He leaned close to her and tried to get her to look at him. "I couldn't see the fear past the love in her eyes for my children."

She sniffled. "I do love your children."

"And they love you."

She finally looked up at him and was startled by the look in his brown eyes.

"I love you, too, Marjorie."

"You do?" she whispered.

"More than I ever thought possible."

She couldn't hold in the truth any longer. "I love you."

He put her hand to his lips. "I hoped you would say that."

"But I'm scared, John. Scared of so many things."

"Then that makes two of us."

"What are you scared of?"

"I'm scared I'll lose you." His hand came up to her cheek and he wiped away a stray tear. "I have something for you." He reached inside his coat and pulled Petey's airplane out of the inner pocket.

"Why do you have Petey's airplane?"

"I stopped there to tell the children about Charlie before coming here and Petey asked me to give this to you." He extended the metal airplane.

Marjorie took it in her hands, holding it like it was the most precious item in the world, and at the moment, it was. "Why?"

"He asked me to give it to you, so you would have to return it to him." He studied her face. "He doesn't want you to go, and neither do I. None of us want you to leave."

Marjorie examined the airplane, thinking of the quiet little boy who loved it. Had he finally accepted her? She wanted nothing more than to take him up in her arms at this very moment.

"I want you to be my wife," John whispered beside her. "Not because I need a mother for my children, but because I want you by my side for the rest of my days."

"What about Camilla?"

He shook his head.

"You're not marrying her?"

"It never even entered my mind."

A great burden lifted from Marjorie's heart at the news.

"You once told me you are afraid that you could never complete anything," John said. "So I'm asking you to finish something right now."

"What is that?"

"You said you couldn't leave until you found me a wife—so become the wife I need, and finish the job you set out to accomplish." He reached inside his coat once again, and this time he pulled out a small velvet box. "This isn't from Petey. This is a gift from me."

He opened the box and a beautiful diamond ring sparkled in the sunshine pouring into the depot. "It's my mother's ring. Unlike Petey's gift, I don't want this back. I want you to keep it and wear it forever."

Father's words ran through Marjorie's head once again. *You're a quitter, Marjorie, and you'll never change.*

This time, she wouldn't quit. She would spend the rest of her days loving John and his children—their children. Marjorie couldn't contain the grin. "Yes."

John offered her a stunning smile. "Yes?"

She nodded and allowed him to slip the ring on her finger.

It fit perfectly.

He let the box fall to his lap and then he kissed her, right there in front of Mr. Turner, the ticket agent and a whole host of strangers.

His kiss was soft and loving, yet it held promise for passion, adventure and a dose of whimsy.

John lifted his lips from Marjorie's and offered her another smile as he shook his head.

"What?" she asked quietly, a smile playing about her mouth, her dimples glowing.

"The day you walked into my home, I never imagined I'd be asking you to stay forever."

"Neither did I."

"But now I can't think of anything better than this."

She put her arms around him and pulled him down to kiss him once again.

A train whistle filled the depot and they both looked toward the bank of windows. A hulking locomotive pulled into the station.

"Westbound train," the ticket agent called out.

Marjorie looked away from the train and toward John. "Can we go home now?"

John grinned. "The children will be excited to hear our news." He glanced down at her bag. "Is this one yours?"

"Yes."

He lifted her bag and offered his arm, but then he stopped and stared out the window. A familiar figure strode away from the train and toward the depot, wearing a dark wool coat and matching fedora. "It looks like we have another guest."

Marjorie followed his gaze. "Who is he?"

John grinned. "That's Dora's fiancé, Jeremiah Watkins."

Her brow rose high. "Did Dora know he was coming?"

"I don't know. Do you mind if we give him a ride?"

"Of course not. I'm eager to meet him."

They waited near the door for Jeremiah to enter the depot.

"Hello," John said, snagging the young man's attention. "Merry Christmas."

Jeremiah's blue eyes registered his surprise. "John! Merry Christmas. What are you doing here?" His questioning gaze lingered on Marjorie.

"I came here to pick up my fiancée, Miss Maren." John couldn't hide the pride in his voice. "Marjorie, this is a good friend of mine, Dr. Jeremiah Watkins."

Jeremiah grinned at Marjorie, and John could tell his friend approved. "It's a pleasure to meet you, Miss Maren."

"The pleasure is mine." Marjorie smiled back at Jeremiah and then took John's hand in hers.

"It's a pleasant coincidence running into you," John said to Jeremiah. "Would you like a ride?"

"Yes." Jeremiah's face showed his appreciation. "It would save me the trouble of hiring a cab." He clutched a single satchel in one hand. With the other, he clapped John's back. "Do you think Dora will be happy to see me?"

"A little surprised, but very happy."

The three walked out to John's sleigh and were soon swishing through town, toward East Broadway and the

Scotts' home. On the way, John told Jeremiah all about Charlie's illness.

"How long will you be in town?" Marjorie asked Jeremiah.

"Just as long as it takes to make Dora my bride."

"I plan to get the preacher to my house in the morning," John said, giving Marjorie a wink. "You're more than welcome to join us."

"I might, at that, if she'll finally say yes!" Jeremiah laughed, and the sound matched the ringing of the jingle bells on the harness.

John stopped the sleigh in front of the Scotts' home and helped Marjorie out.

"I'm nervous," she said to John quietly as Jeremiah climbed out of the back.

"Why?"

"It sounds silly, but I feel as if I'm meeting your children for the first time." She touched her hair. "Do I look all right?"

John could finally allow the truth to shine from his eyes. "You're the most beautiful woman in the world."

"Miss Maren!" Lilly's voice carried over the snowy lawn as she jumped up and down on the front porch, waving with all her might. Petey appeared at her side, a grin on his face. "Hurry. We've made more gingerbread men!"

Marjorie grinned and started toward the house, her skirts gathered up in her hands as she climbed over snowbanks to get to the children.

John chuckled. It did his heart good to see their excitement for one another.

Dora appeared at the door, a dish towel in hand, and her eyes grew wide at the sight of Jeremiah. She rubbed self-consciously at the flour on her nose.

Jeremiah followed in Marjorie's footprints and met Dora at the door, just as John came up behind them.

"Merry Christmas," Jeremiah said to Dora.

"Merry Christmas—what are you doing—?"

John walked around them and into the foyer, just as Jeremiah kissed Dora.

John closed the front door to give them privacy.

"Papa!" Lilly said as she tugged on his arm. "You brought Miss Maren home."

"And she brought my airplane," Petey said from Marjorie's arms. He flew his airplane over Marjorie's head and Marjorie used the opportunity to kiss his cheek. Instead of pulling away, Petey wrapped his arms around Marjorie's neck and squeezed her tight.

Marjorie turned to John, a smile on her face, even as tears filled her eyes.

Mother Scott entered the foyer holding Laura in her arms. Her gaze swept over Marjorie and disdain filled her face. "I see we aren't done with her."

It was time to share their news. Mother Scott needed to realize that Marjorie would stay, whether she liked it or not.

"Mother Scott. Children." John put his arm around Marjorie's waist. "I've asked Marjorie to marry me."

"You're going to be our mama?" Petey asked.

"Not our mama," Lilly corrected. "Our stepmother."

Petey's little brow furrowed. "What does that mean?"

"It means she's going to take your mother's place," Mother Scott said with a gravelly voice. "It will be as if Anna never existed."

"That's the last thing I want to do." Marjorie looked toward John, dismay on her face. She set Petey on his feet. "I will do everything I can to keep Anna's memory alive. I wouldn't dream of taking her place." She turned her green eyes toward Mother Scott. "I love John and the children, and I know my love for them would not be possible if Anna's love had not come first. I will never replace her. I will simply carry on the legacy she began, and hope I can do her proud."

Mother Scott harrumphed and then handed Laura over to Marjorie. "I suppose I don't have a say, so what does my opinion matter?"

"Mother Scott." John took a step toward his mother-in-law and put his arm around her shoulder. She stood stiff and unyielding. "A great deal has changed in the past few months, and I know how difficult it has been for you. You're the children's grandmother and you'll always have a special place in their lives. But…" He looked at her closely, his voice serious. "Marjorie will become my wife, and if you cannot treat her with love and respect, you will not be welcome in our home."

Mother Scott looked from John to Marjorie and back again. "I would never dream of being disrespectful."

John wanted to roll his eyes, but instead he offered her a hug. "Please join us for supper tonight."

She nodded, wiping at her eyes. "I'll be there." She looked around John, her tears already forgotten. "Who's that on my front porch? Is that—" She put her hand to her chest. "Is that Dora *kissing* a man right out my front door?"

"That's Dr. Jeremiah Watkins." John laughed. "And I do believe he is kissing your daughter. Pretty soundly, by the looks of it."

"Why, I never! Right there, for everyone to see?" Mother Scott moved toward the door and peeked through the window. "Is he the young man who has been writing to Dora?"

"I believe so."

Mother Scott grabbed the doorknob before John could stop her, and she opened the door. "Dora, what is the meaning of this?"

Dora turned to her mother, her cheeks pink, but she didn't leave Jeremiah's arms. "Mother, this is Jeremiah, and I'm going to marry him."

Jeremiah grinned at Dora, but Mother Scott's mouth sagged. "You're going to what?"

"I'm going to marry him. Tomorrow." Dora laughed, and the sound made everyone but Mother Scott smile.

Instead, Mother Scott's mouth hung open as she stared at Dora. "And when were you going to tell me?"

"I've been trying to get up the courage for weeks now."

"Why were you afraid?"

"Because I'll be moving to Minneapolis after we're married."

Mother Scott didn't say anything for a long time, and the children seemed to sense the magnitude of the moment, not saying a word. Finally Mother Scott nodded once and then climbed the stairs without looking back.

Dora glanced at Jeremiah, her smile gone.

"It will take her some time," John said.

Dora bit the inside of her bottom lip and nodded, though John could see a glimmer of moisture in her eyes.

"Can we go home now?" Lilly asked, tugging on John's arm again.

"Later." John took Laura from Marjorie's arms and lifted the baby in the air. He was rewarded with a giggle and a stream of drool from her little mouth. "For now, I must check on Charlie and let him rest. Marjorie and I will come back for you in a few hours when supper is ready."

"I hate to leave the children so soon." Marjorie put her arm around Lilly's shoulder. "We've only just been reunited."

"I'll take good care of them." Dora took Laura from John's arms. "The children will be ready when you come for them."

John looked at Jeremiah and then back at Dora. "Are you sure?"

Both Dora and Jeremiah nodded, so John offered Marjorie his arm and they kissed the children on their cheeks before walking out the front door.

They went back to the sleigh and John drove it around to the carriage house. Together, he and Marjorie rubbed down the horse and wiped the sleigh, sharing smiles as they worked. When the tasks were complete, he kissed her soundly, and then they walked toward the house, hand in hand.

John pushed open the back door and they stepped into the warm hall. "Will you be ready for the preacher in the morning?"

She offered him a dazzling smile. "I'd be ready by suppertime, if I needed to be."

"Tomorrow morning, then?"

She nodded. "I can't wait."

They took off their coats and hats and walked up the stairs to Marjorie's old room.

Mother and Paul were sitting in the room with Charlie, who was awake. Mother was spoon-feeding him steaming broth and Paul was reading the *Little Falls Daily Transcript* in the chair. All three looked up when John and Marjorie entered the room.

"Merry Christmas," Marjorie said to them all.

"Miss Maren!" Charlie's dull eyes lit up and a smile played about his tired mouth. "You came home."

Marjorie sat on the edge of Charlie's bed and put her hand on the side of his face.

Charlie lifted one hand to touch hers and he looked happier than John had ever seen him.

"I'm back, Charlie, and I'm not ever going to leave again. You must promise to get well and stay well."

"I will."

John put his hand on Marjorie's shoulder. "Marjorie is going to marry me."

"Congratulations, John," Mother said, rising with the bowl of broth in her hands. "I'm so happy."

Paul also rose and extended his hand to John. "Congratulations."

Mother set down the broth and gave Marjorie a hug and a kiss. "Welcome to the family, my dear." She held up Marjorie's left hand and admired her ring. "It never looked lovelier."

"Thank you."

Charlie watched the whole scene unfold with a quiet smile on his face. "God has given us a gift, hasn't He, Papa?"

John knelt beside his son, but his eyes were on Marjorie. "He has indeed."

Chapter Twenty-One

Marjorie reached into the back of her wardrobe and lifted the green silk gown off the hook. She pulled it forward and heard a sigh behind her.

"It's just as beautiful as I remembered," Lilly said from the edge of Marjorie's bed.

Charlie had been moved to the guest room after supper the night before, and Miss Ernst had returned and cleaned the governess's room so Marjorie could sleep there on her final night before becoming Mrs. Orton.

Now it was the morning after Christmas, and Marjorie was getting ready for her wedding.

"Are you happy to marry my papa?" Lilly asked.

Marjorie laid the gown on the chair and then turned to the bureau mirror where she looked at her reflection. She noted her flushed cheeks and her shining eyes. "Yes. I'm very happy."

"You're not sad you won't be in the movies?"

Marjorie lifted the dried rosebud Charlie had given her on the first day she arrived and she tucked it into her blond curls. "I'm not even a little sad. Because I know my life will be even better than the movies. It will be full of love, adventure, comedy and plenty of drama."

Lilly stood and walked over to Marjorie's gown. "Do you think I could wear this dress someday?"

Marjorie glanced at her reflection once more and, seeing she could do nothing else with her appearance, turned to Lilly. "I would love for you to wear it someday, but I have a feeling when you're old enough to wear it, the dress will be out of fashion and you will be ready for something new."

Lilly blinked up at Marjorie, her blue eyes filled with love. "Will you be there? When I'm all grown up, I mean."

Marjorie took the little girl in her arms and held her tight. "God willing, yes, I will be there."

Lilly squeezed her back. "I'm glad."

"Are you almost ready?" Mrs. Orton asked, knocking at the door.

"Come in," Marjorie called. "I'm just about to put on my gown and then I'm ready."

Mrs. Orton stepped into the room, already wearing her best dress. "Shall I help?"

Marjorie nodded and allowed Mrs. Orton to help her slip the gown over her head and then button up the back.

"It's even prettier on," Lilly breathed.

"Let's hurry," Mrs. Orton said. "Everyone is waiting downstairs. The other bride and groom have already arrived."

Mrs. Orton walked out of Marjorie's room, followed close by Lilly and then Marjorie. They crossed the upstairs hall and began their descent down the steps.

Mrs. Orton and Lilly hurried ahead of Marjorie into the parlor, so Marjorie stood alone at the bottom of the stairs.

She took a deep breath. This was it. The moment had

come. Once she said I do, she could never walk away again. There would be no quitting this time.

John appeared near the parlor entrance. He wore a black evening coat tailored to fit his body to perfection. His dark brown hair was combed to the side, and his brown eyes sparkled with love. He walked toward her, and her heart quickened in her chest.

"You look stunning, Marjorie." He offered his hand.

Marjorie didn't even hesitate. She placed her hand in his. "Thank you."

"Are you ready?"

She couldn't help lifting her eyebrows. "Are *you* ready? You do recall all the trouble I cause?"

He pulled her into his arms and hugged her. "How could I forget? It's why I fell in love with you."

"Because I cause trouble?"

He kissed her forehead. "Because there's no one else like you."

"Stop that, now!" Mrs. Scott said from the parlor arch. "You haven't said your vows."

"Shall we?" John asked Marjorie.

She nodded, unable to contain the shiver of excitement that raced through her body.

They walked into the parlor arm in arm. The room was festive with Christmas decorations. The tree still stood in the corner, decorated by the children just before Charlie had become ill. All the candles had been lit, offering a gentle glow. Mistletoe hung from the ceiling in the center of the bay window where Dora and Jeremiah waited with the preacher.

Charlie had been brought downstairs for the ceremony and was lying on a sofa with a blanket around his legs. His pale cheeks were a reminder of the ordeal he had been through. Though he wanted to be present for the wedding, John insisted that he be brought back to bed the moment the ceremony was over. The grin on his face indicated he was feeling as good as could be expected.

Lilly stood in a beautiful red dress with a matching ribbon in her hair. Petey wore his blue sailor suit, his hair slicked down and his airplane firmly grasped in his hand. When he saw Marjorie enter, he ran to her side and wouldn't budge. Even Laura had been dressed up in a white gown, a red ribbon encircling her downy head. She sat in Mrs. Orton's lap, cooing to anyone who would pay attention.

"Are you the other bride?" the preacher asked.

Marjorie nodded at the jolly little man. "I am."

"Good." He lifted his hands. "Everyone, please find a seat."

Paul and Mrs. Scott took a seat near Mrs. Orton and the children—all except Petey, who continued to stand by Marjorie's side.

Jeremiah's parents, Mr. and Mrs. Watkins, had come on the morning train and they sat on the other sofa. Mrs. Gohl and Miss Ernst had also been invited, and they stood near the door.

Marjorie wished her parents could be in attendance. Hopefully, one day, they would find it in their hearts to forgive Marjorie and embrace her new family.

"I'll have both couples face me," the preacher said as he opened his Bible.

Marjorie caught Dora's eye and they smiled at each other. Dora wore a pretty blue gown, and Marjorie couldn't help thinking how much she looked like Anna. Was this how Anna had looked eleven years ago when she married John?

It felt good and right to sense Anna's presence today.

Marjorie looked at the four children, all of them smiling at her, and knew that Anna was with them, and would always be with them.

John watched Marjorie. "You look happy."

"I am happy."

He squeezed her hand. "So am I."

"Dearly beloved," the preacher began, "we are here today in the sight of God and man to join these two couples in holy matrimony. Marriage is an institution ordained of God, and it is not to be entered into lightly or unadvisedly, but reverently, deliberately and only after much consideration, for in coming together in marriage you are committing yourselves exclusively, the one to the other, for as long as you both shall live."

Marjorie looked at John once again, and he smiled down at her.

"Knowing this," the preacher continued. "I ask you this question. John, do you take Marjorie to be your lawfully wedded wife, to have and to hold, from this day forward, for better or for worse, in sickness and in health, until death do you part?"

John studied Marjorie, his eyes filled with a deep understanding of the vows he was committing to. "I do."

"And, Marjorie, do you take John to be your lawfully wedded husband, to have and to hold, from this day forward, for better or for worse, in sickness and in health, until death do you part?"

Marjorie looked at John, and then at Charlie, Lilly and Laura on the sofa. Her gaze went to Petey, who looked up at her with adoration. She touched his little chin and then turned her full attention to John. "I do."

John smiled at her and then took her hand as they listened to Dora and Jeremiah speak their vows.

"Then, by the authority granted to me by God and

the State of Minnesota, I now pronounce both couples husband and wife." The preacher closed his Bible. "Gentlemen, you may kiss your brides."

John took Marjorie in his arms and kissed her thoroughly. When he pulled back, his gaze was filled with love and hope.

There were congratulations all around, with many hugs and kisses for the brides and grooms. Only Charlie remained seated, though he watched everything with a smile on his face.

Marjorie leaned down and picked up Petey while John took Laura from Mrs. Orton's arms. Together, they went to the sofa to join Charlie.

Lilly nestled next to Marjorie. "What will we call you now, Miss Maren?"

"We shall call her Mommy," Petey said with finality.

Marjorie put her arm around her daughter. "You may call me whatever you'd like, Lilly Belle."

"But not Miss Maren," John said with a wink.

"Why not?" Charlie asked.

"Because she's no longer Miss Maren. Now she's Mrs. Orton."

"But we can't call her Mrs. Orton," Lilly said.

"Let's call her Mommy," Petey said again, this time with a bit more force.

"I like Ma," Charlie said.

"And I like Mom," Lilly said with her arms folded.

John sat on Marjorie's other side, and he took her free hand. He leaned over and whispered in her ear, loud enough for the children to hear, "I shall call you My Love."

Charlie rolled his eyes and Lilly wrinkled her nose.

Marjorie offered him a kiss and then looked at the

children, her heart full. "I don't care what you call me, as long as you call me yours."

Lilly leaned her head against Marjorie's shoulder and played with the new ring on Marjorie's left hand. Petey placed his cheek over her heart, clutching his airplane close to his chest. Charlie grinned from his place on the sofa, his eyes wandering to the rosebud she had placed in her hair, and Laura reached for Marjorie's necklace.

But it was the look in John's eyes that brought her the sweetest joy. He quoted from Proverbs thirty-one. "'Her children arise up, and call her blessed; her husband also, and he praiseth her.'"

Large snowflakes began to fall just outside the windows as Marjorie snuggled on the sofa with her new family, content to stay forever.

* * * * *

Dear Reader,

Thank you for joining me on the banks of the Mississippi, in my hometown, during the year 1918. Little Falls, like many other American communities, experienced the devastating effects of the Spanish flu. It infected nearly five hundred million people worldwide, but little was known about its cause or cure. At the time, our local newspaper mentioned cinnamon oil as a treatment, so it only seemed appropriate for Dr. Orton to advocate this method. I don't know how well it worked, but many still use it for the same purpose today.

This is my first Love Inspired Historical, and I had so much fun writing this story and creating the cast of characters. I shared a glimpse of my four children in the Orton children, and there was a little of my husband, Dave, in John's character. That would leave Marjorie to me—but, alas, I'm much more like Anna.

God bless!
Gabrielle Meyer

REQUEST YOUR FREE BOOKS!

2 FREE INSPIRATIONAL NOVELS
PLUS 2 *FREE* MYSTERY GIFTS

Love Inspired® HISTORICAL

YES! Please send me 2 FREE Love Inspired® Historical novels and my 2 FREE mystery gifts (gifts are worth about $10). After receiving them, if I don't wish to receive any more books, I can return the shipping statement marked "cancel." If I don't cancel, I will receive 4 brand-new novels every month and be billed just $4.99 per book in the U.S. or $5.49 per book in Canada. That's a saving of at least 17% off the cover price. It's quite a bargain! Shipping and handling is just 50¢ per book in the U.S. and 75¢ per book in Canada.* I understand that accepting the 2 free books and gifts places me under no obligation to buy anything. I can always return a shipment and cancel at any time. Even if I never buy another book, the two free books and gifts are mine to keep forever.

102/302 IDN GH6Z

Name _____ (PLEASE PRINT) _____

Address _____ Apt. # _____

City _____ State/Prov. _____ Zip/Postal Code _____

Signature (if under 18, a parent or guardian must sign)

Mail to the **Reader Service:**
IN U.S.A.: P.O. Box 1867, Buffalo, NY 14240-1867
IN CANADA: P.O. Box 609, Fort Erie, Ontario L2A 5X3

Want to try two free books from another series?
Call 1-800-873-8635 or visit www.ReaderService.com.

* Terms and prices subject to change without notice. Prices do not include applicable taxes. Sales tax applicable in N.Y. Canadian residents will be charged applicable taxes. Offer not valid in Quebec. This offer is limited to one order per household. Not valid for current subscribers to Love Inspired Historical books. All orders subject to credit approval. Credit or debit balances in a customer's account(s) may be offset by any other outstanding balance owed by or to the customer. Please allow 4 to 6 weeks for delivery. Offer available while quantities last.

Your Privacy—The Reader Service is committed to protecting your privacy. Our Privacy Policy is available online at www.ReaderService.com or upon request from the Reader Service.

We make a portion of our mailing list available to reputable third parties that offer products we believe may interest you. If you prefer that we not exchange your name with third parties, or if you wish to clarify or modify your communication preferences, please visit us at www.ReaderService.com/consumerschoice or write to us at Reader Service Preference Service, P.O. Box 9062, Buffalo, NY 14240-9062. Include your complete name and address.

LIH15

SPECIAL EXCERPT FROM

Love Inspired HISTORICAL

*Sheriff Shane Timmons just wants to be left alone,
but this Christmas he'll find that family is what he's
always been looking for.*

*Read on for an excerpt from
THE SHERIFF'S CHRISTMAS TWINS,
the next heartwarming book in the
SMOKY MOUNTAIN MATCHES series.*

"We have a situation at the mercantile, Sheriff."

Shane Timmons reached for his gun belt.

The banker held up his hand. "You won't be needing that. This matter requires finesse, not force."

"What's happened?"

"I suggest you come see for yourself."

Shane's curiosity grew as he followed Claude outside into the crisp December day and continued on to the mercantile. Half a dozen trunks were piled beside the entrance. Unease pulled his shoulder blades together. His visitors weren't due for three more days. He did a quick scan of the street, relieved there was no sign of the stagecoach.

Claude held the door and waited for him to enter first. The pungent stench of paint punched him in the chest. His gaze landed on a knot of men and women in the far corner.

"Why didn't you watch where you were going? Where are your parents?"

"I—I'm terribly sorry, ma'am" came the subdued reply. "My ma's at the café."

"This is what happens when children are allowed to roam through the town unsupervised."

Shane rounded the aisle and wove his way through the customers, stopping short at the sight of statuesque, matronly Gertrude Messinger, a longtime Gatlinburg resident and wife of one of the gristmill owners, doused in green liquid. While her upper half remained untouched, her full skirts and boots were streaked and splotched with paint. Beside her, ashen and bug-eyed, stood thirteen-year-old Eliza Smith.

"Quinn Darling." Gertrude's voice boomed with outrage. "I expect you to assign the cost of a new dress to the Smiths' account."

At that, Eliza's freckles stood out in stark contrast to her skin.

"One moment, if you will, Mr. Darling," a third person chimed in. "The fault is mine, not Eliza's."

The voice put him in mind of snow angels and piano recitals and cookies swiped from silver platters. But it couldn't belong to Allison Ashworth. She and her brother, George, wouldn't arrive until Friday. Seventy-two more hours until his past collided with his present.

He wasn't ready.

Don't miss
***THE SHERIFF'S CHRISTMAS TWINS* by Karen Kirst,**
available wherever
Love Inspired® Historical books and ebooks are sold.

www.LoveInspired.com

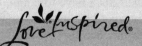
She leaned back in the seat and covered her face with her
hands. "I am angry. I'm mad because I don't know what to
do for Colby. And the person I always went to for advice
is gone. Grant is gone. I think Colby and I were both in
a delusional state, thinking they would come home. But
they're not. I'm not getting my brother, my best friend,
back. Colby isn't getting his parents back. And it isn't
fair. It isn't fair that I had to—"

Her eyes closed, and she shook her head.

"Macy?"

She pinched the bridge of her nose. "No. I'm not going
to say that. I lost a job and gave up an apartment. Colby
lost his parents. What I lost doesn't amount to anything. I
lost things I don't miss."

"I think you're wrong. I think you miss your life.
There's nothing wrong with that. Accept it, or it'll eat
you up."

Tanner pulled up to her house.

"I miss my life." She said it on a sigh. "I wouldn't be anywhere else. But I have to admit, there are days I wonder if Colby would be better off with someone else, with anyone but me. But I'm his family. We have each other."

"Yes, and in the end, that matters."

"But…" She bit down on her lip and glanced away from him, not finishing.

"But what?"

"What if I'm not a mom? What if I can't do this?" She looked young sitting next to him, her green eyes troubled.

"I'm guessing that even a mom who planned on having a child would still question if she could do it."

She reached for the door. "Thank you for letting me talk about Colby."

"Anytime." He said it, and then he realized the door that had opened.

She laughed. "Don't worry. I won't be calling at midnight to talk about my feelings."

"If you did, I'd answer."

She stood on tiptoe and touched his cheek to bring it down to her level. When she kissed him, he felt floored by the unexpected gesture. Macy had soft hair, soft gestures and a soft heart. She was easy to like. He guessed if a man wasn't careful, he'd find himself falling a little in love with her.

Don't miss
THE RANCHER'S TEXAS MATCH by Brenda Minton,
available October 2016 wherever
Love Inspired® books and ebooks are sold.

www.LoveInspired.com

LIEXP0916